SEDUCTION

A Novel by

C.L. BLUESTEI

SEDUCTION series • Volume I

Copyright © 2015 by Carol L. Bluestein
C.L. Bluestein Books
A Division of Bluestein Publishing
Slingerlands, NY

ISBN ePub July 2015 ISBN: 978-0-9966210-0-7

ISBN Print July 2015 ISBN: 978-0-9966210-1-4

s

2015 First Edition

Editor: Anne Frazier Walradt

Cover design: www.FYSenterprises.com

DEDICATION

With my love and gratitude to and for
my late husband, Michael R. Bluestein,
our children Sandra, Mark, and Lisa,
and their families

They are my inspiration.

ACKNOWLEDGEMENTS

First and foremost, I'd like to thank my family whose support never wavered despite a bit of healthy skepticism. My daughter, Sandra Bluestein Carrk read and edited every version for logic, consistency, and grammar. She has supported me through this amazing journey.

I thank family who have passed but, in their own way, made my journey possible: Roslyn and Noah Levine, Alynne Levine Sharp, and Jack D. Main. And, last but not least, my late beloved canine companions, Sugar and Sam, who were by my side as I worked on draft after draft.

My general readers and their input helped keep the book on track. Thank you to: Judith Prest, Leiah Bowden, Sylvie Bergere, Leslie Tabor, Lisa Van Avery, Joan Levine, Janet Tanquay, Pat Pinchback, and Richard Levine. Judith Rodwin and Barbara Traynor contributed to my final editing process.

My monthly writing group, Women Who Write, listened and critiqued chapters with open hearts and generous suggestions which contributed to the refining and truth-telling process.

Thank you to my teachers and friends at The International Women's Writing Guild (IWWG) who opened my eyes to the wonderful world of expression. In particular, these women worked with me directly at the time I was ready to listen: Zita Christian re: character development, Lynne Barrett re: plot, Paula Chaffee Scardamalia re: story. Judith Searle re: dialog, Alice Orr re: manuscript development, Linda Bergman re: pacing, Lauren B. Davis re: show don't tell, and Marj Hahne re: wordsmith.

Special mention to my teacher "Humor is good writing too," friend, and editor Anne Frazier Walradt for her tireless editing and belief in me and my project.

Finally, the patience award goes to Cooper, my rescued schnoodle. I'm sure he was looking for a raucous little boy yet has adapted with joy and sweetness to his spoiled and exalted positions of snuggler, walker, jester, kisser, listener, and protector.

Contents

SEDUCTION

Chapter 1
Harlem, New York City

From his double-parked Lincoln Town Car, the driver scanned the Harlem neighborhood for anomalies. None. Across the street seven local gang members camped out on crates and frayed beach chairs—all eyes on him.

The chauffer's hat sat low, touching the rim of dark aviator glasses. On the passenger's seat lay a two-month-old edition of *The Daily News,* ALLEGED TEEN KILLER OF 2 GIRLS RELEASED. He folded the paper, stuck it under the seat, slid on driving gloves, and exited the vehicle.

He adjusted his jacket covering the Chiappa Rhino Snub-Nose .357 Mag in the small of his back, shot his cuffs, and centered his black tie's half Windsor knot.

He turned, walked to the decrepit brownstone, climbed the chipped cement stairs, and pressed the 2A buzzer—twice.

A window opened above him. Charlotte Jenny Mays stuck her head out. "Be right down."

The driver returned to the curb and waited, his body balanced like a karate sensei.

In apartment 2A, the strident buzzing startled the seventeen-year-old man-boy in the back room. "Shit. Fuck."

"Jamal Henry Johnson. Time to go. The PRAISE car's here."

"Not going," said Jamal, better known as Shooter. He had five kills by age twelve. This year, during a turf war, two little girls were collateral damage. He'd be on death row if the cops had found even one credible witness.

Shooter sat on the edge of his stripped clothing-strewn bed, phone in hand. His fingers texted gang leader, BigGee, his best friend, "*going.*"

Charlotte appeared at his door. "Stop messing around, Jamal. I've got a good job and you're going to college. No way we're turning that down."

"Mama, I can't go," Shooter said without looking up. His phone dinged, "*u needed here.*"

"You stay and you'll be dead in a week."

Silent, he texted BigGee, "*she all i got.*"

"Jamal, put that phone down or I'll take it."

"Mama...." The phone dinged. "*kill the bitch.*"

Charlotte grabbed the phone and looked at the message. "You listen to me, *boy*. You've been waving your gun around since you were eight."

Jamal's jaw dropped.

"Don't look so surprised. Just because the police

didn't arrest your ass doesn't mean I didn't know."

"Mama...."

"Those two little girls, Jamal. How could you?"

"I don't..., didn't...."

"Not listening, boy. I'm not in the mood. Move your ass and pack.... Now."

Shooter texted BigGee, *"no fucking way,"* and stood up. He repositioned his low slung jeans, went into the empty closet, pushed on a piece of wallboard, and retrieved his gun. The safety was on.

"Jamal," Charlotte called from the living room. "Where are you, boy?"

He grabbed a T-shirt from the bed, wrapped it around the gun, and carried the package to the open window. He stuck his head out. The alley was clear. Shooter dropped the package into the half-full garbage can two stories beneath his window.

"Jamal!"

He closed the window. Shooter dumped his clothes into the suitcase, zipped it, and dragged it into the living room. When he saw his mother, he smiled. Charlotte wore her Sunday best royal blue suit with a blue and scarlet wide-brimmed hat perched atop her coiffed hair.

"I'm not going to miss this place," she said. "No, I'm not. Not for one little itty bitty second."

Shooter glanced around the room. No matter how many times she made him patch and paint the place, the ancient cracks and discolorations always bled through. Peeling metal cabinets and broken appliances added to the despair. Only his mom made this place a home. He wouldn't miss it either.

He glanced out the front window. His crew stared back from across the street. Shooter texted BigGee, *"baby in can."* BigGee looked at his phone and nodded to skinny ReeTree, who took off in a dead run.

Charlotte opened the apartment door. "Ready?"

He nodded the lie.

"Good boy."

Charlotte opened the door for him. Shooter started down the stairs. Four days before at the church supper, he was sitting next to her when she received The PRAISE Foundation Community Service Award. He'd kept her from falling when she heard the award included a new job at triple her current salary, a college scholarship for him, and her own home in Atlanta, Georgia. It had turned his life upside down.

When he opened the front door, the driver came forward, took his luggage, and escorted him to the car. Shooter ducked into the backseat and reached for a soda on the courtesy bar.

Thud. Shooter sat upright as the town car trembled.

Thud. The car rocked.

The noise was right behind Shooter's head. He twisted his neck as his hand reached for the gun that wasn't there. "Shit." ReeTree and two other gang members stood with their palms on the car's roof.

"Gentlemen," the driver said as he grabbed ReeTree's hand and executed a swift wrist lock twist. ReeTree screamed and dropped to the pavement. The two others backed up a step. "This vehicle is equipped with the latest in surveillance technology." He jerked ReeTree's wrist upward and ReeTree screeched in pain.

"If you persist," the driver said, "I'll have your collective asses thrown in jail." He paused. "Do we have an understanding here?"

The two kids still standing said, "Okay. Okay," and, hands held high, walked backward to safety.

"Thank you for your cooperation," the driver said. He turned his attention to ReeTree. "And you. Do you understand?"

ReeTree, his face stained with tears and snot, nodded several times in quick succession.

"Good." The driver let the boy's wrist drop. ReeTree scrambled to his feet and ran—his twisted arm hanging by his side.

Shooter, jaw tight and temple vein throbbing, punched the seat cushion several times, and reached for the door handle. Too late. Charlotte entered the backseat and sat down next to him.

"Jamal, did you see that? Those dumb-ass boys had it coming. Maybe next time they'll think twice before messing with a stranger."

Head down, he said, "Uh-huh."

She patted his knee. "Don't worry. You're going to be fine. You'll see."

Shooter crossed his arms and mumbled, "Fuck. Fuck. Fuck."

The driver finished packing the trunk and entered the vehicle. He put on his seat belt and lowered the courtesy window. Looking into the rear-view mirror, he said, "Ready?"

Charlotte said, "Yes, sir." Shooter, shoulders hunched, looked at his sneakers and remained silent.

"Good. Lean back. Relax. We'll be at the airport in no time." He raised the courtesy window, locked the doors, pushed the radio button for the soothing classical sounds of WQXR, and entered the stream of traffic.

After the first turn and several blocks, he pressed the first button under the console. Vents in the rear compartment opened and nitrous oxide seeped into the air. His passengers drifted into a light sleep. Fifteen minutes later, he pressed the second button and added the more potent anesthetic, sevoflurane gas. Charlotte and Shooter entered a comatose state.

The driver knew the route. He had driven it in four different cars and walked it in three different disguises over the past two months. He knew where every traffic and security camera sat and whether or not they were operational. He triangulated their ranges and identified the blind spots.

He chose these areas to alter the car's appearance by changing license plates, as displayed on the modified LED monitor, and altering placement of maps, coffee cups, packages, and similar items in the front and back window. To alter his appearance, he used a combination of hats, wigs, facial hair, and glasses. He further maximized visual confusion, as recorded by traffic cams, by driving next to other black cars as he wove through traffic to the warehouse district.

As he neared the row of three buildings he owned under a legal corporate labyrinth, he used the remote. A garage door opened, he drove in, and it closed. The overhead lights revealed the windowless space— where all his targets ended their journeys.

In the large room, on the wall opposite the garage doors, were two circular iron doors—much like those of a coal furnace, a stainless steel surgical table, and an industrial six-foot double door cabinet. On the left hand wall, about two thirds of the way down its length, was an EMS gurney, a tablet—hung like a monitor over another surgical table, and a closed door.

He had, over time, developed efficient, painless procedures to induce death and remove all trace of each seduction with respect to target, the car, and his person. The entire process, as well as wireless connections, was programmed into the tablet affixed to the wall. He exited the car and walked over to the tablet. He turned it on and started the program.

Tap. The cabinet doors popped open. A locked white box sat on the top shelf. The bottom three shelves were filled with cleaning supplies—several packages of HAZMAT suits, a stack each of face masks and paper bags, and a box of vinyl gloves.

The driver stripped, except for the small silver heart dangling from the silver chain around his neck, dropped his clothing into a paper bag, and put on a HAZMAT suit, face mask, and vinyl gloves. He retrieved the white box and set it on the small table. Inside were several syringes and bottles of potassium chloride. After filling two syringes with the chemical, he entered the car and injected a lethal dose into each body.

While he waited, he collected all items from the car, including the luggage, Charlotte's purse, the courtesy bar's contents, and the folded newspaper under the front seat.

Tap. The incinerator door popped open. Everything went down the chute. Roaring flames fed on the garbage. He closed the door and returned to the car.

He checked Charlotte and Shooter's carotid arteries for a pulse. None. He encased the bodies in heavy duty plastic bags and used the EMS gurney to transport them one at a time, from the car to the second iron door.

Tap. The second door popped open. He loaded each body into the portal. Holding the plastic bag's closed end, he let gravity do its work. One at a time, the bodies slipped from the bags and down a one-story shaft into a dehydration chamber. He shut the iron door.

Tap. The Dehydrator Application started. The tablet showed visuals of the chamber and its contents.

Tap. The chamber vibrated until the bodies aligned. Tap. The chamber closed and the lid locked. The tablet visual disappeared and statistics came up— estimated fourteen-day desiccation time based on weight. Tap. The green light showed, "Process Initiated."

He spent the next hour detailing the car. Tap. Both body bags and all cleaning rags and vacuumed debris, from the car and the garage floor, went down the incinerator.

He closed and returned the white box to the cabinet's top shelf and the unused cleaning supplies to a lower shelf. Then he stripped and tossed the HAZMAT suit, face mask, and vinyl gloves down the incinerator.

Tap. A red light glowed. "All Locks Secure." His work was done for now. He'd return to use the crushing hydraulic press when the process was complete. Once the bones resembled grains of sand, they'd join the others in the confluence of the East River, the Hudson River, and the Atlantic Ocean. The uncrushable went into the furnace.

Naked, except for the silver heart necklace, he stood in front of a steel three-hour fire door, lifted the keypad cover, and punched in the code. The door slid open, he stepped over the threshold into the adjoining garage, and the door closed.

A BMW 650i Coupe Frozen Silver Edition occupied this space. He ran his hands over its sleek, smooth finish— the fender reflected his arousal. "Be right back," he said aloud. He opened the door on his right and entered a stark one-room apartment. The only adornment, a photograph of a man around fifty years old with his arm around a young man, perhaps eighteen years old, hung on the wall next to a full-length mirror.

After a cleansing shower, being careful to brush under his nails and double wash all exposed areas of his body, he dressed—buffing his shoes on his pants. In front of the mirror, tying his tie, he looked over at the picture of himself with his mentor, Philip Vanderhagen. "Another successful seduction," he said aloud, as if the man were present. "You'd be proud of me—if you only knew."

Back at the mirror, he shrugged his shoulders to set his jacket, shot his cuffs, and straightened his tie. He put his hand over the hidden silver heart and looked heavenward. "Saving lives in your honor. I love you, Brenda."

He closed his eyes for a moment and then returned his gaze to the mirror. The reflection showed a thirty-five-year-old man in his prime—a dedicated humanitarian, founder and PRAISE Foundation CEO.

Again, talking to the photograph, "I know. I'm sorry about Mrs. Mays. But it's excruciating to live with the images of a lifeless, tortured, discarded body of a loved one. Her death was my gift to her."

He opened the door, grabbed his car keys from the hook, smiled at the familiar jingle, and walked out, locking the apartment door. He slid onto the BMW's leather seat, activated the garage door, and drove across town to his office.

Detective A.J. Simmons took the call.

"This is Abby Mays. My sister's missing."

Simmons picked up a pen and took down the information. "Charlotte Jenny Mays and her son, Jamal Henry Johnson, are missing. They were supposed to be here in Atlanta four days ago. I figured she had to finish her reports at work. But four days is too long. Way too long. I got worried. Now, I can't reach her or Jamal. Something's wrong. Very wrong. You need to get over there right now."

The detective entered the interview information into the computer tracking system and searched. Results showed Charlotte Mays was clean. However, Jamal Johnson had a record of petty thefts and had been a suspect in several gang-related murders. Despite a huge case load, he checked the electronic lists of the city morgue, area hospitals, precinct holding areas, and homeless shelters. Nothing.

Thirty minutes later Simmons and his partner stood in the Mays's empty apartment. They walked down the hall to check the two bedrooms. In the back bedroom closet, Simmons investigated the cut-out wallboard. Empty.

Returning to the living room, Simmons glanced out the window. Seven young men stood across the street with eyes on the apartment. He nodded to his partner and tilted his head toward the window. His partner shrugged and followed Simmons outside and across the street.

As the detectives approached, all seven pairs of eyes focused on the sidewalk.

"Okay, boys, assume the position against the wall."

A continuous chorus of, "We ain't done nothing," rang out as the boys moved slower than old men on crutches.

Simmons approached each one, dragged him off to the side, and shoved his back against the wall so his head bounced off the brick. Then he whispered: "Where's Shooter?" All he got was a vacant stare.

The fourth kid followed suit but added a mumble.

"What?" Simmons said. "Speak up, kid."

"Shooter's with his mom."

Over the next few days, the detectives interviewed neighbors, church members, and Charlotte's co-workers. They viewed all the street videos and caught the limo turning onto the avenue but lost it in the heavy traffic. They checked financial records and traced phone calls. Their last stop was the PRAISE Foundation.

An unscheduled onsite interview with the foundation secretary came up empty. Yes, Charlotte Jenny Mays was in their system. She had received and cashed their award check. No, they had not sent a driver. If the foundation name was used for any other purpose, it had to be under false pretenses. And, yes, with a warrant, their files would be made available to the police for review.

Simmons got the warrant. No leads. He notified Abby Mays, placed the open case file on his desk, and entered Charlotte Jenny Mays and Jamal "Shooter" Henry Johnson into the National Missing and Unidentified Persons System.

Chapter 2
White Plains, New York

"What!" Rachel Allen slapped the computer desk with both hands and jumped out of her chair. She strode across the room, shoving chairs out of her way, offering, "Excuse me," to jostled people, and entered the computer geek's lair.

Hidden behind his tinted glasses, shoulder-length brown hair, and earphones, the man seemed oblivious. Rumor had it that Fox News had gotten access to the campaign system and this computer guy was here to fix it.

Hands on her hips, lower jaw thrust forward, brown eyes flashing, Rachel said, "Listen up, computer genius, I've had it. Stop screwing around with my login permissions."

He took off his head phones, raised his eyebrows and said, "Is there a problem?"

"I know you know there's a problem," she said. "The first day, you said the problem was in the new update. The second day, you said the problem was corrupted data. Today, my login sets off fireworks. Enough, already. I have work to do."

"You're a high school senior summer intern."

"You're deliberately wasting my time. Stop screwing around."

"Ah," he said. "So, you didn't like the aquarium or hot air balloons. And now, no fireworks." He rested his elbows on his desk and brought his face closer to hers. "What about elephants, orangutans, or cheetahs?"

Rachel said, "Are you kidding me?"

He said. "Just a static image then. How about Mt. Rushmore?"

Rachel stepped to the side, put her hands on the desk top, and leaned in close to him. Through clenched teeth, she said, "If you make me lose 'Intern of the Month' because I don't finish my daily assignments, I will personally wreck your life forever."

With a wry smile, he said, "I'm intrigued."

Rachel straightened. "Don't be. I can be downright insidious."

He laughed. "Well, we can't have that, can we?"

"Good decision."

"Why don't you use workstation three. That way, you won't have to move your stuff." He turned back to his monitor and put on his headphones.

Rachel said, "You knew! I knew it." It fell on deaf ears. She turned away and mumbled, "Creep."

Two hours later, she took a break. She filled a cup from the water cooler and, instead of moving forward, she turned and crashed into the computer guy. The water splashed down the front of his jeans.

"Oh, no," Rachel said, grabbing a fistful of paper towels. "I'm so sorry."

The paper towels were within an inch of his crotch when he stepped back. "It's okay, Rachel. I'm fine. Really. It'll dry."

"No, no," Rachel said. "It's my fault. I'll fix it."

He caught her hand. "Rachel, give me the paper towels. I'll take care of it."

She raised her eyebrows. "Why...." When comprehension dawned, her face burned, turned scarlet. "I... er... here." She thrust the paper towels into his hand.

"Thank you," he said, with a broad smile. "No big deal."

Rachel nodded and backed away—into the cooler. She spun around, grabbed the rocking jug of water, steadied it, and fled back to her desk.

Seated, she dropped her head into her hands and muttered, "I'm an idiot."

The computer guy was gone the next day. To her surprise, Rachel missed the fireworks.

Chapter 3
Freeton, Greene County, New York

Four years later, Rachel Allen was set to graduate *summa cum laude* from Freedom College. She had a job starting in the fall and a summer vacation that included a trip to Europe and a trip to Seattle to visit her sister. Life was good—even though her fiancé cancelled their engagement and tabled a Fulbright Scholarship, taking off for the unchartered Australian outback. A month after he left, she found she didn't miss him. *So much for true love.*

It was dark when she skipped down the library steps, books and notebooks cradled in one arm, and phone to her ear. "Just finished.... Will do. Be right there."

Several students she knew were hanging out by the benches, but Rachel didn't stop to chat. She had to meet her friends back at the dorm for a Saturday night on the town—a late movie and a snack at The Liberty Bell Bar and Grill.

Motion-sensor mercury lights blinked on to light her path. Instead of her normal route around Commons Square, she took the shortcut between the woodland garden and the science lab's foundation plantings. As she turned the corner, lights didn't go on. *Odd.* She paused, put-off by the darkness. Lights glowed less than twenty yards ahead. Late already, she swallowed her concern and kept going.

Passing the first doorway on her right, Rachel smelled liquor and cigarettes. She hesitated. Before she could react, a hand covered her mouth and an arm encircled her neck. The pressure cut off her breath. Papers, folders, purse, and phone flew out of her hands. She clawed at the forearm as she struggled. The attacker's strength jerked her off balance. His weight dragged her down. Bushes broke her fall. Branches dug into her back. He sat astride her, his hand muffled her screams. She fought against containment until a flash of light bounced off his knife blade.

He slid the weapon across her cheek. "Shut up or I'll fucking kill you."

On the far side of Freedom College's campus, alumnus Ted Donovan attended a dinner honoring his gift—the Theodore Xavier Donovan Chair in Human Rights Studies. The small elitist (one had to apply for an invitation to apply) institution in upstate New York promised to imbue its students with vision, initiative, and enterprise. As a result, graduates were among the world's top movers and shakers—like Ted.

After dinner, the awards ceremony, and the obligatory "good-bye's" and "thank you's," Ted stepped outside. His sandy-colored hair, combed straight back, exposed his high forehead and accented his ice blue eyes. If all else had failed, Ted could have made his living as a model and landed the cover of the *New York Times'* Male Fashions supplement.

He adjusted his jacket, tailored to follow the lines of his athletic six-foot-two-inch frame, shot his cuffs, and centered his tie's half-Windsor knot. It moved a millimeter. It was time to go back to New York City, but he couldn't resist a last look at the campus.

Dr. Isaiah Youngman approached Ted and said, "Beautiful, isn't it?"

Ted turned to acknowledge the older man. "President Youngman. Yes, it is. I was just remembering my time here."

"You have more than fulfilled your promise, Ted. When I said you were an eminent alumnus, I meant it. Your philanthropic PRAISE Foundation has poured millions of dollars into needy and displaced populations throughout the world."

"Thank you," Ted said. "I'm happy to give back to the college that encouraged me to think outside the box. I hope the Chair in Human Rights Studies will send many others down similar paths."

"We will never forget you or your generosity," Dr. Youngman said.

Ted smiled and his hand slid into his pocket and jingled the Freedom Bell medallions. He withdrew his key chain and showed it to Dr. Youngman. "Do you remember these?"

"Of course. It was your dedication and bravery that elevated the Student Safety Aide Program from an escort service to a major player in our campus security measures."

"Thank you," Ted said. He smiled and then laughed. "Sorry, I had the recollection of my first visit to the school's security office. I faced twelve other applicants for the safety aide jobs. Two girls sat in silence and stared out the window. The ten boys bragged about all the dates they'd get. They had no idea what they were in for."

"I read all about it in your file. You established a boot-camp-like training program."

"I probably over-reacted to the lackadaisical girls and clueless boys. I had no interest in a dating service. My girlfriend was raped and murdered at age fourteen. My personal mission was, and is, to keep people safe. I'm glad it worked out for the college as well."

"Three Freedom Bells, Ted. One for each co-ed you rescued," Dr. Youngman said. "Copies of the letters from their grateful parents are in your folder."

"I'm glad I was able to help," Ted said. He took a deep breath and changed the topic. "The air up here is clean. Much better than the chemical laden New York City air, I assure you."

"Perhaps you'd like to stay a little longer? We have room."

"No, thank you. I've got to get back. Duty calls."

The men shook hands and Dr. Youngman went inside.

Ted walked toward the parking lot. His rubber-soled Italian leather loafers gripped the stone pavers in silence. On the way, the spring night sounds changed. He stopped, gripped by uneasiness. He turned his head in micro-increments to locate a sound or movement. A branch rustled. Again. Instinct sent him off to his right.

At the corner of the science building, he stopped. Nothing. Something. An ominous rhythm of silence and sound electrified him, engaging his primal hunter instinct.

Movement. A bush. To his left. Ted sprinted. Stopped. A gasp. A cry. A grunt. Another. Ted jumped over the plantings. He landed next to a rape in progress. He grabbed the assailant, one hand on his collar and the other around his neck, and hauled him off the woman. Before the asshole could react, Ted had him in a hammer lock.

While his prisoner fought, the woman's body moved. Relieved, Ted eased his grip for a moment. The rapist wriggled loose and made a grab for his pants, which handcuffed his ankles. Ted caught his arm, spun him around, and delivered a punch to the guy's solar plexus. As the rapist doubled over, Ted knocked him out with an upper cut and a right cross. The man landed spread-eagle on the sidewalk. Ted kicked him a few times to make sure the son-of-a-bitch was out cold.

He turned his attention to the woman. Ted knelt beside her and called 911. The co-ed's brown eyes were wide and wet. Dark-haired wisps framed her face. Her low moans cut through the night.

In the available light, the woman's exposed body showed scratches and thin lines of blood against white skin. She saw him and, like Eve in the Garden of Eden, she realized her nakedness. Her shaking hands tugged at her ripped clothing.

"Shhh," Ted said. "I'm here. You're going to be fine. Shhh."

Another moan.

"Here, let me help you. Can you sit up?" He bent his arm in front of her so she could grab it for leverage. "Use my arm. That's it. Okay, good." The woman was sitting. "Now, I'm going to take my jacket off and put it around your shoulders. Is that okay?"

She didn't say no.

Ted removed his jacket in one fluid motion and draped it over her shoulders. She clutched the jacket and withdrew into its shell.

"Don't worry," he said. "I'll make sure nobody hurts you again. I'll stay with you as long as I can. I've already called for help. You're...."

Lights, sirens, and voices filled the night. People raced toward them.

Ted said, "There are people here to help you. You'll be fine."

The police were the first to reach them. One team cuffed the rapist and marched him over to an EMT truck for evaluation. Another team asked Ted to move. A detective tried to question the woman while the EMTs hurried to her side.

Ted backed away, into the shadows. The EMTs were great. They removed his jacket, gave it to a policeman, and wrapped her in a blanket before they placed her on the gurney and wheeled her to the ambulance.

Ted walked up to the officer who remained at the scene. "May I have my coat?"

"Sorry, sir. We need it for evidence." The officer handed the jacket to a CSI who placed it in a plastic bag. Then, the officer pulled out his notepad and addressed Ted. "May I have your name and your statement in regards to the incident?"

Ted nodded. After the last question was asked and answered, the officer's phone rang and he took the call.

"Mr. Donovan, the detective in charge would like you to come down to the station."

It took five minutes to drive to the police station. Ted sat in the back seat, seething. He hated police stations and detested interrogations. Tonight, despite being the hero, he'd be treated to both.

When they arrived, the officer escorted Ted to the waiting area and said, "We have located your vehicle. It will be in the station lot in five."

"Good. I'd like my spare jacket hanging in the back and my toilet kit which is in the glove compartment."

"I'll get it while you are with our CSI people. They'd like to collect any evidence that might be under your nails or clinging to your clothing. We want to nail this guy."

An hour later, all CSI'd, Ted washed up and, escorted by an officer, entered an interrogation room. It smelled of fear, vomit, and arrogance. There was crud on the table and a pool of fluid on the chair. Before the officer closed the door, Ted said, in a voice loud enough for the whole station to hear, "Please have someone come and decontaminate this room."

The officer said, "Take it easy. I'll take care of it," and closed the door.

Ted waited for an interminable ten minutes before a man with a roll of paper towels and a spray bottle of disinfectant arrived. Under his direction, the cleaner cleaned. Afterwards, Ted sat in the chair with an impassive expression, knees crossed, hands resting on his thigh, and head held high, staring at the two-way mirror.

The knob turned, the latch clicked, and the hinges squeaked. An average-sized man with a scruffy beard, in casual dress, stepped into the room and closed the door. He placed several folders on the table.

"Mr. Donovan, I'm Detective Peter Voss," he said and sat. His round face and dark hair were set off by graying temples and a fighter's nose.

"Why am I here?"

"Details, Mr. Donovan. Details."

"It's all in my statement."

"I'd like to hear your story first hand." Voss leaned back in his chair. In a pleasant conversational tone, he said, "Tell me again, Mr. Donovan, why were you on campus?"

"As I said, Detective, it's all in my statement."

"Indulge me."

Ted lifted his chin and peered down his nose at Voss. "I had dinner with President Youngman. I'm sure he'd be furious if he knew I was here."

"Ah, here it is." Voss pulled out his notebook made a show of reviewing his notes. "So, right after dinner you heard the attack?"

"I heard a faint noise on my way to my car."

"Is it your habit to investigate every sound you hear?"

"I used to be a trained safety aide on that very campus."

"Twenty years ago. Right?"

"I'm not sure where this is going," Ted said, shifting in his chair. "There was no wind and I heard a bush rustling. A good thing, right? I saved a woman's life."

Voss changed the subject. "Trouble seems to follow you, doesn't it?"

Ted didn't answer—his eyes trained on the cement floor.

Voss leaned forward, put his notebook down, and opened a file. "I'm sorry about Brenda Underwood. Says here she was raped and murdered. Says you were at the scene and saw her body." He looked at Ted, who returned his gaze and remained silent.

Voss returned to the file. "I see the man responsible for her murder is also dead. He died while in transit for trial." He looked up.

Ted remained impassive said nothing.

"And, two years later, your parents died. In a car crash. Just a few miles from your home." Voss looked up. "Ruled an accident. Left you a wealthy man."

Ted brushed invisible lint from his slacks.

"Psychologist report says you didn't have a meaningful connection with your folks. You didn't exhibit normal loss behaviors."

"This is all old news and public record, Detective Voss. What's your point?"

"The point is, Mr. Donovan, you ruptured a young man's spleen, broke his jaw, and put him in intensive care. I want to know if you are prone to violence."

Ted stood up. "If you're not going to charge me, I'm leaving."

Detective Voss leaned back in his chair. "The young man in question is the son of a foreign diplomat. We can't touch him."

Ted paused.

"My job is to get the facts straight so this does not escalate into an international incident and that you, Mr. Donovan, do not get charged with assault."

Ted returned to his chair and sat down. "What are you saying?"

"I'm saying that after the kid recovers, President Youngman assured us he will undergo mandatory therapy and face campus disciplinary charges."

"That 'kid' raped a young woman and cut her with a knife," Ted said, his voice even, each word emphasized. "He should rot in prison."

Voss said, "Agreed. But, as I said, it's not my call."

"So that's it? Are we done?"

"No. That's not it, Mr. Donovan." Voss leaned forward and referred to another file. "I see you've been involved with three other attempted rapes on campus. The first incident happened on your way back to the dorm. It says here that you saw four males transport a limp female body up a set of stairs in a fraternity house and called security. Is that right?"

Silence.

"The second one happened while you ran laps on the outdoor track. You reported that you heard a scuffle in the trees and the words, 'No. Stop.' You vaulted a four-foot chain link fence and collared the rapist. You're quite an athlete, Mr. Donovan."

Ted put his hand in his pocket and fingered the Freedom Bells.

"The third incident occurred in your senior year. You were the residential advisor and just happened to be in the hall when a co-ed cried out. You kicked the door open, assaulted the perpetrator, and then called security, correct?"

"Are we done?"

"Including tonight, Mr. Donovan, you've put four young men in the hospital."

"I believe the correct interpretation is that I saved four women."

"Mr. Donovan, I find it hard to believe that you, a civilian, happened to be in the vicinity of four rapes. And, by vicinity I mean close enough to capture the perpetrator. The odds of that happening are astronomical."

"Detective Voss," Ted said. "I have dedicated my life to serving communities. I don't have to stage situations." Ted got to his feet and buttoned his jacket, shot his cuffs, and straightened his tie. "If you're done, I'm leaving."

Detective Voss closed the manila file and stood. Staring at Ted, his skepticism leaked out in a low growl, "You can go...for now."

Chapter 4
Greene County General Hospital,
Freeton, New York

In the emergency room, after the doctor and nurses stabilized Rachel, a police woman entered. Through small talk and kindness, she calmed Rachel and, in time, began her interview.

"I know this is painful, but do you think you can tell me what happened?"

"I... I was hurrying to my dorm. To meet my friends. I passed a guy from class. I can't even remember his name. Anyway, to save time, I used a cut-through. It was darker than usual. But it was only a few feet and I was late. So I kept going." Rachel paused. "Oh, my God. I'm so stupid. I should've...."

"None of this is your fault. Don't blame yourself."

Rachel blinked back tears.

"What happened next?"

"I smelled something and stopped. The next thing I knew I was down on the ground with him on top of me, branches dug into me, my head throbbed from the impact. I tried to get up, push him off. He was too heavy. When I tried to talk, he hit me. That's when I saw it."

"What? What did you see?"

"The flash of a knife." She broke into tears.

The officer calmed her. "Stay with me, Rachel. We need your help to put this guy away for a long, long time." She grabbed a box of tissues from the counter, set it down on the bed, pulled out a few, and handed them to Rachel.

Rachel wiped her eyes and blew her nose. "I must've screamed because he put his hand over my mouth and spit out the words, 'Shut up or I'll fucking kill you.' That's when he cut me. I saw the bloody blade. Felt him wipe it on my cheek. Then nothing."

"You're doing great. We're almost done."

"I tried to resist when I felt him tearing at my clothes but he hit me and must have knocked me out since I don't remember much after that."

"If you do, please let me know." She clipped her business card to the patient file. "You've been very brave and very helpful. Remember, none of this is your fault. Now, I know this is difficult, but it is the last step. May the doctor come in and administer a rape kit?"

"Will you stay?"

"For as long as you want."

Ten hours later, Rachel Allen's eyelids fluttered in the darkened hospital room. When her vision stabilized, she saw drawn shade edges outlined by the sun's rays.

"Mom?"

The recliner straightened with a bang. Helene Allen jumped to her daughter's side. "Rachel. Honey. I'm so glad you're awake." Helene, finger-combed the hair out of Rachel's face and fussed with her covers. "Would you like a drink?"

"Dad?"

"Don't worry, Baby. Your father will be here any second. He went down for some more coffee." Helene leaned over and kissed Rachel's brow. "You had a rough night. How do you feel?"

Mad. Sad. Violated. Afraid. Lucky. Vulnerable. Anxious. Furious. Victimized. Pissed off. Terrified. Rachel swallowed and said, "I'm okay, Mom." But she knew she would never be the same. Not ever. Then she broke down. "Oh, Mom. I'm so sorry."

Helene wrapped her arms around her daughter and rocked her, "You're going to be okay, Sweetheart. You're going to be okay."

Rachel wasn't so sure.

Chapter 5
Greene County General Hospital, Freeton, New York

"Mr. Donovan," the nurse said as she touched the dozing man's arm. He woke with a start. "Sorry, sir. I just wanted you to know Miss Allen's awake, but it'll be some time before you can go in."

Ted picked up his cup of coffee, took a sip, and gagged. His stomach growled. He had to eat. But first, he made a call to Electronic Private Investigations (EPI), one of several companies he used for background checks.

The EPI investigator said, "Mr. Donovan, what can I do for you?"

"File on a Rachel Allen, student at Freedom College. Mother Helene. Father Harry."

"When?"

"ASAP," Ted said, ending the call.

In the hospital cafeteria, he ordered the breakfast special. Despite his careful instructions, the cooks did it their way. Ted paid the cashier and sat down at a table in the far corner. From his vantage point, he observed staff and visitors as they came and went.

While the coffee was on par with Starbucks, the eggs were hard and the toast rubbery. He swore under his breath but consumed the meal anyway. The bad taste in his mouth reminded him of the police station.

Ted didn't like Detective Voss. He didn't like his motives questioned. It was goddamned insulting. Resigned to enduring the folly of others, he got up, dumped his tray into the garbage, and headed for the elevators. His phone buzzed and he checked his email from EPI.

"Rachel Allen, Scarsdale, NY, is the daughter of housewife/interior decorator Helene and CPA firm partner, Harry. She has an older sister in Seattle— married, four kids, visual artist.

"Subject is twenty-one, graduated from high school in the top two percent, Freedom College Human Rights club president, Student Council secretary, staff editor for *Freedom News*, works twelve hours a week on campus, and graduates the end of this semester. She has one speeding ticket and one credit card. No sorority. No current boyfriend.

"Copy of license, campus ID card, social security, reported part-time work history and internships below."

Ted closed his phone and put it in his jacket pocket. He took the elevator to Rachel Allen's floor, sat down in the waiting room, and picked up a copy of *Newsweek*.

"Mr. Donovan?" a woman's voice said.

He stood. "Ted, please."

The woman smiled. "I'm Helene Allen, Rachel's

mother. And this is my husband, Harry."

Ted shook their hands. "How's Rachel?"

"She's okay," Harry said. "However, before you see her, I want to thank you for everything you did for Rachel."

"I'm so sorry your daughter got hurt, Mr. Allen. But I'm glad I could help."

Harry said, "I heard you were here all night."

"I wanted to see Miss Allen before I left."

Helene said, "Mr. Donovan, Rachel has had a rough time, but she's calm now. I told her you were here and what you did. She's very grateful and has agreed to see you."

"I've got to make a few calls," Harry said. "Nice to meet you, Mr. Donovan." He gave Helene a kiss. "See you later, Honey. I'll bring coffee."

Ted followed Helene down the hall to Rachel's room, past the buzz at the nurse's station—unintelligible voices surrounded by beeping machines, blipping monitors, and hissing oxygen pumps.

Rachel lay motionless—eyes closed and crossed hands resting on her abdomen. At bedside, monitors showed Rachel's status, machines regulated several drips and her blood pressure cuff. On the opposite side, purple iris, yellow chrysanthemums, and red roses rose from a cut-glass base.

Helene patted her daughter's hands. "Rachel, honey. Mr. Donovan's here."

Rachel woke and managed a partial smile.

Helene said, "Are you comfortable?" Rachel nodded. "Want me to stay?" Another nod. Helene gave Rachel a kiss, walked around the bed, and sat in the recliner.

Rachel looked at Ted. Rachel looked at Ted. "Thank you, Mr. Donovan."

"I'm glad you're okay. May I do anything else?"

Rachel shook her head, the motion almost imperceptible. Her eyes filled with tears. Before her mother could move, Ted handed Rachel a box of tissues.

After several false starts, Rachel spoke. "I'm sorry. I… um…."

"It's okay," Ted said. "You don't have to explain. I understand." He plucked two business cards from of his left jacket pocket. "I know it's going to take some time to heal. I want you to have my contact information. You can reach me here any time for any reason." He placed one card on the portable bed tray and gave one to Helene. "I have many resources, which I am happy to make available."

Helene said, "Thank you. I'm sure we'll be okay."

Ted said, "I think so too. But you never know." He paused. He looked first at Helene and then at Rachel. "I only make this offer because I am deeply moved." He paused, cleared his throat, and squeezed his eyes shut for a heartbeat. "You, Rachel, have an uncanny resemblance to someone I loved and lost a long time ago. Please call me if you need anything— anything at all."

Rachel nodded and drifted off.

Ted paused at the door, looked at Rachel, then Helene, and left.

In his car, he put his hands on the wheel and rested his head. Seconds later, he leaned back, pressed his hand over his heart and the silver charm, and closed his eyes for a moment.

His brow furrowed, his jaw tensed, and his mouth tightened into a grimace. He said, "Damn Voss. Damn Youngman," and hit the steering wheel with both hands. "Shit. Therapy, my ass."

Chapter 6
East Side, New York City

Ted Donovan entered his East Side penthouse apartment at noon. By twelve-fifteen, stripped, showered, and exhausted, he got into bed and welcomed sleep. It didn't come.

He got up and put on a blue silk kimono. In the living room, he poured a double Scotch and took a sip. He plopped down onto his favorite chair and turned the TV on to CNN. Another sip. The anchor, flanked by the pictures of two men, identified them as wanted by the FBI. "And now to Bob Splain, what can you tell us about the fugitives?"

"Thanks, Jeff. I'm here in northern Georgia with Jeremiah Mercer, the sheriff of Overlook Valley. Sheriff, I understand you know Jocko Smith and Little Fred."

The sheriff stared at the ground for two long beats

before he spoke. "Yep, I know the boys. They grew up around here. They grew up around here. It's a small town. I'd guess everybody knows them."

"Did they skip town to avoid prosecution?"

"Don't know. Last I heard, they'd won a trip to Las Vegas."

"When did you realize they were missing?"

Sheriff Mercer lifted his eyes to the sky as he remembered.

Wayne Galt, the local white supremacist group leader, waved as he entered the sheriff's office as though he owned the place. He took the chair across from Mercer, spun it around, straddled it, and sat. He folded his arms and rested them on the chair back. He stared at the sheriff for thirty seconds and said, "Something's wrong in Deacon Hollow."

"Really?" Mercer asked with naked disinterest. It had been a very quiet several weeks, and the sheriff liked it that way. It gave him plenty of time to get in some serious fishing in the creek less than one hundred feet away from where he sat.

"We've got a situation building, and I can't reach Jocko."

"A situation?"

"There's a family of...." Galt stopped before he got started. "Look," he said. "That's not why I'm here."

The sheriff leaned back in his chair as if ready to trade stories with his best friend rather than this piece of shit. "Why *are* you here?"

"I can't find Jocko or Little Fred. They won some gambling trip and should've been back by now. But they're not. Their truck's gone and their house collapsed in the last storm."

"Think they're inside?"

"Nothing smelled bad so I didn't go looking."

"What do you want me to do?" As far as Mercer was concerned, the town was better off without them.

"Investigate. Find them." Galt jumped to his feet and leaned on Mercer's desk, face redder than a cock's comb. "I love those boys like they're my own."

"Come on, Wayne. Take it easy. Sit back down," Mercer said. "You know they could've gotten up and gone anywhere."

"Without a phone? Jocko lived by that phone. Hell, when that cell tower went up on the mountain, he celebrated for a week."

Mercer remembered. That celebration caused three separate fender benders and a ruckus at the county fair. Took Jocko three days in jail to sober up and the first thing he asked for was his phone. Galt was right. Maybe he did have a reason to be concerned.

The sheriff sat upright, found a pad and pen, and made a few notes. "Okay. I'll check Jocko's cell phone record and let you know. Here." He pushed a pad in front of Galt. "Write down his phone number. And Little Fred's, if you know it."

Galt jotted down the phone numbers.

He pushed the paper back to Mercer. "There you go."

Mercer unsnapped the holster safety and said, "Wayne," and slapped his gun on the desk with a loud thud.

Galt stared at it. "Hey, Sheriff, what's that for?"

"Since I'm doing you a favor, do me one."

"What?"

"No situations."

Galt's gaze shifted from the gun to Mercer's unblinking cold eyes. Wayne Galt nodded and pointed a finger at the sheriff. "You find them." He paused for effect, turned, and marched out of the station.

Galt had broken the day's tedium, so Mercer took the case rather than give it to a deputy. He called the phone company and checked Smith's phone record. Jocko had closed the account. When he reviewed the last ten numbers on the phone's call record, all were local except the last, which was untraceable.

Mercer rode out to the hollow, to the house Jocko and Little Fred shared. A tree had fallen on the roof, and the shack had collapsed like a house of cards. He got out of the police car and walked around. No discernible signs of life. No smells of rotted corpses or food—just a couple of broken liquor bottles by the foundation. He walked the immediate area. He looked for signs of a fight, a killing, or a burial—any kind of a clue as to the missing men's fate.

"What're you looking for, Sheriff?" Old Sam Tracy leaned on his branch cane. With deep lines on his face, unkempt beard, and feathery white hair, he looked like an ancient wood sprite.

Mercer turned to Tracy. "Have you seen Jocko and Little Fred?"

"Not for a while," Tracy said. "Last I saw, them boys had visitors. Come in a shiny black van."

"How many?

"Three men."

"Did the boys go with them?"

Old man Tracy stroked his chin. "Yup. The very next day. Looked happier than pigs in shit."

"What happened to Jocko's truck?

"Don't know. Didn't ask."

"Anything else that might help me find it or them?"

"Nope." The old man turned and disappeared into the shack he called home.

Sheriff Mercer took off his hat and rubbed his head. In this particular hollow, high end tourists were unusual. Sure, there was tourist trade in town, but in the backwoods? Out here? No. Not a chance. He checked with the other neighbors. No one knew more than the old man.

Back at the office, with the open file on his desk, Mercer forwarded the information to the National Missing and Unidentified Persons System and the FBI.

"A friend reported them missing," Sheriff Mercer said. "After I investigated their disappearance, I sent my report to the FBI."

The reporter said, "And that report triggered the warrant?"

"Yep. Seems the FBI matched their fingerprints to several arson cases in neighboring states that killed nine people."

"Tennessee and Arkansas?"

"Yep. That's right."

"Thank you, Sheriff." The reporter faced the camera and pictures of the two fugitives covered the screen with a phone number. "If you have seen these men, please call the number at the bottom of your screen."

Ted shut the TV off and finished his drink. Jocko Smith's successful seduction calmed him. He took the glass into the kitchen, cleaned it, and placed it back on the shelf. Returning to the bedroom, he got into bed and slept.

Three days later, a package arrived from Freedom College. It contained a letter from President

Youngman and a velvet covered tie-tack-sized box. Ted opened it. Inside, wrapped in tissue paper was a gold plated Freedom Bell award with his name on it. He added it to his keychain and spread the four bells into a fan. He smiled and put the keychain on the entry table.

Next, he read the letter, handwritten on Youngman's personal stationery.

"Dear Ted:

I want to thank you on behalf of the college and the Allen family for your act of courage and bravery. I want you to know that, on the advice of counsel, I have taken steps to admonish the alleged perpetrator, Hannes Svensson. He is suspended indefinitely until he successfully completes a prescribed course of intensive therapy and anger management. The rest I must turn over to the justice system which, in this case, must abide by the foreign diplomat courtesy rules. As of this writing, Mr. Svensson is out of the country for an extended stay.

Please find enclosed a small token of acknowledgment.

Thank you again.

Warmly,

Isaiah

Ted crumpled the letter and threw it across the room. With clenched fists, he walked to the windows. Outside, cars streamed across the Brooklyn Bridge and tugboats towed barges on the river below. The scene's monotony and rhythm calmed him, as it always did.

He turned and retrieved the letter from under the curtains and studied it. In an effort to be thorough, Youngman had included the student's name and home address in a post script.

For the rest of the afternoon, Ted did an online international public records search on Hannes Svensson Jr. and his father, Hannes Svensson Sr., a Swedish diplomat who listed residences in Stockholm, New York, Washington D.C., and Paris. The father was clean, but young Svensson had been in trouble before. He'd incurred criminal charges inside and outside of Sweden, and his father's status saved him every time.

Ted pulled out his phone. He took a picture of the letter, emailed it to Lucy Kilmer, his expediter, and called her.

"Ted. How nice to hear from you. Where've you been?"

"Cut the small talk, Lucy. Did you get the letter I sent? I need you to do a job for me."

Lucy laughed. "What happened to the charming boy who seduced me in grad school almost twelve years ago?"

"We never…."

"Call it what you want. You lured me into the coffee shop. Flattered me. Called me brilliant and precise. Called me Lucy instead of Lucille. Softer, you said. More accessible. Remember?"

"Of course. That was…."

"That was the day you told me about Positive Response with Action to Insure a Safe Environment, better known as the PRAISE Foundation. Asked me to evaluate my moral compass as it related to the greater good."

"Lucy...."

"Did I ever thank you for meeting my exorbitant price point? I'm not sure I'd have found a job this challenging on my own."

"Enough. This is serious. Track one Hannes Svensson Jr. I want a full report. The little shit raped a college co-ed. He is under the protection of his diplomat father. In effect, he is free to rape again and again. It's all in the letter."

"Got it."

"And Lucy," Ted said. "Nice job down south."

He closed his phone. He'd hear from her within the hour. Lucy was that good.

Lucy called back forty-five minutes later. The Svenssons had left the country six days ago and were at their flat in Paris, France.

Ten days later, the junior Hannes Svensson fell under a bus in front of the Parc des Princes after a Paris Saint Germain soccer game. The coroner ruled the death an accident. Svensson happened to be in the wrong place at the wrong time—a casualty of a mindless spectator victory celebration. The small story appeared in *Le Parisien,* buried on page eight.

Chapter 7
Paris, France

Three days after the bus accident, Ted arrived at the Vanderhagen home, a renovated townhouse that predated World War I. Ted used the ornate lion's head brass knocker that graced a single width oak door with a small shuttered security window. At one time it opened to vet callers. Now, it remained shut, retrofitted with a security camera.

The door opened and the butler ushered him into the foyer.

A round table with a bouquet of flowers centered on its glass top graced the large entry. Delicate waves of gray and burnt sienna wove through the white marble floor. The walls featured mahogany wainscoting and green silk brocade. A four-tiered crystal chandelier hung from a ceiling worthy of the Château de Versailles. The staircase on the right, carpeted in cranberry wool with a small gold *fleur de lis* motif, wound its way up four floors.

On Ted's right, the library door swung open, and Philip Vanderhagen stepped into the foyer with his arms open wide. "Ted, my boy. So good to see you again." Trim and well-dressed, Vanderhagen possessed an enthusiasm for life that belied his seventy plus years. He gave Ted a big hug and a couple of thumps on the back for good measure. "It's been too long."

"I'm glad to be back," Ted said.

Vanderhagen nodded to someone behind Ted, and the dinner chimes resounded through the house. The entry filled with adults and children. Thirty-year-old Sarah spotted him first and gave him a warm embrace. "Ted! What a nice surprise."

James, Vanderhagen's son and Sarah's father, appeared right behind her. "Come on, Sarah. Share Ted with the rest of us."

Sarah gave Ted a kiss on the cheek and said, "Sit next to me at dinner."

Ted smiled. "Of course."

More greetings as the family gathered. The butler opened the dining room doors. Vanderhagen, with Ted in tow, led his family into the room. Once they were seated, conversations from the arts to government to travel erupted around the table—"Did you read about...?" "Did you hear that...?" "I couldn't believe...," and "What do you think?"

Ted felt truly at home. He did not miss his parents' endless pedantic conversations.

"The toaster's broken."

"It's only fifteen years old. Fix it."

"I threw it out. I'm getting a new one."

"Two or four slices?"

"What do you think?"

"Up to you."
"Why is it always up to me?"

This, and variations on theme, caused horrific fights that kept them cold and distant.

The Vanderhagens, in contrast, encouraged each other, sought out opinions and advice, and appreciated spontaneous wit and humor.

If and when his parents spoke to him, it was to accuse or demean, and then turn a deaf ear. In the end, Ted had the last word—"Good-bye," as they drove down their driveway for the last time. He smiled. It was the second best day of his life.

"What's so funny, Teddy?" Sarah said.

"I was thinking about that ten-year-old irrepressible child I met the first time I was in Paris." He turned to face her. "I don't think you've changed a bit."

After dinner, Ted and Vanderhagen retired to the library with its impressive and extensive collection of books. Vertical and horizontal surfaces without volumes were covered with framed photographs of Vanderhagen with notables from television and the newspaper, including François Hollande and Segolene Royal, Barack and Michelle Obama, Jean-Paul Belmondo, Queen Elizabeth and Prince Philip, George Bush and Saudi King Abdullah, Sean Connery, and Pennsylvania congressman, Franklin Sandford.

"Have a seat," Vanderhagen said.

Ted sat on the leather couch and glanced at the picture on the side table—Vanderhagen with three Africans, two men and a woman.

Vanderhagen walked over to the picture, picked it up, and said, "Their names are Kwanh Ebu and Adebowale and Opeyemi Okoro. Nice people. Her father was the Menanandu chief, a nomadic tribe in that area. She was full of fire—him, not so much. I met them in the early nineteen-nineties when I toured the southeastern corner of the Democratic Republic of the Congo to scout mineral deposits and mining options." He put the picture down and sat down opposite Ted.

"I hope that went well."

"It did. My friends and I were able to buy several very lucrative mines," Vanderhagen said. "By the way, how were those soccer seats? I had to call in a favor since the stadium was sold out."

"Very much appreciated. Thank you."

"Ted, you hate soccer. My friends had the other half of the box. They said college students were in your seats." Vanderhagen slid a picture onto the coffee table. "Here are the boys."

Ted shrugged. "I couldn't make the game. A scheduling problem."

"Too bad one of them died." Vanderhagen placed the newspaper article, with the boy's photograph from healthier days, next to the picture. "Did you know him? The paper said he went to your Alma Mater—Freedom College."

Ted shook his head. "No."

"Come on, Ted," Vanderhagen said. "I can always tell when something's up with you." He got up and walked over to the bar and asked, "The usual?"

Ted nodded. "Please."

When they both had their drinks, Vanderhagen said, "What'd he do?"

Ted focused on his drink and took a sip. "I understand he raped a woman and got off with diplomatic immunity. Wasn't his first time. He had a history of behavior problems."

"My God," Vanderhagen said. "Despicable."

"I agree."

"Was the young man's death accidental?"

"I have no idea." Ted raised his glass. "To the women free of his clutches."

Vanherhagen said, "Hear, Hear," and they sipped in unison.

"Ted, you know I'm proud of you and your accomplishments, don't you?"

"I do, Sir. Your support has made all the difference."

"For that reason, I have a new opportunity for you to help people on a larger scale."

"PRAISE is already international, thanks to you. How much larger could it get?"

"This is not about PRAISE. It concerns a more personal involvement on a political and confidential level." Vanderhagen paused and sipped his drink. "James and I would like you to intercede on our behalf."

"You know I've kept an apolitical stand so PRAISE could remain bi-partisan. I'm not sure how I could help."

"This is not about PRAISE. This is about a few individuals impeding critical legislation essential to world economic progress."

"There always are," Ted said. "It's called the political process."

"Perhaps," Vanderhagen said. "However, these individuals are interfering with a complex global plan for an equitable distribution of wealth, jobs, and general economic recovery. As a result, progress is at a standstill and people are suffering."

"This complex plan, is it yours?"

"Initially, mine and a small group of like-minded individuals. But now, the best minds in the world are on board, ready to lend their expertise on a strategic and implementation level. We believe our initiatives will benefit humankind in ways only, heretofore, imagined."

"Sounds utopian—in an Orwellian way."

"We have done our due diligence. Committed leadership is a pre-requisite to our success."

Ted took another sip and looked at his mentor. "Again, I don't see how I can help."

"To move our agenda forward, we work behind the scenes as counsel to the world's top government officials, all of whom influence policies and laws. We support them financially through donations and opportunities."

"And yet people still stand in your way? I find that hard to believe."

"I'll ignore your sarcasm," Vanderhagen said. "As you know, not everyone has vision. Fear of change can be very powerful. To neutralize this fear, we must increase our persuasive response, using any means available to us. The efficiency of your seduction model is a most attractive alternative."

Ted put his glass down and sat up straight. "I'm sorry. My seduction model?"

"Yes, Ted. In our game plan, you will be our knight."

"I'm afraid I don't understand. I don't...."

Vanderhagen held up his hand. "Son, I have at my disposal the best information systems in the entire world. I can find a snowball in Alaska. More to the point, I found you."

Ted's face twisted in confusion. "In Paris? At the Louvre?"

"No, that's where we met. My people track unusually high intellects. So you came to my attention when you took your first national standardized test."

"In the second grade?" Ted stood up. Walked

behind the couch and turned toward his new nemesis.

Vanderhagen took another sip. "You didn't jump into focus until your emotional disconnect around the time of Brenda Underwood's death."

Ted, body rigid, clasped his hands behind his back. While his face remained stoic, his knuckles were white. "Really. And why was that?"

"Your grades never faltered. Your test scores never dropped even though your withdrawn demeanor morphed into a lackadaisical playboy.

"Then, at sixteen you cleverly seduced the corner bully and drug dealer with boxing gloves loaded with potassium chloride. In your senior year, you ingeniously messed with the air filter on your parents' car, causing the accident that killed them. No one suspected you in either incident."

Ted's nails bit into his palms. "Is that when you decided to meet me?"

"Yes. Your skills impressed me. At our first encounter, I liked you right away. Bright, charming, and comfortable in your own skin. It's been a pleasure watching you grow-up and maximize your potential with PRAISE and other endeavors."

"Meaning what?""

"I know all about your seductions, warehouse operation, and Lucy Kilmer."

Ted took a deep breath, dropped his arms to his side, returned to his seat on the couch. He leaned back and sipped his drink. "Why didn't you report me to the police?"

"To what end? You developed an effective process to excise the lowest form of scum from society. I saw nothing inherently wrong. Besides, I knew that down the line, your particular set of gifts would benefit my own goals."

"You want me to be your personal killer?"

"Not exactly. I'd like you to neutralize—seduce—the enemies of world progress."

"By enemies, you mean people who don't agree with you."

Vanderhagen smiled. "Ted, I don't understand your reluctance. Killing is killing. Dead is dead. What's the difference?"

"What's different is that these people haven't hurt anyone. They haven't jeopardized their community's safety or stomped on human rights."

"Yet," Vanderhagen said. "These people haven't hurt anyone—yet. My intent, with your help, is to be proactive. Prevent them from *ever* hurting anyone."

"I can't. This goes against everything I believe in. I won't do it."

"You will," Vanderhagen said. He stood and walked over to his desk. "And you'll do it willingly." Vanderhagen held up a thick folder. "I have enough information to have you executed in any number of states. Don't make me use it."

Ted held out his hand. "I'd like to see that folder."

Vanderhagen shook his head and put the folder down. He walked over to Ted, sat on the couch's arm, and placed his hand on Ted's shoulder. "Ted, you're a son to me. I've always supported you. Now, I'm asking you to expand your sphere of operations and become part of our family's business. Join our team. Work with James and me."

Ted shook his head. "How could you set me up to use me like this?"

"How could I not?"

The men stood, facing each other. In the silence, Vanderhagen offered his hand. Ted paused before returning the handshake.

Outside the home turned prison, Ted hit the sidewalk in long strides, burning off the explosion of suppressed rage. Three miles later, he felt calmer. He pulled out his phone, removed the SIM cards and battery. He stomped the battery and threw it and the phone into a nearby fountain. After paying cash for a prepaid phone card, he stepped into a public phone booth and called Lucy. "All access security breach. Paris. Initiate protocols."

Vanderhagen did what he always did after every meeting. He walked over to the lamp on the side table and upended it. In the base was a digital recorder. He removed the thumb drive and put in a new one. He went over to his desk, labeled the used drive, picked up the folder, and slid a bookcase panel aside to reveal a safe. He opened it, placed the folder on a shelf and the drive in the nearest box of recordings.

Within a year, a Palestinian activist suffered from a non-specific illness, fell into a coma, and died. The data surrounding his illness and death was and remains a mystery. Although a close friend stated: "I have no doubt that he was assassinated. The toxic material in his blood was not represented in the normal toxicology table."

The following year, a Sudanese politician and leader who stood against child-slavery died in a helicopter crash.

Eighteen months later, an American politician from the Midwest broke ranks with the Republican Party on a key funding bill and died at home following an accident in his woodworking shop.

Six months later, a Mexican politician who served in the president's cabinet and denounced plans to open the Mexican side of its northern border died in a plane crash during an inspection tour.

Fourteen months after, a nationalistic Indian politician who wanted to limit the number of foreign companies usurping the Indian talent pool died during a ceremonial bathing in the Ganges.

A year later, a Spanish activist and international reporter was trampled to death during the Running of the Bulls, ending his fight against the poisonous fallout from aggressive industrial complexes.

Chapter 8
215 Gramercy Avenue, New York City

At International Computerized Universal Inc., headquarters were on the second and third floor of the five story apartment building. Christopher Mark Gregory, owner and chief designer, sat working in his office. His team of specialists worked on the floor below.

Chris, a third generation Massachusetts Institute of Technology graduate, held twice as many patents as his grandfather and father combined. A child prodigy, he built and programmed computers by the time he hit seven.

By the age of sixteen, Chris launched Electronic Private Investigations Inc. (EPI). At twenty-one, with his doctorate in one hand and an undetectable spyware program equipped with data recognition and cypher modules in the other, he started International

Computerized Universal Inc. (ICU). Now, at thirty-five, he was the top security programming guru for the Fortune 500, governments, and organizations around the world.

He and his team were preparing the next version of his system for rollout. He'd targeted the upgrade to be released in four months, and they were right on schedule.

He took a sip of coffee while he studied code on the monitor. He could make it better. He set the coffee aside and revised, his fingers flying over the keyboard.

Ping.

Chris was oblivious to the computer chime until his monitor background went red. He pushed away from his desk and flew downstairs. He burst into the techs' office. "What do we know?"

The techs were checking the servers and isolating the problem. "We have a new intruder," one called out. "Paris, France, server."

Chris said, "Put it up on the big screen." The seventy-two-inch screen lit up with the three dimensional image of ICU's world-wide servers and their connections. Like a spider's web, each link was sensitive to touch by an outside computer. Every instance was cause for investigation and evasive action. The team maintained a record for every intrusion—how, who, where, when, and reason. "Can you tell what address it's checking?"

More typing. A customer file popped up in the lower right hand corner.

"That's not good." Chris was quiet for a minute. "Have you located the origin?"

A tech's fingers were flying over the keys. "It's new. Coming through as a search. Location hidden. Tracking now."

Chris said, "Use the dummy server and load with vanilla info. See if our intruder is cruising or digging."

One tech said, "On it."

Another added, "Yeah, and I'll tag the IP addresses and put them on our Watch List. Will get a name while I'm at it."

"Good," Chris said. "Let me know when all that's done. Then, downgrade the threat level to orange for the time being. Also, alert the client to threat. Recommend he initiate his phone back-up and archive. On our end, randomize his IP address with each internet access and ramp-up his firewall." He turned toward the door. "I'll be upstairs. Send me the info as soon as you can."

Less than an hour later, the results were in. The intruder, still unidentified, was digging. They were trying to access multiple sources through multiple servers. The user, now known as "Red Fox," was familiar with security techniques and looking for a backdoor. Two techs nullified each attempt and, in the process, strengthened the security codes.

The pings were insistent for the next few days, coming into ICU's secure servers from various directions. In all cases the threat was neutralized without revealing ICU's identity. Red Fox was elevated to a level red threat which appeared once a month at irregular intervals. Every time the techs identified the source, it changed.

Hide-'n-seek with Red Fox became a part of ICU's normal operations.

Chapter 9
Scarsdale, New York

Six years after her attack, twenty-seven-year-old Rachel Allen was tired. Tired of her life and her surroundings. Tired of herself and her endless list of shortcomings. Seated at her desk, she wanted to work on her overdue manuscript but couldn't put a coherent sentence together. Her meds were off.

Rachel stared out the window. The outside beckoned between the rivulets of rain that ran down the pane, but she had neither the energy nor desire to go. The empty driveway, bordered by mowed grass and small stands of evergreen shrubs, stretched to the street. When the occasional car went by, puddles of water erupted like the wings of eagles, only to crash and return to their former innocuous state. Just like her life.

Tears welled, again. Sobs rose from her core and

caught in her throat when her cell phone rang. Her finger hovered over REJECT as she read the Caller ID-"Ira." She'd avoided her agent for weeks because she couldn't write. She didn't want to deal with his wrath. But now, at rock bottom, whatever he said couldn't hurt her more. She took the call.

"Rachel?" Ira said.

"Yes."

"Finally. Do you know how often I've tried to get in touch? No, of course you don't. Doesn't matter. We're talking now. Tell me, how's the book?"

"Book?"

"Don't mess with me, Rachel," Ira said. "You've got a contract and I've got a family."

"Sorry."

"Sorry isn't acceptable. This is part of your book deal. The publisher needs your manuscript by December. Otherwise, we have to give back the advance, which we don't want to do, right?"

"Ira."

"Rachel, don't 'Ira' me. Stop screwing around."

Rachel pressed END.

A second later, Ira called back.

She answered and put the call on speaker. "What?"

"I'm coming up," he said. "I'm leaving now."

"Don't. It won't help."

"Rachel Allen, you listen to me. Pull yourself together and focus. This is not just *your* life you're playing around with."

Rachel stared at the phone.

"I know what it is," Ira said. "It's that isolation room of yours. It has sucked out all your ideas. You need more stimulation. You need life in your life. It's time to make a change. Move to New York City where I can keep an eye on you. You must take charge and reclaim your mind and energy. Do you hear me?"

No answer.

"Listen to me, Rachel. Get out of there—now!"

She ended the call without answering. She stood up, took two steps, collapsed on her un-made bed, and thought about Ira's words.

Her room used to be stimulating. Nothing had changed. The "eclectic office" style featured a huge white board, a magnetic green board, and a cork board—all covered with notes, time lines, and lists. Her book shelves were filled with reference materials and print-outs instead of storybooks and biographies that fed her young imagination and spirit.

On the top book shelf next to her bed sat her two published books and a framed picture. In the picture, a smiling seventeen-year-old Rachel Allen stood next to Presidential Candidate Barack Obama. Underneath the image, the inscription read, "Campaign Junior Intern of the Month."

Her first book, *"Rape: Power, Control, and Healing from a Woman's Perspective,"* Rachel wrote while in psychotherapy, as she'd dealt with the emotional trauma of her attack. She remembered those days when she seemed to be getting better, stronger. She even took private karate lessons with a local sensei. It gave a sense of control but didn't allay her fears.

Rachel's book had touched many readers, who'd reached out to her through emails and letters. Their support gave her strength. Her book made the required book list in women's studies courses around the country. As the demand for speaking engagements and book signings increased, she ventured out, eager to please her agent and publisher.

At her third book signing, a fight broke out in the crowd and she panicked. Separated from Ira and her parents, she stood on a chair to look for them. Someone recognized her, pointed, and screamed "Rachel Allen!" Mob mentality took over. Arms and hands—reaching, grabbing, pulling, pushing, touching, made her feel raped all over again.

A terrified Rachel fought back until the writhing human mass overwhelmed her. Her strength ebbed. She couldn't breathe. The darkness had begun to envelope her when the light appeared. The circle widened and she heard, "It's okay, Rachel. I've got you."

Her father pulled her to her feet and, along with her mother, hustled her out of the store and into the car for the forty-five minute ride home. Rachel shook for two days.

The experience sent her back into therapy and into the safety of her room. For her second book, *"Women and Human Rights: Not an Option,"* published eighteen months ago, she never left the house. She did all the research on-line, by phone, email, and snail mail. Once the book was out, she refused all public appearances.

Seven months ago, her shrink advised her to make a move, reconsider her options, and reach for the life she wanted.

"Bullshit," Rachel said, and quit.

Today, she realized it wasn't bullshit. She longed for the life she imagined—a life full of power, promise, invincibility, and love—and that life did not live here. Ira, damn him, was right. She had to change right now, or die where she lay.

It was time.

Decision made, Rachel's mind filled with all the complications of apartment hunting, packing, transportation, furniture, medical support, food shopping, notifications, clothes, and God knows what else. She was overwhelmed and exhausted before she'd flexed one muscle toward her goal. Her heavy eyelids closed and she slept.

Two hours later, Rachel woke up. New plan. One step at a time. First, she had to have a place to go. She went on-line and checked New York City apartment rentals and their neighborhoods. Between the income from her books and her grandmother's trust, she knew she could afford whatever she wanted—if she could find it.

Each time she found a possibility, she printed it. By the time she went to bed, Rachel had half a ream full of information.

The next morning, Rachel brought her printout and laptop to the breakfast table and sat down. Her mother seemed preoccupied as she washed dishes at the kitchen sink.

"Coffee?" Helene said without turning around.

"Sure. I didn't think you heard me come in."

"You were up late," Helene said and dried her hands. "Toast or bagel?"

"Bagel," Rachel said. "I *was* up late."

"Were you working?" Helene opened the refrigerator and retrieved cream cheese, butter, marmalade, and milk for the coffee. She put it all on the table.

"Sort of."

Helene brought two cups and the coffeepot to the table. After pouring the coffee, she pulled two bagels from the toaster oven and placed one in front of Rachel. She sat down, put the bagel on her plate, and placed her hands around the coffee cup.

Helene nodded toward the stack of paper and said, "What'd you bring down?"

Rachel had a sudden pang of doubt. She looked away from Helene, down at her food, and out the window. "I'm leaving."

Once the words were out, she looked at her mother.

Helene's eyes met Rachel's. "Leaving what?"

The answer exploded from Rachel mouth in one breath. "Leaving here. *This* time, I mean it. I'm going to New York City, move into an apartment, and make a new life for myself."

Rachel lowered her head and braced for her mother's tirade with all the reasons this wasn't going to happen. She had heard it all before. She waited, her heartbeat thundering in her ears.

Helene raised her eyebrows and peered at her daughter. She picked up a bagel, added a little cream cheese, and took a bite. After washing it down with a sip of coffee, she said, "Since when?"

Surprised at the reprieve, Rachel turned to her mother. "Since yesterday afternoon. After Ira called, I knew I had to do something." She touched the stack of paper. "These are apartment listings and neighborhood reviews." Rachel saw her mother's half smile. "Mom, this time is different. This time, I'm really going."

"Rachel, sweetheart," Helene said. "You do realize you haven't been out of the house more than ten times in the past few years, including the backyard. And now, you're moving to New York City?"

"I know. I know. I'm terrified."

Helene folded her arms and leaned back in her chair. "New York is filled with all sorts of people."

"I'll watch them from my windows. Practically everything can be ordered on-line and delivered. I'll figure it out because I have to."

Helene leaned forward, elbows on the table. "Rachel. Come on. What are you really talking about? What's wrong?"

"I'm...." Rachel's tears came unbidden, flowing down her cheeks. "I'm dying...," she said, using her fist to tap her heart several times, "in here."

Helene stared at Rachel, nodded, and called her husband. "Harry, I'm making chicken salad for lunch. When will you be home? ... Good. Uh-huh ...On your way, will you please bring home all the New York papers.... Those too....All of them.... Uh-huh. I'll explain when you get here."

Helene put the phone down and said to Rachel, "Your dad will be home in two hours. While you get dressed, I'll go over your research. When you come back, we'll compare it to this morning's listings."

Rachel got up and hugged her mom. "I love you."

Three and a half hours later, the Allen family had scrutinized the real estate rental sections of all the newspapers and magazines that Harry had brought home. The ones they liked, they checked out on Google Earth.

Rachel was about to give up when Helene handed her a folded newspaper. "Did you see this one?" She had her finger on an ad. "I don't remember it from any list and it's not circled."

The ad read:

> e38, 1000 sqf, 4fl apt w/scrty, gd
> nbrhd, cbl rdy, full ktn, w/d, 2br,
> 2 bth, 1 mo dpst, $5000/mo., ref
> req. Avail in 30 dys.
> 555.579.6083

"Nice, but a little expensive, don't you think?"

"If you want nice and safe, you'll have to pay for it."

"It's probably gone," Rachel said.

"Call anyway. You don't know if you don't ask."

Rachel picked up her phone and made the inquiry. "One minute, please." She covered the mouth piece and said, "The apartment is available and we can see it today."

Helene looked at Harry and he said, "Do it."

Rachel made the appointment, hung up, and called J&J Security. Jay and Jack arrived in their black mini-limo in less than half an hour. They made it to 215 Gramercy Avenue by four-fifteen. Jack found a parking space in front of the building. Jay escorted the two women to the stoop. A man in workman's overalls, dark T-shirt, and sneakers opened the door before they could knock. He stepped aside so they could enter. Rachel caught Jay's eye and held up her hand. He recognized the "I'm okay signal" and returned to the car.

Rachel figured the man at the door was in his fifties based on his salt and pepper hair. About six feet tall, he had broad shoulders, large rough hands, kind eyes, and a warm smile, punctuated with a gold tooth. His quiet confidence put her at ease. So much so she was ready to sign for the apartment sight unseen. But she knew better. Helene Allen had the last word.

As the door closed behind her, Rachel sighed and looked around. She and Helene stood in a small lobby decorated with black and white checkerboard floor tiles, two red Eames molded chairs, and a black iron side table. A desk and chair sat on the right. There was a coffee bar with a small sink in the back.

"I am Nikolai," the man said, as he sat behind the reception desk. Rachel heard a distinct middle-European accent. "Sit," he said, and gestured toward the two chairs. "I will tell Mr. Gregory you are here."

Chapter 10
Gramercy Avenue, New York City

For fun and profit, Chris Gregory had bought and rehabbed three contiguous five-story apartment buildings eight years ago. All were outfitted with his security systems, and he considered them the safest buildings in the city.

The first floor of 215, the middle building, served as the concierge for all three. ICU occupied the second floor, Chris's private office was on the third, and he lived in the duplex above that.

This afternoon, he was relaxing in his office, musing on a new system. His phone rang, and he answered without looking at the caller ID. On this line, it had to be Nikolai. He put his feet up on the computer table, crossed them at the ankles, leaned back, and said, "Hey."

"Excuse me?" a female voice said. "Are you the

person with an apartment for rent?"

Goose bumps popped out on his arms. "I am."

"Is it still available?"

His hand shook. "It is."

"My name is Rachel Allen. I'd like to make an appointment to see the unit. Today if possible."

He jerked forward but his ankles locked. He lost his balance and almost fell on his face. Regaining control of his body, he said, "Yes. Uh. Today would be fine."

"Good. We'll be there around four."

Chris hung up, stared at his phone, then at the framed picture on the wall beside his desk. The image showed first-time presidential candidate, Barack Obama, surrounded by the interns and the volunteers, Westchester main office. The names were on the bottom, left to right. He was in the back row, twenty-five and already a millionaire. Rachel Allen, high school senior, was in front. He smiled and held the picture. "Okay, Rachel Allen. Looks like I'll get a second chance."

To take his mind off their imminent meeting, he dove into code and lost track of time. He jumped when his phone rang. The ID said, "Nikolai."

"Your four, make that four-fifteen, appointment is here."

Chris saved his work, grabbed his tablet, and made it down to the lobby's back door in record time. He paused, ran his fingers through his hair, took a deep breath, and entered.

"Hi. I'm Chris Gregory."

The women rose in unison and smiled. "I'm Rachel Allen and this is my mother, Helene Allen."

Chris froze for a moment. The woman in front of him was "his" Rachel. Compared to his runway models, she was short at about five-foot-seven inches with curves. Her wavy brown hair, with its red highlights, provided an asymmetrical frame around her face. He looked into her deep brown eyes and returned her beautiful smile with his own.

He cleared his throat to make sure it worked. "I'm pleased to meet you both." He went over to the desk and picked up a file folder with a rent application, an apartment description, and floor plan. "Follow me, ladies," he said. "The apartment is on the fourth floor in the building next door, 213 Gramercy. And," he nodded toward the older man, "Nikolai is the indispensable concierge, manager, and handyman for this building, yours, and 217."

Nikolai said, "Enjoy the tour. We'll talk when you're done."

To enter 213 from the street, Chris swiped an access card and held the door open for the women. They stepped into the eight by ten glass vestibule, mailboxes to their right and a narrow table on the left. Chris crossed to the far side and used the keypad. The inner door opened to the interior lobby. Chris said, "And now we wait."

Rachel heard a soft hum. "What's that?"

"The elevators are programmed to scan the area and record images of anyone in the inner lobby before the doors open," Chris said. "If a face is hidden, it will wait until whoever it is looks up to check on the elevator's progress. It's another building security feature."

Once inside, the elevator doors didn't shut until Chris entered his key into the lock beside the numeral four. Seconds later, they were in the fourth floor hallway in front of the apartment. Chris unlocked the door with the same key he used in the elevator. The apartment door swung open and they entered, women first.

Chris said, "Would you like the grand tour?"

Helene said, "If it's okay with you, we'd like to check it out on our own first."

"No problem. I'll wait here," he said. "Um. Miss Allen, I have to ask. Are you Rachel Allen, the author?"

Rachel looked surprised. "I am. Have you read my books?"

"I have." Chris smiled. "And were you a high school intern for Obama's campaign?"

Rachel's eye brows went up. "I was. But how…."

"I'm the computer guy. Remember the fireworks? I was lucky to get out of there alive."

She smiled. "You're right. I could've killed you."

Helene took her daughter's arm, "C'mon, Rachel. Let's look at this apartment."

While they were gone, Chris activated his tablet and did a search on "Rachel Allen, author."

Rachel Allen had made the Ayatollah's hit list. It seems the spiritual leader did not like the references to Islam and Islamic beliefs in her discussion regarding the unacceptable treatment of women in the Arab world. After his death, many names (hers included) were downgraded but not discarded. Her book remained on the forbidden list, and the call went out to boycott her public appearances, if any.

As the women approached him, Chris said, "So, ladies, what do you think?"

Rachel said, "I like it."

Chris said, "Do you have any questions?"

Helene said. "The rooms are small. Can we lose the interior walls and go with an open space concept?"

"Yes," Rachel said. "Mom's right. I'd like to be able to see the whole apartment when I walk in—no nooks or crannies. Would that be possible?"

"Of course," Chris said. "Does that include the two bedrooms?"

"Oh, Mom's not moving in," Rachel said. "Just me."

"Excellent." Chris smiled. "Okay. Give me a second. I'll pull up the floor plan."

Helene stood by the window and looked up and down the street. She said, "There's no doorman. That's a deal breaker."

"Mrs. Allen," Chris said. "Besides the best security system in New York City, we have Nikolai. He is responsible for all non-tenant access to the building. Deliveries and pick-ups all go through him. For all tenant requests, he can either do it or arrange to have it done. We keep a list of very reliable workmen and service providers."

Rachel turned to face her mother, so Chris could neither see nor hear her.

Helene focused on her daughter and said, "Not so fast." To Chris she said, "What about the renovation cost and time frame?"

Rachel said, "Mr. Gregory...."

"Chris, please."

"Chris," Rachel said. "I don't want to lose this apartment, but the cost and time is a factor. How soon could you give us the figures?"

"Uh...."

Helene said, "Humph." She forced a shallow smile and raised an eyebrow. "Sometime today would be nice."

"I need a few minutes to pull up the floor plan and study the structural elements," Chris said. He removed several pieces of paper from the folder and slid them toward the women. "While I do that, look over these rental forms and agreements. If they're okay, fill them out. Don't sign until we go over the changes you'd like and I give you a rough estimate.

"How rough?" Helene said. "We don't want any surprises."

"I understand," Chris said. "I'll be right back."

He walked into another room and returned five minutes later. "Are you ready?"

Together they modified the apartment, and Rachel signed off on the changes and signed the contracts.

Rachel said, "I love it!" and gave her mother a hug and a kiss. But her mother wasn't finished yet.

"When will the apartment be ready, Mr. Gregory?"

"Three weeks to four months. But don't worry, Mrs. Allen. I'll make the renovation my top priority."

With a hint of a smile, Helene tilted her head slightly and shifted so her body leaned toward Chris. She stuck out her hand and crooked her first finger at him several times. He leaned toward her. As his ear came close to her lips, she said, "Sooner is better."

Nikolai watched the women leave. Chris came through the front door and dropped the rental folder on the desk. Nikolai opened it. "Hey. What is this?"

"It's a rental agreement."

"Where are the standard reports like the credit check, the financials, proof of income, personal references, and psychological profile? And as manager of this complex, I have not interviewed them yet."

"Her. Just Rachel Allen."

"Fine," Nikolai said. "*I* have not interviewed her yet."

"No need. If she wants to rent one of my apartments, she's got it. In fact, if she'd suggested I move the whole building three inches to the left, I would've agreed. It's a no brainer. I'm not letting her go again."

"Do you know how illogical you sound? I am not used to it. I need a couple of hours, on the clock, to adjust."

Chris laughed. "Don't even think about it."

"Does she know how you feel?"

"No. She didn't even recognize me. I had to remind her that we'd met ten years ago."

"That does not sound promising."

"Right now, all that matters is she's here, and I'll give her the apartment she wants."

"Which is what," Nikolai said, "exactly?"

"Um. Uh. About that."

Chapter 11
Gramercy Avenue, New York City

Three weeks and four days later—a New York City record—the apartment was ready. Rachel moved in the following Saturday.

Nikolai, under specific orders from Chris, made sure Rachel's move didn't encounter any problems.

"The truck is empty," Nikolai said. "I made sure before I gave them your check."

"Thank you. You've been a great help."

Nikolai removed the music pod's ear phones and let them rest around his neck. "Not so difficult," Nikolai said. "I have seen worse."

Rachel, with a furrowed brow, stood by the window and surveyed the apartment. She held her left arm around her waist while her right hand stroked her chin.

Nikolai said, "What is wrong?"

Rachel said, "Mom and I spent days on my floor plan and now that I see it, it feels all wrong."

He spoke, using his hands for emphasis. "Do not worry, Miss Allen. I will stay until you are happy."

She stared at him for a moment, dropped her arms, and smiled. "Okay, Nikolai. Let's do it."

Together they cleared the space and manipulated the main living room pieces until the arrangement pleased her. In the dining area, Rachel tripped on a throw rug and fell against Nikolai, who was facing away from her. He was knocked off balance, and she slid to the floor. He recovered first, ear pods hanging on his chest, and offered his hand to Rachel.

She waved him away. "I'm okay, thanks." She got up and cocked her head. "What's that music?"

Nikolai looked at his ear-pods and smiled. "Gypsy folk music. My family is Roma. Although that term refers to all those of my culture, we *are* from Romania. However, as Gypsies we wandered all over middle Europe and Russia. Sadly, many were gassed in concentration camps during the Nazi's ethnic cleansing campaign." With that, he dry spat three times. "A curse upon them and theirs."

"I'm so sorry." Rachel paused. "Ummm. I have an odd request. Would you be open to listening to one of my dream sequences? I'm having trouble understanding what it means."

"Of course. My mother and her mother and her mother's mother were dreamers and interpreters of dreams."

"Here's how it works with me. When my conscious or subconscious mind gets hold of an impression, I tend to dream. It often takes two or more for the dreams' essence to reveal itself. In this case, for reasons I don't understand, I've dreamt about you since we met."

"Maybe I have dazzled you with my gold tooth," Nikolai said, smiling, "and my Baltic charm."

"Maybe," Rachel said. "But the dreams weren't charming. The first few were non-specific. In the last one I saw you alongside a caravan. I heard music—the same music you're listening to now.

"When the music ended, green forests turned black. Smoke filled the air. It swirled around your body as you walked toward me. It was you and it wasn't you. Does that make sense?"

"It is your dream. What do you think?"

"If I had to interpret, I'd say you fought in a war, although I didn't see a uniform. The smoke camouflaged you. So you were an unseen soldier. My guess is that you fought in the resistance. Is that true?"

Nikolai's face darkened. "I do not talk about this. It was a terrible time. Friend against friend. Neighbor against neighbor. Terrible atrocities. All best forgotten."

They stared at each other for a moment. Rachel nodded. "I understand. I'm sorry."

Nikolai rubbed his hands together, smiled and said, "Come. We still have much to do."

Pre-Rachel Allen's occupancy of 213-4, Nikolai had the same schedule every morning.

Upon arriving at work, he made a cup of strong coffee and took it to his desk where he checked his email for instructions or requests from Chris and the tenants. He added the information to his work schedule, detailed on the calendar he shared with Chris.

In the quiet aftermath, he drank the rest of his coffee and leaned back, closed eyes, hands resting on his stomach—his ten minutes of yoga-like meditation before wrestling with the day's agenda. And then Rachel moved in to her apartment, and Chris moved into the lobby.

Every morning, with prescient timing, Chris slouched in as Nikolai finished his updates. Chris got a cup of coffee, feigned interest in the work schedule, and then asked about Rachel. In the past two days, he'd even come down at lunch time.

Today, Chris had dark circles under his eyes. His hair, at best, was finger-combed. He wore the rumpled version of yesterday's clothes. He shuffled over to the coffee machine. He filled a stoneware mug and added creamer. Cup in hand, he shuffled over to the closest guest chair, sat down, crossed his legs, and stirred his coffee. No "Hello." No "Good Morning."

The concert of non-linear cacophony began at the first clink of metallic spoon against ceramic cup.

Nikolai's face scrunched up at the nerve-wracking noise. He swiveled in his chair to face Chris. "Sorry. I did not hear you come in."

Chris stared at his coffee cup and said, "Bullshit." He looked up. "So, what's on the schedule today?"

Nikolai pursed his lips and forced a smile. "It is on the calendar."

Chris stirred his coffee. "Good."

Nikolai grimaced. "Chris, why are you here? You should be upstairs working. You have a big project, right? With a deadline."

Chris didn't answer or look up. Nikolai left his desk and took the seat next to his friend. "Or maybe you want my job?"

Without humor, Chris said, "Very funny."

Nikolai said, "So tell me, what is it? What can I do?"

Chris shook his head. "It's Rachel. She treats me

like a stranger." He looked at Nikolai. "Does she ever talk to you?"

"Well, yesterday I delivered two packages and she invited me in for tea."

"Did she mention me?"

"Let me think," Nikolai said. He rubbed his chin while he inspected the ceiling. After a few seconds, he looked at Chris and said, "No, not you. However, she did call me cute, sweet, charming, helpful, handy, and perceptive."

"Did you tell her you're married with three children?"

Nikolai slapped his forehead. "You know, that never came up."

Chris didn't laugh.

"Come on, Chris. You must stop moping around. Just do it. Ask her out. Pretend she's one of those society women you used to date."

"I can't. She thinks I'm a jerk. She doesn't trust me or talk to me."

"Ridiculous. What is the real reason?"

"I feel like a tongue-tied ten-year-old with a crush on my teacher."

Nikolai made a fist and punched Chris in the shoulder. "Time to man up, Chris. Go do it."

"Ouch!" Chris rubbed the offended area. "I just said I can't."

Nikolai put his hands together and shook them. "Please. I beg you. Do it for me. You make us both crazy."

"Man-up, huh." Chris set the cup down on the table. "Maybe you're right. God knows I've got to do something."

An hour later, Chris was showered, shaved, and

dressed in pressed khaki pants, white shirt, and tie. He knocked on Rachel's door. The red light blinked on the security camera.

The door opened. Rachel, dressed in sweats, had a pencil tucked behind her ear and a legal pad in her hand.

Before she could say anything, in an officious tone of voice, Chris said, "Greetings. I'm here for your quarterly appliance check."

She didn't smile. "Sure. Okay." She turned her back on him and left the door open.

The first time he'd tried this, it was for a security check. She had followed him all over the apartment with her phone in hand and Nikolai's number on screen. Her thumb remained over CALL for his whole visit. She did the same thing for the window-door check and the plumbing check. Chris smiled at this change of behavior.

He followed her into the apartment. Ignoring him, Rachel sat on the couch, pulled the pencil from its perch, and commenced writing on the yellow pad. He stopped at the kitchen area and looked at her. She didn't look up. He was on his own.

He opened and closed the refrigerator door and the freezer door, shutting them both with more force than necessary. The sound was absorbed by the rubber gasket. He opened the oven door and let it snap close. It didn't. It had the soft-close feature. He opened the microwave door and swung it close—click. Each time he made a noise, he waited for a reaction from Rachel. She didn't seem to notice.

His *coup de grâce* was the dishwasher. He opened and shut it with a push. Another slow close. He turned it on. It was so quiet that even he was surprised. Rachel remained oblivious. Only the washer and dryer remained and they were across the apartment, in the bathroom. He was half way there when Rachel spoke.

"Where are you going?"

He turned to her, eyebrows lifted in surprise. "I didn't mean to interrupt you. I'm going to check the washer and dryer."

"They're fine."

"It's my job."

"Maybe, but it's my mess in there."

"I don't mind."

"I do."

"Fine. But if there's a problem…."

"I'll call you," Rachel said and returned to her writing.

Chris walked over to the couch. "When?"

"When what?" She looked at him.

"When will you call me?"

"When I meet my publisher's deadline, clean the bathroom, and the washer or dryer breaks down." She returned to her writing.

He sat down in the chair closest to her. "This week?"

She gave him a quizzical look, put her things on the coffee table, tucked one foot under her, leaned back, and said, "So what's going on with you and appliances?"

He laughed, leaned forward, elbows on knees. "Six great answers just flashed through my mind, but I want to be honest. I'm here because of you." He took a deep breath. "Would you go out with me?"

Rachel's face changed from surprise to fear, warm to cool, open to closed, in a micro second. Chris shook his head and stood. "I'm sorry. I didn't mean to upset you. I just had to ask." He headed for the door.

Rachel got up and took two steps toward him.

"Wait, don't go."

Chris turned.

"I'm flattered. Really. But it's complicated. The simplest explanation is that I've become sort of an agoraphobic hermit."

Nervous laughter caught in Chris' throat. He searched her face. She wasn't kidding. "You don't go out and you don't date?"

"Exactly. Otherwise I'd say yes."

"Okay, let me think," Chris said, walking toward her. "Umm, how about if I get take out and we have dinner here? As landlord and tenant. See if we can progress to friends. Does that work for you?"

Rachel looked down at her hands, "Yes, if that will end all these apartment checks?" She lifted her eyes to his.

Assuming his inspector persona, he said, "Well, Miss Allen, I can't make that promise. Who knows what will need checking? And when?"

Chapter 12
Gramercy Avenue, New York City

Six weeks later and now good friends, Rachel and Chris shared a take-out dinner from the local Indian restaurant and watched *Masterpiece Theater*—she curled up on the side chair, he stretched out on the couch.

Chris picked up the remote, pressed the pause button, and got to his feet. "Ready for some ice cream?"

"Sure," Rachel said. "And after, we need to talk. Or, more accurately, I need to talk to you."

Chris sat down, angling his body so he faced her. "Sounds serious. I don't like to put off important conversations. If you want to talk, let's do it now."

Rachel looked down. "This is hard. I've never had to explain myself before." She paused for a few seconds before she looked up at him. "Are you sure about the ice cream? I could use a hit of hot fudge right about now."

"Come on, Rachel. Spit it out. Once it's out in the open, we can deal with whatever it is."

"Okay. You're right." She played with her fingers. "Chris, you've become very important to me."

"Ah," he said. "First, the good news."

She didn't laugh. "That makes this even more difficult because I don't want to waste your time."

"I'm listening."

Rachel stared at him as she tried to get the words out. Uncertainty and fear muted her attempt. She flew off the couch and into the kitchen. "I need a drink." She poured a shot of vodka and downed it. Sighing, she put the glass on the counter, stood up straight, and returned to her chair.

She looked at Chris, took a deep breath, and said, "This is hard for me."

Chris nodded encouragement. "Tell me anyway."

Without taking her eyes off him, her fingers explored her cuticles and picked at rough edges. "Okay, here goes." She cleared her throat. "You know how I'm always a little distant? Never getting close—physically?"

"Of course," he said. "But for some, it takes time." When Rachel didn't answer right away, he sat a little taller and leaned forward. "I hope you don't think I'm rushing you."

Rachel shook her head, "It's not you." She paused, focusing on her clasped hands, fingers tightening and releasing. "I was raped near the end of my senior year at college."

"Rachel...."

She looked up, eyes wet. "Please, don't talk. Let me get this out. It's emotional and difficult. Unfortunately it's the only way to get past it and not let it suck the life out of me—out of us. Okay?"

Chris nodded.

The words tumbled out. "Freedom College is a 'green' campus. That includes outdoor lighting activated by motion sensors. One April evening, I took a short cut from the library to my dorm. The lights didn't go on as usual. I didn't realize it right away. When I did, I stopped. At that moment, someone grabbed me. He dragged me into the bushes and threw me on the ground.

"My attacker was a student. I recognized him from my classes. He had asked me out, but I'd refused. I had just broken up with my fiancé and wasn't ready to date. I never gave it a second thought. He must have carried the rejection around for weeks and weeks. I had no idea he would come after me.

"At first, when I realized who it was, I tried talking to him, but it didn't help. He was angry and brutal. He hurt me, inside and out. The bruises healed but I lost my sense of control, invincibility, and safety. Since then, I've lived in isolation. As for the rapist, he died several weeks later in a freak bus accident outside a Paris soccer field."

Chris reached out to her.

Rachel held up her hand. "Please, don't. Let me finish." She licked her dry lips. "Even though that happened seven years ago, I still suffer from random flashbacks, which cause panic attacks. The sound of ripping fabric, the smell of mulch or the mix of cigarettes and alcohol or the flash of a knife can trigger a total physical and mental recall. When I'm outside this apartment, I become hyper-vigilant. My anxiety level hits the roof. My head looks like a lighthouse on speed. I jump at every sound.

"I'm lucky. I can afford to hire Jay and Jack, my security team. They behave like my friends, but they run interference and make sure I'm safe. With them around, I can almost relax.

"Another fallout from the rape is that I have major trust issues. Any invasion into my personal space sets me off. I recoil if I'm touched or grabbed." Rachel paused. "I may look normal here in my apartment, but I have a lot of baggage which may never go away." She looked up at Chris.

"I'm so sorry," Chris said, jaw muscles flexing. "No one should go through that. No one. It makes me want to rip the guy's heart out with my bare hands."

"I know. Believe me."

Chris said, "You've come a long way."

Rachel nodded. "I've gotten a lot of help from my therapist and on-line support communities dealing with the same issues as mine. We help each other by sharing our stories and our recovery process."

"I applaud your fight for normalcy, whatever that means."

"I *have* come a long way. But, Chris, I still have a long way to go. I know I'll never be the person I was. And I can't promise I'll overcome my fears."

"I understand," Chris said. "Thank you for telling me. I'm touched by your trust." He relaxed against the back of the couch, never taking his eyes off her. He took his time. "Now I've got a confession."

Rachel rearranged her body, resting her arms on the chair and placing both feet on the floor. If he was going to walk, she wanted to be ready and strong. With an intake of breath, she braced for the words she didn't want to hear.

"Rachel, you're the first woman I've ever wanted to spend time with, to really get to know. I'm not walking away so fast. I get that you have challenges, but we'll face them together and see how it goes. I've got a good feeling that in the end, it will be well worth the wait."

Rachel let her breath out and smiled. "Me too."

"On one condition."

Rachel lifted her eyebrow. "What condition?"

"Ice cream sloppy sundaes. You make sure you always have the fixings on hand, and I'll make sure your freezer's stocked."

She laughed. "Deal."

Chapter 13
Gramercy Avenue, New York City

Three months later, despite working long hours to meet ever looming deadlines, Rachel and Chris managed to find a lot of together time.

They shared take-out dinners, picnic-style, and the evening's entertainment—TV, either the news or "G" rated movies, Scrabble, thousand-piece puzzles on her dining table, or crossword puzzles on his tablet.

He'd often send her a text and show up with lunch or knock on the door to come in and talk. On his birthday, she gave him a large vintage brass skeleton key, which she identified as the symbolic key to her apartment.

One morning after her workout, Rachel showered and, instead of her usual sweats, she put on jeans, a silk T-shirt, a casual jacket, and low-heeled wedges. She had plans. When she emerged from her dressing room, she saw Chris in the kitchen with coffee and bagels.

"About time. Coffee's almost cold," he said without looking up. When he did, he whistled. "Nice outfit. You look great. Your mom in town?" He sat down at the table.

"No. I'm going out. Have some shopping to do."

"Out? Really? Shopping? What kind of shopping?"

Rachel sat down and unwrapped the bagel he brought from Alfie's, the restaurant and take-out place across the street. She took a bite and reached into her pocket, extracted a piece of paper, and handed it to him.

Chris scanned the handwritten list and looked at her. "You're shopping for a new computer, printer, and phone?"

"I am," Rachel said. "My system is too slow. As I type, it seems the words aren't even formed on the screen by the time I've finished the sentence. I print and it feels like I could paint the apartment before the printer engages, much less prints. It's driving me crazy. Plus my phone contract is up. I'm going to upgrade the whole antiquated mess today."

"I'm coming," Chris said, and he started to bag the garbage on the table.

"Stop," Rachel said, putting her hand on the wrapper in front of him. "Not necessary. I've done the research. I know what I want."

Chris looked at her. "You do know I'm one of the top Fortune 500's 'go to' tech guys, don't you?"

"Of course."

"So, tell me, how would it look if I let you buy less than the best? It'd ruin my reputation if word got out." Chris slumped in his chair with his head in his hands, Rachel's list sticking out from his splayed fingers. "All those years of hard work down the drain.

Gone. Kaput. I'll die an ignominious death."

Rachel laughed. "Very dramatic. I promise I won't tell anyone I know you." She plucked her list out of Chris' hand. "I'll be fine."

Chris jumped up. "I'm going. What time?"

"Jack and Jay will be here in thirty minutes."

"Wait for me. I have to clear my schedule and change. I'll be back in twenty."

An hour later, with Jay riding shotgun, Jack idled the car at the curb in front of Best Buy. Jay got out, circled the car, and waited outside the rear door with his hand on the handle.

"Rachel," Chris said. "Are you sure you want to do this? There're a lot of people here. We could order all this equipment on-line. And I bet it'd be cheaper."

Rachel hesitated. "I know. This is not about money. I've been feeling pretty good and wanted to get out. It might be overwhelming, but maybe this time I'll get through it. In any case, it's time to try. Besides, I'll have Jack and Jay."

Chris raised his eyebrows. "And..."

"And you," she said, laughing. Rachel looked at Jay through the window, watched him scan the area. Done and satisfied, he opened the door.

Rachel entered the store with Chris in front of her and Jay behind. As they walked the aisles, the men, in silent agreement, kept Rachel between them. It didn't help. Her earlier resolve and bravado caved as the sight and sound pandemonium took its toll.

People talking. "Don't touch that!" "Frank, where are you?" "I was here first." "I told you only the stuff on sale!" TV screens blaring. "Giants on the one yard line." Music playing. "Let it go, Let it go...." "All about that bass...." Screechy announcements over the loud speaker. "Electronics please pick-up. Electronics."

Eyes wide, heart pounding, Rachel surged into hyper-vigilant mode—head turning side to side, eyes darting here and there, unable to focus, and short breaths escalating to hyperventilation. Her pace slowed and Jay bumped into her as Chris forged three steps ahead. Jack appeared and caught her as she stumbled.

"Do you want to sit down?" he asked.

Rachel shook her head and called to Chris, "Not so fast." He rushed to her side. "I can't breathe," she said in a whisper. "I need a minute."

Jack said, "We'll stay with her. She'll be fine."

Chris said, "Is that okay, Rachel?"

She nodded, unfolded her fingers, and dropped the damp crumbled sheet of paper into Chris' hand.

He took it and said, "Don't worry. I'll take care of everything."

Rachel turned to Jack, "I'm feeling sick."

He produced a paper bag, snapped it open, and formed a collar at the top. "Here. Breathe."

A few breaths later, Rachel felt better. Jack and Jay escorted her to the Ladies Room. Removed from the chaos, she cooled her anxiety with cold water and paper towel compresses to her wrists and the back of her neck. The panic subsided. She splashed cold water on her face, ran her fingers through her hair, and adjusted her jacket. She stood for a minute in front of her reflection. She nodded her head and said, "Let's do this."

Accompanied by Jack and Jay, Rachel went to the computer section. Chris met them and said, "Follow me." The small parade wove through several aisles until they stood in front of an array of laptops.

Chris said, "This is the one you picked. But, if I may, I suggest you get the model next to it. It has more power, more memory, and a faster processor."

Rachel said, "I don't see a problem. They seem to be about the same size and weight."

Chris said, "Why don't you test the keyboard while I get a cart."

When he came back, she said, "I'm okay with your suggestion, but it's way more powerful than I need."

Chris checked the shelves, found the box, and put it in the cart. After they chose the printer, Chris led them to the accessories section. He selected a stylus for the laptop's touch screen, several thumb drives, and three digital external hard drives for rotating full system backups.

Next they went over to the phones. Somewhere between the cameras and the mobile phones, Rachel experienced a glint of light. "Knife." She started to shake. "He's got a knife." Jack and Jay sandwiched her.

"We've got this, Rachel," Jack said. "You're safe."

She pushed them away as she pivoted, eyes darting, perspiration dripping down the sides of her face. "Where's the knife?" She looked at Jay and then at Jack.

"There's no knife," Jack said. "You're safe."

"Where is he?" She looked at Jay. "Where is he?"

Jay said, "No one's here to harm you."

Chris stepped in front of her. "Rachel, you're with me. Jay and Jack are here. You're safe."

Rachel zoned out—her face lost color, blank eyes widened and narrowed, her head leaned to one side and then the other. "I've got to get out of here."

Chris stepped in front of her and put his hands out to stop her. "Rachel, it's Chris."

She stared at him. As awareness returned, her tremors stopped, color flooded her face, and her fog lifted. She smiled. "Chris. Guys. Why are we standing here?" Three faces, each with one eyebrow raised, looked at her. She laughed. "You look like skeptical triplets." She took a few steps and turned. "I'm fine. Let's go."

At the mobile phones display, Rachel said, "Don't even start." She bumped him out of the way with her hip. "I want the same brand as my old one."

"I think…."

"I know. But I don't want to learn another system."

"Fine." Chris threw up his hands in surrender and checked out the phone extras. He picked out an ear piece, a screen protector pack, and five stands—one for her bedroom, bathroom, kitchen, dining table, and living room table, as well as a clip-on for her treadmill handle.

Chris dumped his selections into the cart and Rachel said, "What's all that?"

He said, "Everything you'll need."

"We'll see," she said. "I think I'm done. May I see my list?" She held out her hand.

Chris didn't give it to her. "We're not done."

"Let me see." Rachel held out her hand.

"Sorry, no can do. I've made some adjustments."

"Chris, come on."

"Follow me." Chris grabbed the cart. He led Rachel and company into the home theater section. "Close your eyes. I'm going to put my hands on your shoulders and move you into position. Okay?"

At the words "hands on," Jay took a step closer to Rachel. He looked at Chris and said, "I'm sorry, no hands." He angled his body to maintain a distance between Rachel and Chris.

Rachel nodded. "Not closing my eyes either."

"Look," Chris said. "All I want to do is surprise you."

"How about I walk backwards?" she said.

"May I put my hands on your shoulders just to guide you?"

"You may try. If I don't freak out, it's okay."

Chris positioned himself in front of Rachel and placed his hands on her shoulders. She didn't flinch but her body stiffened.

"Relax. I've got you," he said. She rolled her shoulders. "Now, three steps to the left. That's it. Back up. Feel the chair? Good. Sit down."

She was engulfed by the soft comfortable chair. When Chris stepped away, Rachel saw the largest TV monitor she had ever seen. "It's like sitting in the first row in a movie theater."

"So," Chris said. There was uncharacteristic excitement in his voice. "Is this not an amazing home theater system?"

Chris sat down on the chair next to her. "I checked it out. It's the newest thing. It'll bring the whole world into your living room."

"Come on, Chris,"` she said, hitting the chair's arms. "Let's go. I already own a TV."

He didn't move. "Too small, trust me. This is a seventy-inch screen. Movies will be amazing."

"Sure, because we'll be *in* the movie."

A runaway train crossed the huge screen and the chairs began to shake.

Chris laughed. "These seats are wired to respond to the noise."

She looked at him as he enjoyed the moment—handsome and full of energy. She must have had an odd look on her face because he said, "I knew you'd be surprised, but you look stunned." His laugh was infectious and she laughed with him.

"You're crazy. No one needs this. It must be a man thing."

"And I'm just the man who wants it." He got up. "Wait here. I'll be right back."

Rachel reached for her phone to check her messages. She didn't get a chance to read even one. He was back with his hand extended to her. "Come on," Chris said. "Get up. No time to rest."

Rachel tried to stand but the pillows held her captive. She offered her hand to Chris. He took it and helped her to her feet. She moved with ease as if they did this all the time. Her hand fit in his like two puzzle pieces. Still, she had to make a conscious decision not to pull away. She glanced at Jack and raised her free hand. She was okay.

Jack and Jay didn't interfere, but they didn't leave them alone.

Chris led them to smaller screens, and they agreed the sixty-inch might be a better choice. Still holding hands, he showed her the Blu-ray players.

"The system comes equipped with WiFi, so you'll be able to stream from on-line services. Still it's a good idea to get one of these. And that," he said, pointing to a box with a picture of a long black rectangle, "is for surround sound." He dropped her hand to put the boxes in the cart. Done, he held out his hand and she took it.

In the electronics area, Rachel watched Chris check the contents of each box and pick out the necessary cords, connectors, cables, and screen cleaner. At last, he announced, "We're done."

Jack said, "I'll get the car and meet you out front. Jay'll stay with you."

Two sales people helped them through check out. Rachel paid for her computer, printer, and phone. Chris paid for the rest.

On the way home, Chris said, "Well, that was fun."

"I could tell. You were in your element." Rachel paused. "I'm glad you came."

"Me too."

After a few minutes of silence, she said, "So, about the home theater system. Where will you put it?"

"In your apartment," Chris said. "I'll sync it with your new laptop and phone. You'll be able to work out on your treadmill and feel like you're in the Alps. Or you can watch the live videos from the Bronx Zoo or opera from the Met or a movie."

"Tell me you're kidding," Rachel said. "I don't need it and it's too big. Chris, please, take it back or use it in your apartment."

"Don't worry. It'll fit. You'll love it."

Rachel put on a pouty face. "You mean you'll love it."

Chris laughed. "Okay, okay. If you don't like it after I get it installed, I promise I'll dismantle it and take it home. How's that?'

"That's an offer I can't refuse."

By dinner time, Chris finished the installation. He integrated all the state-of-the-art electronics. He fell backward onto the couch with several remotes in his hand and patted the cushion next to him. "Okay, Rachel. Let's take this baby for a test drive." She sat down. "Watch this," he said. With a magician's flourish, he selected a remote, pushed a button, and the TV screen lit up with a re-run of *Castle*.

"Amazing."

"All part of the service, Ma'am," he said, a big grin on his face. "Now, how about you rustle up some food for your hungry man?"

"No problem, cowboy." She pulled out her new phone and ordered Chinese. Twenty-seven minutes later, take-out boxes filled the coffee table. They ate while *Hugo*, with all its intricate mechanics, filled the huge screen.

As Chris watched the movie, Rachel watched him—the lines of his face, strong jaw, topaz eyes, and irregular nose. Her fingers ached to experience the texture change from his forehead to his temples, eyebrows to eyelids to eyelashes, down into the sandpaper of his five o'clock shadow. Her lips pursed. His perfect asymmetrical lips, soft and relaxed, made her want to touch them, feel them with her fingers, with her lips. Her nerve ends pulsed. *Stop it! This is going nowhere.*

Chris hit pause. "Ready for dessert?"

"Sure," she said, grateful for the distraction. "There's coffee almond fudge in the freezer."

"Don't get up," he said, putting his hand in front of her. "I'll get it."

As he crossed in front of her on his way to the kitchen, Rachel wondered what he looked like under his loose clothing. *Stop!* She changed position and moved the dinner debris from the coffee table to the take-out box.

Done, she looked up to see Chris at the kitchen counter making the sundaes. She leaned back and tucked a leg under her, hands in her lap. She visualized kissing him, holding him, touching him. But, and that was a big "but," based on years of therapy, could she ever let him "touch" her?

"So, what do you think?" Chris asked, as he handed her huge bowl of ice cream drowned in hot fudge.

It took her a couple of seconds to realize he meant the ice cream. "Oh, my God," she said. "Way too much." She ate it anyway.

At the movie's end, Chris turned off the TV and looked at her. "Happy?"

"Definitely. I'll give you a check in the morning."

"Save your money. I bought this. It's mine and I'm sharing. I know you didn't need it. You were right. It's a 'guy thing,' so I'm guilty as charged." He held up his hands in surrender.

"Well, if you put it that way…"

"Good. That's settled." He stood up. "I've got to get back and do some work for an early teleconference."

Rachel walked him to the door. "Thank you for all your help today. I enjoyed it."

"Me too." Chris grinned.

They both stood there, grinning at each other—waiting.

Now what? Shake his hand? Give him a kiss on the cheek? Touch his arm? His face?

Chris reached for the door handle, as Rachel took a step forward and hugged him with a light touch, her shoulders close to his chest but her body arched away, as she would a casual family friend.

His arms didn't move. An awkward moment gone awry. A heated flush spread from her chest to her cheeks. She released her tentative hold as his arms encircled her, nice at first then tighter than expected.

Without warning, she couldn't breathe. Her hands got clammy and her eyes watery. She dropped her arms and gave a light push on his biceps. He released her. She stepped back two steps and smiled. "Thank you, again, for today."

"No problem. See you tomorrow."

That night, Rachel lay in bed, wide awake. She relived the hug a hundred times. *I'm so stupid. Never should have hugged him. When he didn't respond right away, I should have stepped back and apologized. He'd probably say there's nothing to apologize for. Maybe I'd be so grateful, I'd hug him again. And he'd hug me—really hug me. Then what? I'd have a major panic attack. Well,*

I'm glad that didn't happen. Still, it was so awkward. What was I supposed to do? Well, whatever I did, I did. He probably thinks I can't hug right. I'm so out of practice. Now what, if anything? Another hug? A kiss? Sex?

The thought of "sex" sent an anxious shiver through her body. She clutched the covers for warmth and security. Her breath came in short gasps. Beads of perspiration swelled on her forehead until their weight sent rivulets down her temples and into her hair. Words swirled into images that caused the room to spin. She squeezed her eyelids shut and formed her mantra, "Too soon. Don't start."

She repeated the words. The rhythm dictated her breathing. The anxiety subsided. She fell asleep wrestling with her dilemma—live with her demons or risk her sanity for love.

The next morning, Rachel logged on to her new computer. While it initiated the start-up programs, the screen filled with fireworks.

Chapter 14
East Side, New York City

At PRAISE Foundation headquarters, Ted Donovan prepared for his board meeting. The high profile PRAISE Foundation, well-known for its humanitarian work and prestigious awards, distributed donations to newsworthy and desperate causes throughout the global community. Ted had no doubt that the board would be pleased

In its shadow, Ted continued to carry out successful seductions. Lucy Kilmer, an exceptional Operations Manager, took over the distant and more complex targets as well as the lucrative, privately funded Vanderhagen directives. Working together and without leaving a trace, they improved communities and changed the world.

As he prepared PRAISE's quarterly report, his phone rang—dum de dum dum. He grimaced at the

Dragnet themed ring tone and answered.

"Ted, my boy," Philip Vanderhagen said, his voice warm and inviting.

Ted put a smile in his voice. "Philip, I didn't know you were in town."

"Just flew in. How about drinks at the club around five?" Vanderhagen said. "I'll send a car for you."

"I'll be there."

Ted walked outside at four-thirty. A limousine rounded the corner, pulled up to the curb, and parked. The driver got out and opened the rear door. Ted got in and almost sat on Vanderhagen. "Well, this is a surprise."

The men shook hands. Vanderhagen put his encrypted SATCOM phone on the seat and offered him a drink. Ted accepted.

"Ted, I wanted to talk to you before we get to the club." Vanderhagen reached into his brief case, exchanging the SATCOM for a tablet. "In today's world one can't live without these things." He released the arm rest between them and put the tablet on it. He started the whiteboard application, pressed the setting button, and turned RECORD off. Using a stylus, he wrote, "*New sponsor.*"

Ted nodded. Vanderhagen touched ERASE and wrote, "*Political problem. Imanuela Meyerson,*" and hit ERASE.

Imanuela Myerson, a human rights lawyer and advocate, wrote an editorial for the *New York Times*. In it, she criticized presidential candidate Governor Franklin Sandford's proposed initiatives, calling them ineffectual. With a lot of money and political currency riding on Sandford, his backers, including Vanderhagen, labeled her a threat that needed to be excised.

Ted said, "This is crazy. You can't be serious."

"Please," Vanderhagen said. "Let's not dredge up ideology again. It's the right action for the right reason." He wrote, "*A million cash to you plus expenses and a matching donation to PRAISE.*"

Ted looked out the window. The sidewalks were filled with people that had no idea how tenuous their grasp of reality or their future. "I don't need the money."

Vanderhagen said, "You'd deny PRAISE's largesse to millions of suffering displaced persons based on a technicality? You know we both want to make the world a better place. For that, we need a unified global understanding. And for *that*, the right people must be in the right place at the right time. Need I explain—again?"

Ted held up his hand. "Consider it done."

Later that evening, Ted called Lucy. "We have a new target. Seduce as soon as possible but raise no flags until after New Year's."

"Suggestions?"

"I'll make sure our target gets a PRAISE award. The rest I leave to you and your team. Let me know what you need from me and when."

"And you? I know these political requests make you angry."

"I'll be okay. I've got a date with a pugilistic pedophile."

Chapter 15
Gramercy Avenue, New York City

One April morning, Chris Gregory arrived at Rachel Allen's apartment with a bag of groceries and cooked a big breakfast, a weekly ritual that began New Year's Day. They spent the morning eating and reading the Sunday papers, with CBS's *Sunday Morning* in the background, followed by various newsmakers.

Around one o'clock, Chris got up to leave. He leaned over to give Rachel a parting kiss on her forehead. This time, to her surprise and his, she caught his head with both hands and gave him a butterfly kiss. She released him and waited.

He returned the kiss and pulled her to her feet, and took her in his arms. She yielded, felt him, kissed him deeply.

Chris disengaged. She looked at him. "What's wrong?"

"I just want to be sure that you're up for this," Chris said. "So to speak."

"As much as you are," she said, glancing down and grinning.

"I'm serious," Chris said. "I love you."

"I love you too."

He kissed her. "And that's why I'm leaving. I'm going home to take a cold shower. We are too good together to mess up because we went too fast. Didn't take our time."

She traced his lips with her finger.

He moved her hand away and sat down. He tapped the cushion right next to him and she obeyed, nestling into him. Chris said, "I want you more than you can imagine, but let's do this in stages."

Rachel nodded. "So, I'm curious. For planning and preparation purposes, how many stages do you figure?"

"Hmmm." Chris shifted his body so his legs were stretched out and crossed on the coffee table. "Let's see. We've been through the awkward meeting, getting to know each other, friends, meal sharing, shopping, and big screen TV watching. I think that'd cover stages one through six. Today I'll call stage seven."

"I see," she said. "And you know this how?"

"Read it in *Cosmo for Men*." He mussed her hair.

"I'll bet." Rachel said. "Plenty of quizzes too, right?"

"I don't want to brag, but I'm their top scorer." He grabbed her hand before she could poke him. "Now, pay attention. The next stages require dedication and control."

"Wait." She reached for her tablet. "I'd better take notes."

"Not necessary. I've got this," Chris said. "Stage

eight is clothes on with exploratory light groping. Stage nine is upper body clothes off with extended medium groping."

"I see," Rachel said. "This process is quite technical."

"I have many degrees, including, if you must know, Technical Engineering. So I am equipped, better than most."

"Oh, my," Rachel said. "I had no idea."

"Do not make light of your situation," Chris said and kissed her. "The final stage, if or when you're ready, is what I like to call...." He paused for effect.

Rachel waited. The silence lengthened. She looked up at him. He ignored her, then proclaimed, "Ta-dah!"

Rachel sat up. "What? Ta-dah! Are you serious? That's what you call it?" She burst into laughter. "Don't you mess with me, Chris Gregory."

Chris laughed, took her in his arms, and said, "I can't wait to mess with you."

The next morning Chris returned to Rachel's apartment with his tablet in hand. While she prepared coffee, toast, and eggs, he sat down. "I've been up all night and prepared this schedule based on a series of charts and graphs for us."

"Uh-huh," she said without looking up.

Chris when over each slide in meticulous detail, finishing with, "What do you think?"

"About what?"

"Come on, Rachel, you're not even listening."

"Sure I am. You've entered, compared, and graphed data pertaining to human response times, acclamation studies, experiential autonomic reflex spectrums, and time-motion studies. Right? So, what's the bottom line?"

Chris raised his eyebrows and gave her a crooked smile. "I can't believe you got all that."

"I have secret magical powers," she said. "Now stop stalling and tell me what you've worked out."

"If we work on each stage for two sessions each, it'll take us two weeks. However, it is up to you. If it takes longer, it takes longer."

Rachel set the coffee cups on the table and served breakfast. "So, you figure two weeks." She swept her hand across Chris's shoulders as she slipped into her seat.

"As I said, no pressure."

During clean up, while she washed the few dishes, he leaned on the counter next to her. She dried her hands and swiveled to face him. They kissed.

"Stage eight?" she asked.

"Definitely," he said.

"You're vibrating," Rachel said. "It's kind of a turn on."

"I'm what?" Chris put his hand in his pocket and pulled out his phone. "I've got to take this. Give me a rain check until dinner?"

Rachel nodded and Chris took off.

He returned at six-thirty with East Indian take-out, four jars of hot fudge sauce, and twelve pints of ice cream.

"I think you overdid it," Rachel said, as he stuffed the ice cream in her freezer.

"Maybe for you," he said. "But I'm not sure this is enough for me."

"Come on," Rachel said. "If anybody can do this, we can."

October first, the year anniversary of Rachel's first

day of tenancy, Chris knocked on her door.

"Come in," she said from the couch. Another knock. "Chris, don't make me get up." Knock. She got up, checked the security monitor and cursed under her breath. It *was* Chris. Another knock. She unlocked and opened the door.

Chris, dressed in a suit and tie, said, "Miss Allen, I am here in my official and legal capacity to do a jewelry check. May I come in?" He didn't wait for an answer and swept her aside. "I don't need an escort. I know the way."

Chris, eyes forward, marched in. She followed him into the bedroom and sat on the bed while Chris inspected her jewelry case. Confused but intrigued, she waited as long as she could. "So, Mister Official Jewelry Checker, what's up?"

Chris turned. "In my expert opinion, and without any question, it looks like you're missing a very valuable item."

"What are you talking about?" Rachel stood but Chris gave her the stop signal, so she sat back down. He crossed the room and dropped to one knee in front of her. A small Tiffany blue box wrapped in white ribbon appeared in his open hand.

Rachel's jaw dropped and her hand flew to cover her gaping mouth.

Chris smiled and moved the gift closer to her. Eyes wide, hands shaking, Rachel accepted the offering. She tugged at the ribbon with uncoordinated fingers.

"Let me," Chris said. Taking the box from her, he revealed a three carat oval emerald in a plain Tiffany setting. She gasped.

Chris said, "Rachel Allen, I love you with all my heart. Will you marry me?"

"Yes. Absolutely. Yes!"

Rachel leaned in and kissed him. "I love you,

Christopher Mark Gregory." Then she held out her ring finger and wiggled it—a silent demand for immediate action. Chris freed the ring from its velvet seat and threaded it onto her finger. "It's magnificent," she said. "And so are you."

She fell into his arms. Chris pushed her back onto the bed, tore off his clothes, and gave her the glaring look of a man about to do serious damage. Rachel scurried backwards until the pillows stopped her and then used her arms and legs to claim the bed. "If you dare to invade my space, it will be over my willing body!"

Chris laughed. "Challenge accepted."

"I'm excited," Chris said as he exited the shower and wrapped a towel around his waist. "My whole family will be at Mom's today. My sibs and their families are in from Arizona, Michigan, and South Carolina. They're all coming to meet you. You'll have a great time. I promise."

Rachel, cocooned under the covers, grunted.

"Come on," Chris said. "Get up. Get ready. Turkey. Stuffing. Football. Family. What's not to like?"

Another grunt.

He walked over to the bed and dug Rachel out. "How come you don't look excited."

"You know I love your parents. And I know I promised no security, but I need Jack and Jay. It's just too many strangers in too small a space."

Chris stroked her hair. "You've got me. I'll protect you. Don't you know that by now?"

"It is not the same. I don't expect you to keep an eye on me while you're with your family. These guys will. Plus if I have to leave, they'll take me home."

"So you think I can't protect you *and* you're already planning to leave?"

"I didn't say that. You're twisting my words."

Chris left her side to get dressed. "Look, Rachel. Enough with the security team. We need to start going out on our own."

"I know." Rachel sat on the bed playing with her fingers. "I want to meet your family."

Chris pivoted, pants unbuttoned and his shirt half on. "Then what's the problem?"

"We were only six adults and four children. And they came here. You're talking about a tribe of fifty inside your parents' apartment."

"Honey, we're talking about family." Chris snapped on his watch.

"You're turning me on," Rachel said. "Come to bed."

"Later. No time. Get up. Maybe as I watch you dress, I'll change my mind."

Rachel jumped out of bed and ran into his arms. "I'm sorry," she said. "I love you."

An hour later, Chris looked out the window. "The limo's here. Time to go." He went to the closet and got their coats. "Rachel." He found her pacing around the bedroom wringing her hands. Her face was flushed.

"Come on, Rachel. You're working yourself up over nothing. I'll be with you the whole time. It's not dangerous. It's my family. You'll be fine."

Chris led her to the door, helped her on with her coat, looped her hand through the crook in his elbow, and gave her a big smile. "We're going to do this— together."

Rachel echoed, "Together."

He ushered her into the hall, down the elevator, through the lobby, and into the vestibule. The limousine idled at the curb less than twenty feet away. She disengaged at the building's threshold while he continued outside and stood by the open passenger door. When she failed to materialize, he turned and held out his hand for her. "Rachel?"

"I... I can't," she said, arms hugging her body.

"What?" Chris looked surprised and disappointed. "Are you kidding me?"

"Please, Chris. Let me call...."

"Rachel, come with me." He held out both arms. "No security. Just you and me. Together."

"Chris, I want to."

"No more excuses." His voice became edgy. "You have to try. We're planning a wedding. What were you going to do? Jam our families into the apartment? Take our vows in the kitchen? Book a honeymoon suite for four?"

Rachel's eyes widened and her chin dropped. Chris' expression changed to angry frustration. His jaw clenched. He looked away—up and down the street, up at the sky, and then back to her.

"I'm going," he said. "For the last time, please come with me."

"I can't," she said. "I wish I could but I just can't."

Chris threw his hands up in defeat and jumped into the limo.

With tears rolling down her cheeks, Rachel stared at the car until it disappeared in the traffic. She fled upstairs, torn by her love for Chris, who made her feel normal, and anger at the rapist, who'd forced fear into her life.

It never occurred to her that this incident might be a deal breaker.

Chapter 16
Harrisburg, Pennsylvania

It was the Monday morning after Thanksgiving. President-elect Governor Franklin Taylor Sandford entered his office at four-thirty ready to work.

A young fifty-two, he had salt and pepper hair which framed his square-jawed tanned face, brown eyes, patrician nose, and trimmed eyebrows. He dressed with intent, as a camera might catch him at any moment. Even at this hour, he wore navy slacks, a blue and white striped shirt, and a tie. His studied persona conveyed a relaxed professional who acted with purpose and forethought, his constituency's welfare at the top of his priorities.

Seated at his desk, Sandford sipped his coffee. The photographs on his desk chronicled his journey. A West Point graduate. A decorated officer. Married.

Four children. He looked at each image and

*

smiled, even touching his wife's and each child's face. "I will not let you down."

He had studied all the previous presidents, adopting the traits that made them great and resisting the temptations that brought them down. For those of the flesh, his secret was to surround himself with handsome assistants who deflected the temptresses and kept them happy. It worked like a charm. For those of greed, he delegated negotiations to trusted intermediaries. As a result, he escaped vilification in the press and maintained a squeaky clean, anti-bribe, honest image. The people loved him.

During his run for president, Sandford developed a list of preferential experts and advisors, and solicited suggestions from colleagues. His campaign promise to energize the country, reduce its massive debt, reboot the stalled recovery, fund education, and create jobs got him elected. It was time to deliver on those promises. The men and women who accepted would be the architects of a new government for the people.

With the list beside him, Sandford used a yellow pad and drew a line down the middle of the page. He put available positions on one side and people he wanted on the other. After several hours, he completed his first pass at the pairings, step one in the selection process—done.

He flipped the yellow page and pulled out a list of people who were influential but were not available or acceptable candidates for one reason or another. It included the moneyed, social icons, influence peddlers, fund-raisers, and doers. Sandford needed them involved and committed to him. He only problem was how.

He swiveled his chair to face the windows. Before him, a manicured estate stretched to the Susquehanna's shore. He leaned back and relaxed.

Fifteen minutes later he bolted upright, returned to his desk, and made a call.

"Wendell, my office. I've got an idea."

"I'm on my way," Wendell said. "Be there in five."

Wendell Waters entered less than four minutes later. He looked like a pro-football player gone soft and carried himself with authority and grace. If provoked, the handsome man turned into a menacing tiger. No one wanted to be on his bad side.

Smiling, he sat down in the leather wing chair across from Sandford.

"Mr. President," Waters said, preempting the inauguration. "How can I help?"

"Here, take a look at this." Sandford handed Waters a copy of the appointee list.

Wendell scanned the document. "Good choices." He placed the document on the desk.

"No, keep it," Sandford said. "I'd like you to vet everyone. Make sure they're clear to accept an appointment. We can modify as necessary. But I'd like to present a working list to our inner circle of advisors before I make any offers."

"Will do." Waters retrieved the list, folded it, and put it in his inner jacket pocket. "Anything else?"

Sandford handed him another list. "Look at these names."

Waters reviewed the list. "I know them well from the campaign. Most have well-endowed foundations."

"Correct. I don't want to lose their support. I want to thank them with more than just invitations to the inaugural festivities, a couple of White House dinners, and the like."

"What do you have in mind?"

"Include them in our decision-making process."

"Do you mean policy?" Waters leaned forward. "Didn't we promise to keep big money out of governance?"

"Yes, of course. I'm thinking small high-powered focus groups, think tanks, if you will. They'll develop strategies with viable implementations to meet the specific needs of different segments of our population and our global responsibilities, in keeping with our campaign platform."

"I'm not sure it's a good idea to spend public monies before your January inauguration."

"I agree. So what if we let our friends underwrite the think tanks and, if they want, coordinate the one they fund?"

"I think they'd like the opportunity to have a direct impact."

"Good. Please get started on vetting the advisors, and I'll make the phone calls."

Sandford spent the next three days on the phone. After the last donor agreed, he pushed a button under his desk. A panel slid back to reveal a small well-stocked bar. He got up and poured himself a drink, relaxed in his favorite chair in private celebration before he summoned his Chief of Staff.

"Wendell. Great news. The think tank initiative is a go. Each person I contacted said they'd be honored to participate."

"Let me have the final list. I'll pull a team together and itemize key areas and operational parameters," Waters said. "We should have results back to you within the week. Two, if you'd like suggested participants."

"Two it is," Sandford said. "Thanks, Wendell."

Waters walked to the door. With his hand on the

knob, he turned to Sandford, "Your think tank idea is a stroke of genius. I can't wait to hear about your other innovative plans."

The door closed and Sandford smiled. He swiveled to face the windows and turned on his phone, found the file, and hit play as he stared at the blue sky and mares' tail clouds.

"Ladies and Gentlemen, I give you the next President of the United States, Franklin Taylor Sandford." "Happy Days are Here Again" played in the background while people cheered and clapped. "Thank you. Thank you to my family, my staff, and all my supporters. We are on the cusp of making political and economic history—together!"

He turned the video off and pressed the phone to his heart. "I will honor my promise or die trying."

Chapter 17
Gramercy Avenue, New York City

"Rachel Allen's *Communication Strategies for Peace of Mind: Country and Global Safekeeping* is a must for serious politicos," declared the *New York Times Sunday Book Review* on New Year's Day. "The new operational and philosophical standard for national and international crisis centers.... Allen's theory obliterates the need for weapons through alternative approaches encouraging win-win situations, using concrete proposals to enhance communication and diplomacy, national and global, in the twenty-first century... Her ambitious mission is to eradicate hunger, lack of medical care, and human rights violations endured by refugee and indigenous populations, especially those in war zones throughout the world...."

Rachel beamed. Her "baby" was a hit.

With a knock on the door, Chris entered carrying bagels and coffee from Alfie's. She looked up, stood up with the *Times* in her hand, and a big smile on her face. He glanced at her and walked into the kitchen area. He set breakfast on the table and sat down, head in his hands.

Rachel raced to his side and put her arms around him. "What's the matter? Is someone hurt? Did someone die?"

"No." He released her arms and patted the chair next to his.

She did as he asked and reached for his hand. He withdrew from her touch. "Chris, you're scaring me. Tell me. What is it?"

"Remember Thanksgiving?"

"Of course. Why are you bringing that up? I thought we were past that."

"You," he said. "Not me."

"Wait a minute," Rachel said. "I'm confused. When you called to say how disappointed your family was, we agreed to invite them over for breakfast the next morning—which they all enjoyed by the way. We even have their 'thank you' notes."

"I know. They were gracious, even to Jack and Jay," Chris said. "But I've had time to think."

"Think about what?"

"Think about us and our life together," Chris said. "I thought I could deal with your issues and our isolation. But I can't. It's too claustrophobic. Even though I was furious you didn't come to Thanksgiving with me, I really enjoyed being with my family, with people. I never had the time to be a big socialite, but I did go out to charity events, Broadway plays, museums, Lincoln Center, and Madison Square Garden as well as walks along the river and through Central Park.

"I love you. Still, I miss being outside and a part of the world. I want that for us. Thanksgiving showed me that it's not happening. You're not ready, and it seems to me, not even willing to try. So while it'll probably kill me, I have to go." He stood. "I'm sorry, Rachel. We're not working. It's over." He walked to the door.

Rachel jumped up and grabbed his arm. "Don't go." He stopped. "Chris, please. Let's talk about this. I'll change. I promise."

He looked into her eyes. "When?"

She groped for an answer.

He ripped his arm loose from her grip. "That's what I thought."

"Chris. Please. I love you." Her words echoed throughout the apartment. Chris was gone.

Chapter 18
Gramercy Avenue, New York City

Rachel's emotional world lay in ruins. She placed *The New York Times* article under the glass top of her coffee table, but it brought her no comfort. Her tears made the headline blurry, the letters twisted. It seemed meaningless without Chris.

Rachel's time in New York exceeded her expectations, thanks to Chris. She had a large airy apartment. She felt safe and protected while a part of the neighborhood, thanks to the row of windows on the front and rear walls. She recognized the people who lived in her apartment building and the regulars who populated the streets.

Not their names, of course, but their faces and identifying details. Some had children, some had dogs. Some had both. Some were on their cell phones all the time. Some went to Alfie's for take-out. Some sat at the window bar. Others disappeared into the dark recesses. Rachel knew them all. They were her extended family.

Nevertheless, Rachel never ventured out without her security detail. She kept these forays down to ninety minutes or less. She wore sunglasses affixed with a cycling eyeglass mirror to monitor activity behind her. She kept her hands free. Her wallet hung from a chain around her neck and nestled in her bra. Jack and Jay took care of her, from transportation to security. Rachel never wanted be a target again.

Her life puzzle had fallen into place. She loved her independence—it refreshed her soul. Chris was the icing on her cake. She, of all people, had found love—nirvana.

Then in a split second, her life shattered. No Chris. No engagement. No love. Her ring sat on the coffee table. She picked it up. Rotated it with her fingers as tears streamed down her face.

"Damn you, Chris," she said. "How could you?" She threw the ring at the door and reached for tissues as her nose began to run. She was curled up on the couch, sobbing when her phone rang. She choked back her pain, wiped her eyes and nose, and answered. "Chris?"

"Sorry, Rachel. It's Nikolai. Someone's here to see you."

"Can't," Rachel said, and hit END.

Her phone rang again.

"What?"

"Rachel, don't hang up," Nikolai said. "It's the FBI."

"I don't care if it's Santa Claus," Rachel said. "The answer's no."

"She says she's on special assignment for President-elect Sandford."

"Did you check her ID?"

"Of course. I would never let anyone...."

"I know, Nikolai. I'm sorry. I'm in no shape to see anyone. Please send her away."

A new voice, full of authority and impatience. "Rachel Allen, this is FBI Special Agent Elizabeth Neilson. I'm on special assignment and I must talk with you now."

"You can't.... Who?.... Beth, is that you?"

"You bet. Are you going to let me up or do I have to break down your door?"

Rachel laughed. "No, no violence necessary. Come on up."

Rachel, her mother's daughter, swooped through the apartment and straightened what she could in two minutes. At the sound of the elevator, she went to the door, stopped at the entry mirror, ran her fingers through her hair, closed her robe and tied the belting, and picked up the ring, shoving it in her pocket

At the first knock, she checked the monitor. A trim athletic female FBI agent, about five-eight, with short red hair, heart-shaped face, and blue eyes stood waiting. Rachel smiled and opened the door. "Beth Neilson! My God. Come in!"

The women hugged. Afterward Rachel said, "I never thought I'd see my freshman roomie again. How are you?"

"I'm great," Beth said smiling. "I hoped you'd remember."

"How could I forget! I still get the giggles when I see a role of silver duct tape. Remember how you divided the space in our room?"

Beth said, "Life is all about boundaries."

"Come sit. Can I get something to drink? Coffee? Tea? Water?"

"I'm good, thank you." Beth sat straight, on the

edge of a side chair cushion. "I have to talk to you."

Rachel sat on the couch. "Before we get down to business, I want to say again how sorry I was to hear about your dad."

Beth relaxed and slid into the chair. "My family and I appreciated your note and donation. I took a year off to help establish normal for the family. To save money, I transferred to SUNY Albany. Then I did a stint in the army. Went to Afghanistan. It was a bitch of a tour," Beth said. "As soon as I got home, I applied to the FBI and here I am—Special Agent Elizabeth Neilson."

"Unbelievable," Rachel said. "Congratulations."

"Now tell me," Beth said. "How are you doing? I heard about the incident on campus almost nine years ago."

"I'm fine. My writing keeps me busy."

"You don't look fine. Your face is flushed and blotchy. There are bits of tissues sticking out from your pockets and furniture cushions. It's almost noon and you're not dressed. As a trained investigator, I'd say you're in some kind of distress."

"A small personal disaster," Rachel said. "I'll be fine." She waved her hand to dismiss Beth's concern. "Tell me, why are you here?"

"I've just been assigned to head the FBI Missing Persons division here in New York. At our morning briefing, I heard your name. They needed someone to deliver a message and I volunteered." Beth produced a square envelope from her pocket and placed it on the table. "Ever seen this?"

Rachel picked it up. "Sure. I get these all the time asking for political donations."

"Open it."

Rachel removed a card with a deckle edge and raised lettering.

"The President-elect of the United States,
Franklin Taylor Sandford,
Requests the Participation of
Rachel Allen
in the
Presidential Think Tank Human Rights Initiative,
for the month of February,
Lake George, New York.
RSVP by January 1,
Wendell Waters, Chief of Staff,
202.555.0003 or
wendell.waters.cos@whs.usa.gov."

"Have you seen this invitation before?"

Rachel shook her head. "I worked on his campaign, so I tossed all official looking stuff into the garbage. If I had read it, I would have responded."

"Well, as of today, your RSVP is late."

Rachel looked from Beth to the card and back to Beth. "You want it now? Right now?"

"Yes, if you want to participate. Our standard vetting process takes two weeks."

Invitation in hand, Rachel paced back and forth. "I can't. I'm…. I can't."

"You do realize this is pretty much a presidential order, right?"

"I would love to, Beth. I'm honored. But this is way out of my comfort zone."

"Rachel, you should know I'm not supposed to take 'no' for an answer."

Rachel stopped and began to shake. She put her arms around her body to keep it contained, hold it together. "I…. Beth…."

Beth went to Rachel. "What is it? I had no idea this'd upset you."

Rachel shook her head. "I'll be okay."

"Sit down," Beth said. "Let's discuss a Plan B."

"There is no Plan B. I don't go out."

"Agoraphobic? We can control your environment. The think tank is meeting in an isolated cabin. A few people in a large open space. You'll be fine."

"I've got PTSD. From the rape. My panic attacks are brought about by triggers. It can happen anywhere, at any time. I just can't go."

"Think about it. I'm sure we can figure out something. Let's talk about it tomorrow. I'll call you," Beth said. "Here's my card." She pulled a pen from her inside jacket pocket. "This is my personal cell phone number on the back. You can reach me twenty-four/seven."

Rachel accepted the card and held it. "Thank you, Beth. I appreciate this. But I can't promise anything."

"Tonight," Beth said, "make a list of what measures need to be in place. You'll be staying at the home of a former member of the Joint Chiefs of Staff. There'll be seven other people in the group and one housekeeper. It is both safe and secure."

Rachel read the invitation again. "This would be an amazing opportunity for me to put the principles in my book into action." She looked at Beth. "Is there any more information on this?"

"I'll ask Wendell Waters, President-elect Sandford's Chief of Staff, to forward descriptive material to you," she said, typing on her phone. "Is this your email?" Rachel nodded. "I should have an answer in a few minutes."

Beth's phone pinged and she checked her email. "Waters will send it within the hour."

"I have to say I'm a bit overwhelmed."

"I can see that," Beth said. Her phone rang. She looked at the caller ID. "I have to take this." She got up and walked away for privacy. When she returned, she said, "Sorry, Rachel, they need me downtown. I have to leave. You have my card. We'll talk tomorrow." The next second she was gone.

Rachel tapped Beth's card on her jaw and walked to the window. She watched the busy neighborhood and looked at the card. Tears welled. *Will I ever be free?*

Chapter 19
Gramercy Avenue, New York City

Focused on the think tank invitation, Rachel jumped at the unexpected loud knock. *An unannounced visitor?* She checked the security monitor. Chris. She shook her head, stood up straight, took a deep breath, and opened the door. "What are you doing here?"

Chris brushed past her and searched the apartment. "Where is she? I don't like FBI agents loose in my buildings."

"So you're still talking to me?" Rachel said to his back.

Without turning he said, "Of course, I'm talking to you."

"But you said, 'it's over.'" Her eyes filled. She blinked back the tears.

Chris walked to the window. He appeared to study the street below. She waited, still as a statue, with the exception of her clenching fists, in the heavy silence.

Chris turned to her, arms by his side. "Look, Rachel. I love you. I've loved you from the first moment I saw you eleven years ago. I just can't live with you."

"Why didn't we talk if you were so unhappy?"

"We didn't have to talk. I handled it."

With a deep venomous hiss, she said, "You. Handled. It?" Her tone rose as her throat muscles constricted. "You freaking handled it?" She looked at him through snake eyes, "How dare you? This is not easy for me. I can't turn my triggers on and off. But I'm trying."

Chris ignored her and picked up the card on the coffee table. "What's this?"

"Don't change the subject. How can you stand there and not talk to me."

"I am talking to you...as a friend." He waved the invitation around. "What's this all about?"

Rachel folded her arms across her chest and raised her chin. The vulnerable little girl morphed into the wronged queen. "You read it. Franklin Taylor Sandford wants *me* to serve my country," she said with clipped enunciation. "You see, you have no idea who you're dealing with."

Chris shot her a look, one eyebrow raised. "*They* do not know who *they're* dealing with," he said. "A month away from here? Not happening. You said no, right?"

"Well, no," Rachel said. "Not exactly."

"What does that mean?" He spoke like a father to his unruly daughter.

She uncrossed her arms and put one hand on the back of the nearest chair, a pose worthy of any royal gallery. Chin still raised, she looked down her nose at him. "It means I'm going."

"What?" Chris said, his hands flinging skyward. "We have never been outside by ourselves, and now you're going away for a whole month—to an alien environment with strangers?"

Rachel circled the chair and sat down—legs crossed at the ankles, arms resting on the chair's arms. "I told you I could change."

As soon as the words left her mouth, Chris's energy darkened. His jaw muscles flexed, veins in his temple popped, and his brows dove toward the bridge of his nose. "So, let me see if I have this straight," he growled. "You've changed in two seconds for some guy you've never met, but not in fourteen months for me, the man you supposedly love. Is that it? Do I have that right?" He slammed the invitation on the coffee table.

"First of all, it's not *some guy*. It's Franklin Taylor Sandford, President-elect of the United States. Second, mister-I'll-handle-this-all-by-myself-know-it-all, we've never actually discussed this issue."

"We didn't have to," Chris said. "Your actions spoke loud and clear."

"So did yours." Rachel waved her hand around the room. "You bought all this stuff so we didn't have to go out, remember?"

"A temporary fix," Chris said. "I never thought it'd be forever."

"I'm supposed to be a mind reader? What about trust? This has been on your mind since Thanksgiving, and you didn't or couldn't talk to me." Rachel took a breath and looked at Chris—his face taut and his hands balled into fists.

In a quieter voice, she asked, "What's her name?"

"Who?" Chris looked like he'd been caught with his hand in the cookie jar.

"The woman you've been talking to."

"Are you kidding?"

"Well, if you haven't been talking to me, you must have been talking to someone."

Chris raised his voice. "How could I talk to you? You immersed yourself into your book and your deadlines. I didn't see you for days."

"That's a copout and you know it," Rachel said. "You did more all-nighters than I ever did and got lost in your programming for days on end."

He ran his fingers through his hair, shook his head, and looked away.

"Chris, don't shut me out."

He took a deep breath, rolled his head around his neck and shrugged his shoulders. He sat down on the couch and tapped the invitation with his forefinger. "Where is this place?"

"Lake George."

"Where in Lake George?"

"At the cabin of a former member of the Joint Chiefs of Staff."

"That should be enough. I'll check it out." He got up and went to the door.

"Christopher Gregory," Rachel said and stamped her foot for emphasis. "You turn around and talk to me!"

With his hand on the door knob, he hesitated but didn't turn back. Chris left without a word.

Rachel threw a pillow at the door and stomped into the kitchen. She threw open the freezer door with so much force it closed itself. She kicked the refrigerator and banged on the freezer with her fists.

Calmer, she said, "Sorry, fridge," patting the unit, and filled a mug with two-and-a-half generous scoops of coffee fudge ice cream.

Chapter 20
Federal Building, New York City -
Los Angeles, California

FBI Special Agent Elizabeth Neilson raced back to her office. The phone call was from her supervisor. She was the new lead investigator on the Meyerson case.

Seven weeks prior, an explosion decimated a hotel in Beijing, China. Among the eighty-five people believed dead were prominent California civil and human rights lawyer, Imanuela Meyerson, and four members of her immediate family. The President, a close friend of the Meyersons, demanded an immediate investigation.

The meticulous Chinese authorities, under intense pressure, released vague reports. "We are unable to announce conclusive findings until we finish processing all the evidence and survivor interviews."

The President wanted answers yesterday.

In her office, Beth had the Meyerson file in front of her. She flipped through the material to get a sense of scope. The whole scenario seemed unbelievable and yet the family did disappear. "Don't worry," she said aloud to no one. "I'll find you and figure out what happened."

She read the report cover to cover—family stats, the PRAISE Foundation award, the blast in China, press releases, and the US CIA undercover investigation.

In his report from China, the CIA agent said, "I've got nothing. It's all double talk. The Beijing police said that they found the hotel staff, presumed dead, hiding in fear. They took their statements and released them. As far as the explosion, forensics ruled out a gas leak. For ashes this fine and destruction this complete, it could only be a controlled blast. Someone or some group deliberately bombed this building.

"The hotel staff's reported descriptions of the Meyerson family didn't ring true. I viewed the Beijing Capital International Airport surveillance videos and noted seven families of five. When I showed the images of each family to the hotel staff, they did identify one family as the Meyersons. Went back to airline and interviewed flight attendants and showed them the Meyerson picture. They agreed with the hotel staff. In fact, it is not the Meyerson's picture. See attached comparison images. Thus there is no proof that the real Meyerson family ever got on the plane. Follow-up in US."

Beth looked at the two images. *The imposters looked like the Meyersons. No doubt about it. But why the switch? It meant duplicate passports and altered drivers' licenses. That's a lot of time and money. Regardless, the real questions are where are they now and why?*

Under the CIA report, Beth found the Meyerson dossier. Imanuela Meyerson was a partner in the Los Angeles firm of Worthington, Meyerson & Smith. Her husband, Dr. Steven Meyerson, a top thoracic surgeon, practiced and taught at Good Samaritan Hospital. Of her three daughters, one attended high school and two were in college.

She reviewed the information on the daughters and eliminated them as either targets or suspects. That left the two adults. Dr. Meyerson might be the target of a disgruntled patient or student—except retribution of that kind tended to be close up and personal, not an explosion in a foreign country. Beth made a note for follow-up, just in case. That left Imanuela Meyerson.

A top attorney, Imanuela focused on civil and human rights abuse. She preferred high profile cases that pointed out social injustices or outrageous abuses of power. She wanted others to think twice before emulating such anti-human behavior. She was outspoken, a democrat, and apolitical—respected and feared.

Imanuela Meyerson's human rights work for the United Nations often put her at odds with political agendas. Her last interview criticized presidential candidate Franklin Sandford on his weak policy regarding nations in blatant disregard of their U.N. pledge by denying their citizens basic human rights. If Sandford had made a rebuttal, it wasn't in the documentation.

Beth read the summaries of Meyerson's major cases, past and present, created an interview list of individuals and organizations. She noted awards and recognitions, including the Presidential Award of Freedom, which Imanuela'd received four years ago, and the PRAISE Foundation Humanitarian Award, which she'd received in October. Unfamiliar with this last award, Beth googled it and printed out the page.

Closing the file, Beth studied and prioritized her lists, then created a time line. First priority, the Meyerson home in California. She checked the agents working the Los Angeles area and saw the name of a good friend from her Quantico graduating class. He was her first and only call.

Beth got the text, "*Out front*," from FBI Special Agent Eric Jerrod as she negotiated the passenger arrival terminal at the Los Angeles International Airport.

Emerging from the Passenger Pick-up exit, Beth spied Eric's sandy blonde hair and six-one runner's body by the side of his car. They had been lovers right after the academy, but job necessities stressed their relationship. They ended their brief affair on good terms. He still looked great.

She reached the car, dropped the handle of her suitcase, and hugged Eric. "I'm so glad you found time to help."

He said, "Nice hug, Beth. Good to see you too." He put her suitcase in the trunk and closed it. "It'll be just like old times at Quantico."

Beth looked into his mesmerizing green-gray eyes, determined not to drown in them. She said, "Let's go. We'll talk in the car."

Once they were settled in, he slipped on aviator sunglasses, put the car in gear, and headed for the freeway. She watched him as he drove.

"What are you doing?" Eric asked, glancing at her. "You're making me uncomfortable."

"Just looking at you," Beth said. "It's been, what,

maybe five years since training. You haven't aged a day."

"Just say the word, Beth, and I'm all yours."

Beth blushed. "We had a great time. I loved every minute, but we're just too much alike—dedicated workaholics. Friendship's better." She paused and changed the subject. "Tell me, what'd you find out?"

"So far, I've checked the LAX videos for their day of departure," Eric said. "A Meyerson family did check in and board the plane, but they were look-a-likes. I'm already working on their identities, but so far, no luck."

"You're telling me the real Meyerson family disappeared?"

"That's the problem," Eric said. "I don't know. All I know is that Imanuela Meyerson and family can't be located at this time."

"That's not good news," Beth said. "What's our itinerary for today?"

"First, we're picking up my buddy Victor Zabinsky, a detective in the Los Angeles Police Department," Eric said. "Then, we're going to the Meyerson home, which, at the moment, is occupied by a house sitter and her family."

"Do we have a warrant?"

Eric said, "If we can get access without one, it'd be better. We don't want to raise red flags or alert the press until we have more definitive information. Zabinsky is our front so we're not tagged as FBI."

LA Detective Victor Zabinsky, stocky without an inch of fat, ferret eyes, and silver-laced black wavy hair, waited on the curb with a cup in his hand. When their car pulled up, he tossed the cup into a "Keep Our City Clean" garbage container and jumped into the back seat. Leaning forward over the armrest between Eric and Beth, he said, "Tell me what you've got."

Eric introduced Beth and, as Zabinsky was his friend, took the lead and explained the situation as he drove.

Zabinsky said, "You're telling me there's not one clue?"

Eric said, "Not on either side of the Pacific."

"No way a family disappears just like that." Zabinsky snapped his fingers for emphasis.

Beth said, "I agree."

Zabinsky said, "So they're either kidnapped or dead."

Eric said, "We're keeping an open mind in case they're at home playing gin-rummy."

"Tell me again, why do you need me?"

Eric said, "If they're not home, we'd like a look inside. And, you, my friend, have the best nose in the business for smelling gas leaks."

"Flattery works." Zabinsky laughed. "Besides, I'm always up for a little B and E for a good cause."

Ten minutes later, Zabinsky, with Eric and Beth as his rear guard, knocked on the door of a Spanish-style home in an upscale Los Angeles neighborhood.

"Yes?" the woman said, through the open door constrained by a chain lock. "Detective Zabinsky, LAPD," he said and held up his ID. "With agents Jerrod and Neilson. Are you Imanuela Meyerson?"

"No. She's not here."

"I'd like to talk with you about the Meyersons. May I come in?"

"Only with a warrant. That's what they said." The woman spoke like a dour head nurse—clipped words and haughty demeanor. "That's what the Meyersons said. It's in the contract."

"Ma'am," Zabinsky said, "I'm sorry to have to tell you this, but the family has reportedly died in a hotel fire."

The woman arched her back and set her jaw. "I know. I read the papers. But I'm paid 'til March. So the contract stands." She shut the door.

Zabinsky did an about-face and shrugged. "I'd call her uncooperative."

Eric said, "What do we get if we press the issue?"

Zabinsky said, "Not any useable fingerprints, that's for sure."

Beth said, "But we do get a better understanding of how Meyersons lived, their personal and trip documents, and, if we're lucky, their computer. Any lead is better than what we have now."

Zabinsky said, "True. Let's try." He knocked on the door again.

The door opened with a clunk as the security chain went taut. "Officer, I…."

"Detective Zabinsky," he said, correcting her. "I'd like your permission to check out the house."

"I already told you…."

"May I have your name?"

"Ingram. Mrs. Lena Ingram."

"Mrs. Ingram." Zabinsky said, in a soft, encouraging voice. "If you let us in now, we'll be very, very careful. If we have to come back with a warrant, we'll come back with a whole investigative team." Eric and Beth nodded to support Zabinsky. "Mrs. Ingram, I know from experience these guys will wreck the place, and that'll be on you." He gave her a second. When she didn't respond, he took out his phone.

"Wait," she said. "Five minutes." Mrs. Ingram released the chain, opened the door, and stepped aside.

Zabinsky entered first. He asked Mrs. Ingram to follow him into the living room. "Please sit down," he said and gestured to a chair. "I'd like to get some background information." Zabinsky sat down. "May I have your full name?"

"Lena Wilson Ingram," she said, craning her neck, trying to keep an eye on the two others.

"Do you work?"

"I'm a surgical nurse at Good Samaritan."

"Who hired you for this housesitting job?"

"When my hours got cut back a couple of months ago, one of my kids got sick and my husband lost his job. Before he got another, we lost the apartment. My friend who worked for Dr. Meyerson heard he needed a house sitter and I got the job."

Zabinsky wrote down the names of her husband and three children. He reviewed the woman's work agreement, and asked her to clarify each section. Lena Ingram kept her answers as terse as a hostile trial witness.

While Zabinsky kept the woman occupied, Eric and Beth explored the kitchen where they found the Meyerson itinerary on the fridge. Beth used her phone to snap a picture of it and then bagged it.

They moved to the bedrooms.

Eric said, "The whole place is compromised by the sitter's family."

Beth said, "Let's see if there's an office."

They found it in the rear of the house, with the door locked. Beth said, "Out of sight, out of mind."

Eric said, "Let's hope."

He carded the door. Inside, it was pristine. Eric looked for a wall safe while Beth checked desk drawers and filing cabinets.

Eric said, "If they have a safe, it's not in here."

Beth said, "Looks like they expected to be back."

He said, "What's in the bulky manila envelope on the desk?"

Beth dumped it on the desk. "Mail."

Together they sorted through it.

He said, "I got invitations and professional announcements."

She said, "Medical journals and magazines."

He said. "Standard stuff."

Beth said, "Did you notice there are no computers?"

"Bet they took them on the trip."

"Hmmm," Beth said as she stared at the mound of mail. "I don't remember seeing any bills or bank statements."

They went through the mail again as they repacked the envelope.

"You're right," Eric said.

They looked and pointed at each other. "Follow the money."

Beth, Eric, and Zabinsky left the Meyerson home, split up, and talked with the neighbors. Back in the car, they compared notes on the way to the police station.

All the people they spoke to were friends of the Meyersons. They had attended Imanuela Meyerson's PRAISE Foundation award dinner and her Bon Voyage party. They all agreed the family was excited about their trip. On the day they left, two limousines arrived around seven in the evening. One took the luggage and the other took the family. Since then, no one had spoken directly with any family member. A few neighbors offered copies of their most current Meyerson emails—a total of twenty in all. Others shared the several texts they received.

Eric dropped Zabinsky back at the police station, trading his notes for a latte and box of his favorite doughnuts—for the unit he said, and drove to the FBI Los Angeles Field Office.

"This is going to take some time," Eric said, sitting at his desk. "We'll need a warrant for the Meyerson's financial records."

"I leave that to you," Beth said. "As well as the West Coast list of people to be interviewed, which I'll email to you." She went on her phone and sent the document. "Ok, do you have it?"

"Got it," Eric said, staring at his phone.

"Good. I'll go back to New York and check out the East Coast list, including PRAISE Foundation and its founder, Theodore Donovan. PRAISE arranged the Meyersons' trip."

"Paid for the trip," Eric said. "Not sure who made the arrangements."

"I'll still check it out. Do you want a copy of the itinerary?"

Eric nodded and Beth sent him another email with the image attached.

"We need to trace their phones and emails," Beth said. "Without computers, we need to get our techs on the servers."

"I'll also go to their respective offices. I'm guessing they didn't take their business computers with them," Eric said. "Might find some personal info."

"Unless they carried a laptop back and forth," Beth said. "But it's worth a look. And, please, get their email addresses." She paused. "Do we have their cell phone numbers?"

Eric checked the file. "It's all here."

"Good. Get a warrant for those records, too, starting three weeks before they left."

Eric started typing. Beth walked around the desk and sat on the window ledge. She saw the request forms come up on the computer and asked, "How long do you think it will take before we see the data?"

"Couple of days to a few weeks," Eric said. "Unless…"

Beth finished his sentence. "Unless it's got high priority status. I'll take care of that before I leave. Anything else? If I hurry, I can make the four-twenty-five flight."

"Not that I can think of. I'll take care of my end," Eric said. "Have a safe trip."

Beth hurried toward the elevator but stopped ten feet from the door. She paused, turned, and went back to Eric's office.

As she entered, his green-gray eyes looked up. "Change your mind? You could stay at my place and take an early morning flight."

Beth said, "Tempting, but business first. When you have all the info, let's do a video conference. We'll assemble the profiles together and see what we see. We have to find the Meyersons—and fast."

Beth left. At the elevator, she took one more look down the hall before she entered the lift.

The next day, Beth entered Theodore Donovan's office at the PRAISE Foundation headquarters with her senses on full alert. Donovan, much handsomer than his picture, sat at his clutter-free desk. The room smelled of leather and reeked of wealth, from the mahogany walls to the polished furniture. A number of expensive decorative elements hung on walls and graced dust-free shelves. There were no photographs, awards, or mementos.

"Special Agent Elizabeth Neilson, Mr. Donovan." Beth held her ID in front of her. Ted stood leaned forward to read it as Beth said, "Thank you for seeing me."

"Not a problem. I'm all for law and order," Ted said. He gestured for her to sit down. "What can I do for you, Special Agent Neilson?"

Beth said, "I'm here to inquire about Imanuela Meyerson and her family."

Ted said, "A terrible tragedy. Give me a second and I'll get her file." He picked up his tablet, typed, and placed it on his desktop.

"Did you know her well?"

"No. Not personally. I've met her briefly at various functions. "

"Didn't you interview her extensively before giving her the PRAISE award?"

"What for? Her extensive work and high profile decisions are documented in law cases, journals, and newspapers. Her life's work speaks for her."

"Are you saying that PRAISE Foundation sponsored the trip around the world for Mrs. Meyerson and her immediate family without so much as a face-to-face hello?"

Ted laughed. "You seem to think such largess is odd without a personal association?"

"In my experience, I do."

"Well, as with all our awards, it is not up to me. The PRAISE Foundation board, its advisory board, and donor membership select the awardees and approve the monetary award. My job is to organize the dinner and award for the honorees."

Beth said, "What does that entail?"

"We do a thorough background check. Through interviews with friends and family, we find out what they wish for and fulfill their dreams."

"Did Imanuela Meyerson dream about a trip around the world?"

"Not as such. She wanted to see, without fanfare, how the United Nations Human Rights

Commission's work affected certain targeted areas. You see, she was a U.N. advisor."

Beth said, "Who had responsibility for the trip itinerary and tickets?"

Ted's secretary knocked on the door. He said, "Come in." A woman in her late twenties entered and handed Ted a folder. "Thank you," he said, and she left.

"This is the Meyerson folder," Ted said. He pushed it across his desk to Beth.

It was as thin as Ted's verbal responses. Beth opened the folder and saw several paper-clipped packets of paper. They contained Meyerson's list of accomplishments, the guest list to her award dinner, a list of possible gifts—including the trip, and a list of investigative organizations used to verify and document all the enclosed information. In addition, there was a copy of the board minutes approving the award and a copy of the actual award with a picture of her accepting it.

Beth asked, "Is this it?"

Ted said, "What more do you want?"

"What about correspondence? Her nomination? Her sponsor? Discussions of availability? Her formal acceptance."

"Undocumented. We've never had anyone refuse a PRAISE Foundation award."

"Were you in Los Angeles to see the family off?"

"Not necessary," Ted said. "The Meyersons assured me they had every aspect of the trip under control."

"Again, who arranged the itinerary and the tickets?"

"She did. We gave her a credit card limit that covered the entire trip and any additional expenses. PRAISE paid her receipts."

Ted picked up his tablet, typed, and put it down.

"My secretary will give them to you as soon as you return with a warrant. I'm sure you understand. It's just a business formality to protect PRAISE."

Ted rose to his feet and ended the interview with, "Is there anything else?" He put one hand in his pocket, from which emanated the faint clink of keys.

"Not now," Beth said. She pointed to the folder. "May I keep this?"

"Warrant, remember?" Ted said and smiled.

"Don't worry. I'll be back."

Ted said, "I'll be here."

Chapter 21
Gramercy Avenue, New York City

Rachel couldn't make up her mind. When she met with Beth, she wasn't going to Lake George. After Chris' confrontation, she was going. An hour after he left, she wasn't. The decision rattled around in her brain. About to dive into the freezer for a pint of mint chocolate chip ice cream, she became distracted by the pile of documents faxed by Wendell Waters.

She read the material, looking for any reason to reject Sandford's invitation. When she finished, Rachel knew, in her heart, she had to be a part of this exciting, far-reaching project. The think tank was the ideal venue to explore the win-win concepts from her book, and the chance to create a positive impact on the lives of millions— victims of war and gross neglect.

Her phone buzzed. Chris texted *"Be over."*

He arrived with his tablet.

"Twice in one day," Rachel said. "Should I be flattered?"

Chris ignored her remark. "Got the info on Lake George," he said. "The camp belongs to General Michael P. Portman, retired. The security system is maintained by the Department of Defense, and it's my system."

"And that means what to me?"

"It means you can feel safe. I built and installed the cabin's security system. Nobody can go in or out without triggering the security cameras. The electronic monitoring system will record all communication exchanges."

Rachel said, "So, no random access?"

"Correct—as long as the system's engaged."

"Good."

"So you're going?"

"Look, I know you think this is about you. But it's not. I have to do this. The potential for the United States to curb human rights abuses is enormous."

"You believe this think tank is a world-changer?"

"Yes, I do." Rachel's voice softened as she inched toward Chris. "And if we'd talked …."

"Don't say it." Chris moved to maintain the distance between them.

"Chris." Rachel reached out to him.

"Don't. I'm still trying to wrap my head around this trip of yours."

Rachel backed off. "I'm changing the subject." She looked sideways at him. "Chris, do you remember Ted Donovan, the guy who rescued me?" That got his attention.

Chris said, "Vaguely."

"Well, Ted Donovan's the think tank chairman."

"Small world," Chris said with a smirk. "Bet you'd

go out with him with no security team."

"Stop it. It's just a coincidence. I've not seen nor spoken to him since the rape."

Chris put up his hands in surrender. "Okay. Okay. But even you've said there's no such thing as coincidence."

"Out," Rachel said, pointing to the door. "Go."

"I'm going. I'm going," Chris said as he ambled toward the door. "I'll see what additional safety measures I can put in place. Update the system."

"Fine," Rachel said. "Have fun. Get out."

Before he closed the door, Chris said, "Rachel. I think your—our—problem's not about going, it's about leaving." The latch's click sounded like a shot.

Dammit Chris!

Rachel dashed over to the refrigerator, grabbed a spoon on the way, and dove into the freezer. She took out a pint of coffee ice cream with dark chocolate and almond bits. She ripped off the top, tossed it in the garbage, ran to the couch, and snuggled in the corner. Eyes closed, she put the first spoonful into her mouth—pure food heaven. She let it melt on her tongue, savoring it. She finished the carton.

She felt much better. Now that she had decided to go, Rachel created her list of "must haves" for Beth Neilson. With Chris in charge of electronic security and Ted Donovan on site, personal security and transportation became her main concern. She decided to use J & J to drive her up. They'd stay with her until she felt comfortable, even if it took the whole six weeks. She'd be fine—confined and secure.

The next morning Rachel called Beth about bringing her security team to the think tank.

Beth said, "I'm putting you on hold while I check." Seconds later. "It's done."

It's done. I'm leaving…leaving Chris like he left me.

Chapter 22
Gramercy Avenue, New York City

With the Lake George trip a short three weeks away, Rachel had four yellow legal pad "To Do" lists in her hand. She laid them down on the dining room table and scanned them, again. They were still incomplete. She grabbed a pen and pad, sat down, and started list five. When she finished, she felt the panic rise.

She paced the apartment to work off her flight response. It didn't work. She jumped on her treadmill, increasing the speed until she was exhausted. Dragging herself to the freezer, she put a triple scoop of raspberry-vanilla into a mug and took it to the table. She ate while she tried to create order from endless lists. The ice cream disappeared before she had a plan.

Exhaustion set in and her eyelids slammed shut. Rachel forced them open long enough to reach her bed and dive under the covers.

She awoke to an apartment bathed in moonlight. She turned on the bedside light and saw her tablet on the nightstand. *Okay, I can do this.* Rachel emerged from her cocoon, sat up, plumped the pillows, smoothed out the covers, and retrieved the tablet.

In stream of consciousness mode, she typed a "Top Ten To Do List"—check calendar, clear or change any appointments, decide on clothes to take, replenish toiletries, place orders for essentials, fill prescriptions, call agent, call family, give Nikolai "to and from" dates so he could deal with service people and keep an eye on the apartment.

Rachel reviewed the list several times and decided it was both manageable and doable—a good start to an overwhelming process. After giving herself permission to tackle the list in random order, she decided to make the hardest call first—the one to her agent. He expected chapters for her next book within four weeks, but he'd have to wait.

"Hi, Ira, this is your favorite pain-in-the-ass writer."

"Rachel, tell me the book is done."

"Not exactly."

"Started? Tell me you've started."

"Ira, the incoming President has appointed me to his Human Rights Think Tank for the month of February."

"The president of what?"

"The President of the United States."

"What year?"

"This year."

"Tell him you can't. Tell him you're too busy. Tell him my wife and children will starve because my agency doesn't make one red cent unless my writers give me books."

"As dear as you are to me, you are but a speck in the President's political agenda."

"I'm crushed yet unmoved."

"Look, I will still do the presentation at New York University, and I'm sure I'll have time to get an outline together and maybe even write a few chapters. When I get back, the book will be my sole focus.

"I'm not happy."

"I'll make you happy, I promise."

"Then with a heavy heart, I give you permission to serve your country."

"Such drama—I'll use it in my book."

"Ha! Take care and call me when you get back."

Chapter 23
New York City

Because of the *New York Times* article, Rachel received interview invitations from the media and intellectual forums. She rejected all but those she could do as a teleconference from home, with a few exceptions. To appease Ira, she accepted personal appearances at New York University and an appearance on *Comedy Central's* "The Daily Show."

Tonight, Jack and Jay escorted her to NYU. Jack dressed as a menacing chauffeur and Jay looked like her date. She took Jay's arm as they entered the lecture hall. He sat next to her on the podium while the Dean of Political Science introduced her. Jack stood by the door off to her left. With her team in place, her safety assured, Rachel focused on her presentation.

Two-hundred-fifty people came to hear her speak.

Rachel spoke for an hour on her sources of motivation and inspiration, her passion for her subject, her hope for global change, and read three passages from her book.

"In conclusion," Rachel said, "I would like to thank NYU for inviting me and you for your kind attention. I encourage each of you to identify an injustice, follow your heart, and find ways to generate positive outcomes. We are all in this life together. And together, we can make the world a better place."

Following the applause, the dean stepped forward and monitored a Q and A session. At the end of that, Rachel agreed to sign books. Jay stood behind her left shoulder while Jack monitored the line of well-wishers, to insure they kept their distance.

Rachel's cheeks hurt from smiling, and her fingers ached from scrawling her name on book after book. She wanted to leave after the first twenty-five signings and it was well past that. Faces blurred into one another but she soldiered on, remaining pleasant and polite. So, when the last person in line, a man jingling change in his pocket, stopped in front of her, she didn't even look up. "To whom shall I make this out?"

"Your biggest admirer, Theodore Donovan."

Her pen stopped in mid-air. She looked up. "Mr. Donovan?"

"Ted, please." He smiled. "Yes, the same Mr. Donovan from ten years ago."

"I can't believe it. After all these years, first I find out you're the think tank chairman and now you're here."

"When you confirmed your participation, I thought it'd be nice to meet on a casual level before we get to Lake George. So I decided to surprise you."

"How nice," Rachel said. She signed his book and

gave it to him. "Here you go." She patted the chair next to her. "Come, sit down."

Ted remained standing. "How about we get out of here?"

Rachel hesitated and gripped the desk. Jack stepped closer on her left and Jay moved to her right. If Ted noticed, he didn't show it. "Let's go to some bistro and share a bottle of wine. I know a little place…."

Rachel swallowed, took a deep breath, and stood up. "I don't usually go out. However, if you insist, there's a coffee shop called Alfie's on Gramercy Avenue, right across from my building."

Ted said, "Then, Alfie's it is." He offered his arm. "We can go in my car."

"I have my own driver," Rachel said. "I'll meet you there."

Twenty minutes later Rachel and Ted ordered coffee and two bagel-nova platters. Jack and Jay sat at a nearby table.

"So," Ted said, as he yanked a napkin from the table-side dispenser and began polishing the silverware at his place setting. "How have you been?" He lined the silverware up, bottom edges straight, three-quarters of an inch from the table edge. He placed the crumpled napkin on the table edge for the waiter to clear and snapped another out of the holder. He used this one to go around the rim of his water glass, crumpled it and placed it with the first.

"Fine," Rachel said. "I'm good."

"I can see you have matured into a beautiful young woman."

"You sound just like my dad."

"Not my intent," Ted said. "You know, I did try to get in touch."

"Mom told me," she said. "I shut down...for a long time. I didn't talk much to anyone. Everything I'd ever wanted and the person I thought I was, did a one-eighty. I lost it all."

"I'm sure it was a very difficult time," Ted said. "However, I'm glad you've decided to embrace the life you deserve."

"Let's just say I'm on the path. Two years ago, I left my parents' home and came to New York. And, although it's been rough at times, I've made a life for myself."

"Excellent," Ted said. "I hope you'll let me be a part of your next steps."

Rachel said, "You will be. My next step is the Lake George think tank."

The waiter came with their orders.

After they settled into their meals, Rachel said, "Ted, tell me something about yourself that I didn't read on-line."

"That's hard. PRAISE is my life," Ted said. "Aside from that, I am somewhat of a workaholic with a fondness for the finer things in life."

"Any hobbies?"

"Hmmm." His eyes searched the ceiling before returning her gaze. "Not per se. However, like you, I am concerned with violence and safety, human rights and peace."

The waiter set two cups of coffee on the table. "Can I get you anything else?"

In unison, Rachel and Ted said, "No," and the waiter turned and left.

Rachel laughed. "Doesn't that call for a pinky wish?"

Ted seemed to freeze, his eyes bore into hers, "I've already got my wish." After a heartbeat, he reanimated.

"Good, I'm glad for you. My wish would be to get to Lake George and back in one piece."

Ted said, "Despite your reluctance to go, I think you're going to be fine. Besides, you'll be with me."

"Not to mention two combat veterans." She smiled. "I'm feeling pretty positive about the whole adventure." She looked up as his knife caught a ceiling fixture's reflection and sent shards of light in her direction.

She flinched. The room started to spin. Rachel pushed her chair out from the table, the legs pushing against the floor emitting a deep screech. Jay rushed to her side before she could stand.

He put his hand on the chair's back, leaned over, and whispered in her ear. "Rachel, it's Jay. I'm here and you're safe. Breathe." He said it several times before she responded. As she took deep breaths, the panic subsided.

She looked at Jay. "Thank you."

"No problem." He pushed her chair in and retreated to his table.

"Sorry, Ted. I had an unexpected flashback," Rachel said. She could see the concern on Ted's face. "It happens. I'm sorry. Please continue." She took a bite of her bagel and sipped her coffee.

He said, "There's not much else to tell except we've been a team for quite a while."

"I don't understand."

"Your books have made a huge impact on me and the foundation's board. We have directed many grants to help the causes you advocate."

Rachel's brows dropped and her eyes narrowed as she had an uncensored epiphany-to-mouth moment. "Ted, have you been stalking me?"

"Absolutely not," he said. "I've been more like a guardian angel from afar."

His matter-of-fact response disturbed her. "What does that mean?"

Ted held his hands up in front of him. "Whoa. All I meant was that I've followed your career with interest and appreciation. I knew if you needed me, you had my card." He put his hands down on the table and leaned toward her. "And, if you had called, I'd have flown to your side—from the ends of the earth."

Ted reached to cover her hand with his. Rachel withdrew before he touched her. Ted smiled and let his hand rest on the table. "I understand. I don't talk much about my stint in the army. Got the uniform, gun, and rifle. Went through basic training. Earned an Expert Marksmanship Badge. Within a month of deployment, my unit got stuck in a cross fire. I was one of three who survived, and we all suffered from PTSD. I think I had the fastest armed forces career in history."

Neither spoke for a few minutes. Rachel finished her meal.

Ted broke the silence. "I'm so glad you'll be at Lake George. I know you'll enjoy the people and the challenge."

"Yes, although I'm surprised Sandford asked me."

"I don't know why," Ted said. "I sent Sandford an advance copy of your latest book. He must have been very impressed. He insisted you be invited to participate. Needless to say, I'm very excited that we get to work together."

Rachel sat up straight and stared at Ted. "How did you get an advance copy of my book, much less permission to send it to Sandford?"

Ted smiled. "Not so hard. Your publisher is a generous contributor to PRAISE. We're friends. I should think you'd be pleased. Your ideas are reaching the highest level of government."

"I'm more than a little miffed that I wasn't informed or part of the decision," Rachel said. "I'd appreciate a heads-up if you decide to plan further things to advance my career."

"Certainly," Ted said. "I think we can do great things together."

"Let's see how the think tank goes first," Rachel said. She looked down at her fingers playing with the napkin in her lap. She raised her eyes to his. "May I ask a personal question?"

"Of course. I don't want there to be any secrets between us."

"Back when you visited me in the hospital, you talked about losing someone close to you. A woman. You mentioned we were similar. Do you remember?"

He nodded. "I'm surprised you do. You were heavily sedated."

"Well, the reason I remember is I now have a doppelganger. She visits my dreams every so often. I think she's your friend."

The color drained from Ted's face. "Do you mean Brenda's talking to you from the grave?"

"Oh, no," Rachel said, leaning toward Ted. "I'm sorry. I didn't mean to upset you. I just want to know her story."

"Why?"

"My theory is that she wants me to know about her. And once I do, she'll move on."

Ted seemed to think about that for a second. "Okay." He pushed the plate in front of him to the side and folded his arms, elbows on the table. In a low reverent voice, he said, "Her name is, was, Brenda Underwood—my childhood friend and first love. She died at fourteen. An itinerant psychopath murdered her and dumped her body in the woods. I was there when the police found her. Brenda's death changed my life."

"My God. How awful," Rachel said. "I'm so sorry."

Ted lowered his eyes and brought a hand to his heart. He remained lost in his thoughts for a few beats before he looked up. "She was beautiful, inside and out. And, Rachel, you're the same. You exude the same kind of energy."

"Ted, I'm flattered, but Brenda and I are not the same," Rachel said.

"Nevertheless, I am drawn to you," Ted said as he extended his hand, palm up, inviting her to cement their connection.

"Ted, I can't. I don't think of you in that way. We're virtually strangers."

"Strangers? You can't mean that." His shoulders fell.

He looked so crestfallen that she said, "I'll concede we have a connection. But relationship-wise, let's start as friends."

Ted sat up and his face brightened. "Okay. Friends it is."

Rachel stood and put on her coat.

Ted sprang out of his chair and said, "You're going?"

"It's late and I'm exhausted." She opened her purse prepared to pull out her wallet.

"This is on me," Ted said, putting his hand up to stop her. "My idea. My treat."

"Thank you, Ted. It was good to see you again." She turned and walked toward the door.

"Let's do this again." Ted called out to her back, as the security team fell into step behind her.

Over her shoulder, Rachel said, "Call me."

Chapter 24
East Side, New York City

Later that evening, in his New York City penthouse apartment overlooking the East River, Ted Donovan sat in his favorite arm chair. He gazed at the unobstructed view of Brooklyn Bridge through a wall of windows. A parade of cars crossed the landmark, headlights blazing. He felt like the king of the world.

A glass of Scotch, a plate of crackers and cheese, and a thick scrapbook sat on the table next to him. His tablet rested on his lap. Ted sipped his drink, tapped the tablet several times and scanned his daily reports. He paid ICU Inc. an outrageous sum of money to license a spyware program that reported all electronic searches on his set of keywords. The report showed the key word, the server, the server's owner, the date-time stamp, and, if possible, the individual initiating the search.

Over the years the reports showed very little activity, but this past month was different. The Meyerson debacle initiated increased searches on PRAISE. One searcher was Rachel Allen. She googled him just prior to her acceptance as a think tank member. He typed in additional key words so as to include the think tank members. The results showed she did the same for each—just like she said.

He smiled and sipped his Scotch. What he didn't tell Rachel at Alfie's was that he had called Sandford after sending him Rachel's book and encouraged her appointment to the think tank. The announcement that Rachel was the guest speaker at NYU initiated his attendance and tonight's tête-à-tête.

Returning to the report, Ted frowned when he saw that the FBI searched on his name several times after his interview with Agent Neilson. This, despite the fact that he answered every question and complied with her warrant for the Meyerson file, emails, and the credit card receipts. Why was she still checking him out?

He took another sip of Scotch and turned to his right. Ted picked up the first of three scrapbooks and placed it in his lap. He stared at the cover—Brenda Underwood's school picture. He caressed it with manicured fingers. She had gotten him through each miserable day of bullying. He was short, skinny, awkward, brilliant, and unappreciated. Brenda told him he was smart and wonderful. She'd laugh at his jokes and stories, hold and comfort him when he felt miserable, and encourage him when he needed it. His world centered on Brenda—his mirror, his reason for being—his first and only love.

Donovan's jaw muscles clenched. He took another sip, sighed, and opened the scrapbook. The first section contained images and pieces of Brenda's life, followed by all the newspaper reports of her death. "Local Girl Missing." "Body Found in Woods." "Coroner Confirms Identity." "Underwood Killer Apprehended." "Killer Dies in Custody."

The rest of the book chronicled Ted's seductions including Jamal "Shooter" Johnson. He spent the whole night reviewing Brenda's Book—volumes one, two and three. He searched for that telltale piece of evidence that might give him away.

Unlike *Dexter*, a show that ran for years on Cable TV, Ted did not relish the kill nor revel in gore. Revenge never entered into the equation. He viewed it more like a surgical operation to remove a growing cancer.

He seduced his targets with their dreams—a house in the suburbs, a college education, a month at their sports hero's training camp, a trip to Disneyland, or a paid gambling vacation in Las Vegas. It wasn't hard to figure out what made these thugs happy. They'd tell him in stranger-to-stranger casual conversations as they waited on line at the supermarket or movies. Or their family members would know. He'd meet them at church or PRAISE sponsored community events. Once Ted knew their dream, it didn't take much to convince them to pursue it—money and transportation.

With each seduction, Ted made the world a better, safer place to honor Brenda's memory and give her death meaning.

When finished, he put the three books back on the TL-15 safe's top shelf and picked up Philip Vanderhagen's plain leather-covered book from the bottom shelf. Vanderhagen brokered these seductions through new PRAISE donors who had a vested but not obvious interest in the outcome. While Ted handled the money and connections, Lucy and her team handled the seductions. The last entries in this book covered the Imanuela Myerson seduction. He reviewed them all.

Ted closed the book, sipped his drink. Lucy and her team did a thorough job. No hard evidence connected him or PRAISE to the family's disappearance. He returned the book to the safe and locked it. Standing and facing the pre-dawn sky, he stretched every muscle in his body and then relaxed, tension dissipated.

He was ready for the challenges of a new day.

Chapter 25
Gramercy Avenue, New York City

Rachel exercised on her treadmill and watched the presidential inauguration ceremony on television. Her phone buzzed. Chris texted, *"Come over?"* She answered, *"K."* Minutes later he arrived and sat in one of the side chairs.

He said, "What's going on?"

She said, "Sandford's being sworn in."

"I mean with Ted Donovan," Chris said. "Nikolai reviewed the security footage and happened to mention you'd been out with him several times in the past few weeks."

"Nikolai is now keeping tabs on me?" Rachel kept exercising.

"Just doing his job," Chris said. "Anyway, just to be thorough and because Donovan's going to be at Lake George, I ran his license plate."

This stopped her. Rachel got off the treadmill, turned the TV off, and positioned herself in front of Chris. "Stop doing whatever you're doing. Ted Donovan is not your business. You lost your say in my life when you walked out."

"That doesn't matter. I'm in charge of security around here, and…."

"Of course it matters." Rachel said. "Chris, unless you're here for a conversation about us, I'm not explaining myself and I don't want to hear about Ted."

Rachel moved into the kitchen to get away and calm down. When she flipped the light on, Chris said, "Ice cream? I'll have a scoop."

She did a fast one-eighty spin to confront him. Hands on hips, she said, "Why are you still here?"

Chris remained relaxed and neutral. "I'm reporting in on the Lake George camp security."

"And?" Rachel's voice was clipped and tone arched as she tried to make him feel uncomfortable and intrusive. It didn't seem to faze him.

Chris said, "I've checked with DoD and arranged to run security tests during the think tank residency. With a controlled number of people in and out, it's the ideal testing situation. I'll be able to monitor and even modify the system. You won't be alone."

"That's comforting," Rachel said, the edge still in her voice. Chris gave her such a hurt look, she softened. "No, I mean it. With you and your system in place, I'll feel safer. Thank you."

"You're welcome."

Rachel stared at him.

"What?"

"You're still here?"

Chris looked away—first at the windows and then at his hands before looking at her. "Rachel, you've got to let me tell you about Donovan."

"Stop."

"Don't you want to know?"

"Out." She pointed to the door. When he didn't move, she said, "Now."

As he passed her, Rachel inhaled his strong scent and held it inside her. In the hall, he turned to face her. She swung the door shut, leaned on it, and exhaled his essence with deliberate slowness.

Rachel stretched her arms, flexed her fingers, and went right into the kitchen to get a double, no, triple scoop of ice cream covered in an obscene amount of hot fudge.

I'm going to get a life with or without him!

Chapter 26
White House, Washington, D.C.

President Franklin Taylor Sandford sat at his desk in the Oval Office. Today he intended to solidify his jobs through the education initiative program and set the launch date.

Chief of Staff Wendell Waters entered and said, "Ready, Mr. President?"

Sandford looked up. "You bet." He pushed a button and said, "Nancy, please bring in the budget sheets."

She came right in and gave the president a folder and left.

"Wendell, you did a great job. You've found enough money for the economic recovery program."

"Your cabinet members helped. We're going to discuss specifics at the two o'clock meeting. If we can't find a major problem with it, you're good to go."

"Excellent. We'll start with a media blitz and then

hit the congressional PR trail. Who's going to deny jobs to Americans?"

"No one. I expect it will be a popular sell," Waters said.

"You're my wing-man on this. Catch anyone who starts to undermine this before they gain traction and attention."

"You know I've got your back," Waters said.

A commotion outside the office interrupted their conversation. Sandford had his finger over the intercom button when Nancy burst in and tried to shut the door behind her, leaning on it with all her weight. It didn't help. Uriah Henderson, Secretary of State, pushed his way in. He looked like an exhausted marathon runner crossing the finish line.

Nancy said, "I'm sorry Mr. President. He forced his way in. I told…."

Henderson planted himself in front of Sandford before she could finish.

Sandford said, "It's okay, Nancy. Thank you." He looked at Henderson with his arms crossed as if prepared to address a wayward child. "Uri, what's so important?"

Henderson couldn't catch his breath and gasped, "Mr. President, you've got to read this!"

"Sit down, man. You're among friends here. We'll take care of whatever it is." Sandford left his chair, walked around his desk and guided Henderson to the couch. Waters brought him a glass of water.

Henderson collapsed, released the top button on his shirt, loosened his tie, and chugged the water.

Waters sat across from him. Sandford took the chair next to Henderson and said, "Now tell me, what's the problem?"

Henderson read from his phone. "The country of Tawanda announces the following modification in its international tax and fee structure. As of the first of February, in addition to current taxes on corporations doing business in Tawanda, the company's country of origin will be assessed an Access Permissions Fee in the amount of one one-hundredth percent of gross corporate profits from wholesale and retail sales or trades based on Tawandian raw materials. From the desk of Adebowale Okoro, President of Tawanda."

"The man must be out of his mind," Sandford said. He got up from the couch and paced the room. "Isn't Okoro the head of some upstart group in the Congo that formed Tawanda, a country the size of a bathmat?"

"That's the one," Henderson said. "Okoro was considered a hero in 2000 when he defended the rights of his people against the government. Soon after, he and a consortium of tribes established the state of Tawanda. Okoro's been at war with the Democratic Republic of the Congo ever since. His people are either war refugees or in the army. This announcement must mean he's run out of money."

"What kind of fiscal damage are we talking about?" Sandford asked.

"Our interest in Tawanda is mining," Henderson said. "Copper, cobalt, gold, tin, and zinc are the big metals, and diamonds are their cash cow. The fee could be fifty thousand to a million a month."

Sandford looked at Henderson and said, "I want you to get me a list of US companies currently operating in Tawanda complete with their CEO contact information. We have to know who and how much we're dealing with."

Waters cleared his throat. Sandford looked at him and said, "Go ahead."

"There is no way that the federal budget could withstand such a financial hit. We'd have to pass the responsibility to the companies."

Sandford said, "No matter how we look at this, it will impact our plans for a solid economic recovery." He turned to Henderson. "Get me that information ASAP."

Henderson got up and stepped away from the couch as a courtesy and for privacy. He called his office and ended with, "I want it yesterday! Understand?" He put his phone in his pocket and addressed the president. "Done. I expect to have the information within the hour."

Sandford went over to the bank of windows and looked out. "We have worked hard to be in a position to help this country's economic recovery." He turned to his two advisors. "I'll be damned if I let this little fucker derail us from our goal."

He stepped to his desk and pushed the intercom button on his desk. "Nancy, cancel the cabinet meeting for this afternoon. Please send up sandwiches and cookies—you know what I like—and hold all calls."

Sandford turned to Waters and Henderson. "Let's get down to work. We've got to stop this assault one way or another."

Chapter 27
Gramercy Avenue, New York City -
Lake George, New York

The night before her trip to Lake George, Rachel's anxiety level hit eight on the Richter scale. Sleep was impossible. When pacing didn't calm her, she changed into sweats and jumped on the treadmill.

The TV faded to white noise, drowned out by the circular conversation in her head. *Afraid of leaving. That's what he said. Maybe he's right, dammit. Why did he blame my work? So unfair. He logged more all-nighters than I did. Working because of me or in spite of me? I'm so stupid. Never saw the signs. We never talked. We're both idiots. Shit.*

Rachel upped the treadmill's pace to assuage her guilt. After a grueling twenty minutes, she turned off the machine, showered, and got into bed. She picked up her phone and stared at it. She wanted to call Chris but knew it'd be disastrous. Nothing had changed. She'd have to accept her shortcomings and honor Chris's decision.

At two in the morning, Rachel fell asleep with the phone in her hand.

Five hours later, dressed and ready to go, she sat on the couch, her silent phone on the coffee table.

By eight, J & J's limousine arrived at her building. Nikolai buzzed her. She did a final walk-through of her apartment and, for the fourth time, made sure she packed the chargers for her tablet, phone, and computer. She put her phone in her purse. Someone knocked on the door. *Chris?* She ran to the door. It was Jay.

"You look disappointed," he said. "That could hurt a guy's feelings."

She laughed. "Don't take it personally. I'm more than a little stressed out and didn't get much sleep."

"It's close to a three-hour trip. You can sleep on the way."

Jack drove up the East Side, made it to the thruway and headed toward the Adirondack Northway. Snow flurries started when they passed the Clifton Park exit.

By the time the car took the Lake George exit ramp, the winter storm covered the trees, bushes, and ground with a thick white carpet—shapes defined by shadows.

Rachel said, "Will we see the lake?"

"I can make that happen," Jack said, as he turned onto Route 9 North and then took a right. On her left, Rachel saw the frozen lake with its marshmallow frosting. On her right sat a strip mall bordering the large log gates guarding Fort William Henry.

Minutes later, after snaking up a hill, Jack turned into a private road and stopped at a massive set of iron gates. The engraved metal sign proclaimed

Portman Landing. He used his phone to text a security code. The gates swung open. He drove down a woodland bordered driveway which gave way to stretches of open areas of fields, lawns, and gardens. As the limousine entered the circular drive, Rachel saw the "camp."

Portman Hall's architectural design favored Adirondack-style stone and logs with huge expanses of glass. As they got closer, Rachel counted five chimneys, two emitting streams of white smoke that fanned and curled into the air. The huge cantilevered front porch, with its beautiful carved double doors, loomed into sight.

Jack sat in the driver's seat while Jay removed the luggage and followed Rachel up the steps. He said, "One or both of us will be with you at all times or stationed outside any closed door. You won't have to worry about a thing."

Rachel said, "Thank you. I'm counting on you."

Before she could ring the bell, Ted Donovan, in a blue pinstripe suit, appeared in the doorway and said, "Welcome."

"This is gorgeous," Rachel said as she stepped into the expansive entry foyer. "When's the tour?"

A tall woman with long dark hair plaited into a single braid, black eyes, and high cheek bones walked toward them. "Rachel, this is Yvonne. She runs the cabin—kitchen and housekeeping," Ted said. "Yvonne, this is Rachel Allen. Please take her coat and luggage to her room while we have lunch."

"And," Rachel said, indicating the man at her side, "this is Jay. He and his partner, Jack, will be staying also."

Yvonne said, "We have been notified of the arrangement. Their rooms are also ready."

Ted said, "Good. Thank you, Yvonne." To Rachel

he said, "If you like, I'll give you a mini-tour of the cabin."

"Yes, I'd like that very much."

Ted led her through the main living space, with its four large conversation areas and two fireplaces, to the rough-edged hand-hewn wood dining table set in a large glass-enclosed alcove. For Rachel, it was like standing in the bow of a riverboat, as it moved through a sea of white foam, with trees—spruce, white pine, oak, birch, and maple—like sentries lining the path down to the lake below.

Yvonne appeared. She placed sandwiches and fruit on the table and then returned to the kitchen.

Ted's voice brought Rachel's attention back inside. "Rachel, all drinks from water to liquor are at the dining room bar. The wine rack and refrigerator are under the counter."

"I'm good," Rachel said, and sat. A clock chimed twice. She glanced at Ted. "That grandfather clock has a nice rich tone."

Ted said, "It should. It's a Chippendale. It's worth a second look when you're in the library. It's one of the few things in the house that's not representative of this region."

Lunch was brief and peppered with Ted's commentary on important pieces of art throughout the camp.

Rachel dabbed her mouth with a napkin and said, "What's on the agenda for today?"

"Let's see." Ted pushed his chair away from the table and leaned back. "I expect the rest of our group tonight and tomorrow. Our formal meetings will begin on Thursday. That gives us time for your pre-conference orientation...." He paused and pursed his lips. "Something you missed by ignoring Sandford's invitation."

Rachel jumped to her defense. "Not my fault. It looked just like another campaign mailing."

"Relax. No harm done. You're here and that's what's important." He smiled. "If it's okay with you, let's meet tomorrow morning. I'll to go over the main points of our mission and give you some background on the team. How does that sound?"

"Sounds interesting. I'm looking forward to it."

"Before you unpack, how about a walk around the grounds? Maybe leave your security guy here?"

"Ted, you know I don't go outside alone."

"You won't be alone. I'll be with you and we'll stay near the house. The only other person we're likely to encounter is the groundskeeper and I assure you he's no threat."

Rachel wanted to say "no" but she thought of Chris. *Change starts now.* "Okay. But not for too long."

Ted smiled. "Don't worry. I'll be right next to you." He got up to lead them to their coats.

Rachel pulled back and turned to Jay, "Please follow us at a distance—in case."

Outfitted for the weather, Rachel and Ted stepped into the winter chill. They strolled around the grounds and Ted played tour guide.

"Did you know that this area was inhabited by the Five Nations of the Iroquois—the Mohawk, Oneida, Onondaga, Seneca, and Cayuga people?"

"I'm impressed," Rachel said, glancing behind her. Jay was in sight.

"Don't be," Ted said. "I researched the region once I knew this was our destination. Did you pass Fort William Henry on your way here? It's at the lake's south end."

"I did. The gates were huge."

"During the French and Indian War against the British, Fort William Henry was the site of major battle. It lasted from March through August of 1757. First, the British defeated the French in March. Then the French retaliated in August by laying siege to the fort for six days. Out of patience, they stormed the fort by force and a bloody massacre ensued. After their victory, the French burned the fort to the ground. If all that sounds familiar, James Fenimore Cooper immortalized the whole grim historic episode in his book, *The Last of the Mohicans*.

"You know, it might be fun to watch the movie version since we're here where it all happened?"

"Good idea." Ted sent a text to Yvonne. "Hey, what's this?" He bent down and picked up an object from the ground. He held up a sharp triangular stone, about an inch long, between his forefinger and thumb. "It's an arrowhead—just for you." He placed it in her hand.

"A bit of magic, I think," she said.

"You got me." He smiled. "I saw it in the gift shop and thought you might like to have a souvenir."

"Thank you," Rachel said, placing it in her pocket.

"You know, it could have been a real find," Ted said. "We are standing on the remains of a Mohawk village. Their descendants worked on the construction of this cabin. In fact, Yvonne's father led the framing crew. Normally he's a part of the structure crew for New York City skyscrapers. He helped out here because the architect specified iron for the framing.

"Aside from that, the project manager used local materials. All the exposed beams came from this property. The crew recycled the stone from the foundation excavation and the mountain side. All the glass, experimental at the time, is coated with a compound that absorbs sunlight in winter and reflects sunlight in summer. The passive solar action maintains the cabin's cozy feeling."

"The General was green before green became the only way to build. I like him already."

They walked in silence for a few yards. Rachel was in mid-step when Ted grabbed her arm and jerked her backwards. Jay ran to her side and inserted his body between them, breaking Ted's grip.

Ted raised his arms, open-handed, to calm them both. "Take it easy. No harm meant. I just wanted to alert you to a dangerous area." He pointed. "See the snow-covered picket fence? It surrounds a platform that leads to a set of stairs that goes down five stories to Lake George—an extra feature Mrs. Portman added for lake access."

Rachel saw the break in the woods. It looked different from the dining room view—still beautiful and treacherous.

"Thanks, Ted," Rachel said. "Good to know." She nodded to Jay who returned to his previous position.

She ventured onto the landing and walked over to the fence. The steep staircase led to the dock jutting into the lake.

Ted stood next to her. "From here, you can see why Mrs. Portman placed landings at intervals so people could rest and catch their breath."

"A good thing. That's quite a drop."

"It's built over the Mohawk village's serpentine foot path down the embankment. Word is, General Portman plans to install a mini ski-lift this summer. Says his wife's getting too old for the stairs. In truth and in confidence, his wife told me it's actually for him."

"And people like me," Rachel said. "I don't think I could make it down and back. The incline alone makes me dizzy."

"Well, you don't have to worry. It's hardly swimming weather."

Rachel laughed. "For sure."

Ted said. "Come on. There's more to see."

They walked to the cabin's backyard. Ted said, "So what do you think about the sports complex?"

Rachel surveyed the flat expanse of land between their position and the mountain. "Are you kidding?"

Ted laughed. "In a way. When it's not completely covered in snow, it's outfitted for summer sports— tennis, bocce ball, croquet, basketball, and volleyball. There's even a putting green. General Portman is very competitive and hosts the Portman Olympic Games all summer."

Rachel said, "It looks large enough to land a plane." A gust of wind enveloped them and she shivered.

"Come," Ted said. "Let's go in."

Two minutes later, they were warming themselves by the fire. Ted sat on the circular couch and Rachel on a floor pillow, closer to the fireplace.

"I'm glad you're here," Ted said.

"Me too."

"Would you like a drink?"

"Not feeling very social right now," Rachel said. "I didn't sleep much last night."

"Don't say another word," Ted said. He stood up and offered to help Rachel to her feet. She waved him away, got up on her own, and started for the stairs.

Ted said, "I'll see you for dinner." He raised his voice. "Yvonne." She appeared within seconds. "Yvonne, please show Rachel to her room."

Half-way up the stairs, the clock chimed four times. Rachel paused, glanced down at Ted, and smiled. "I enjoyed the tour. See you later."

Ted clicked his heels, made a slight bow. "My pleasure." He straightened and flashed her a killer smile. "I'm always available—to you."

In her room, Rachel lay down on the four-poster bed and thought about Ted. *Handsome. Magnetic. A sense of self. Exudes confidence. Great voice. A man who knows what he wants and how to get it. But always seems to be holding back. If he were only younger. Maybe.*

Too tired to think straight, Rachel closed her eyes and lost consciousness.

Jay kept watch outside her door.

Chapter 28
Federal Plaza, New York City

FBI Special Agent Elizabeth Neilson sat in her office and surveyed all the data surrounding the Meyerson family's disappearance—phone records, credit card receipts, appointment calendars, interviews, emails, pictures, airport videos, and her timeline drawn on a white evidence board. Nothing yet had produced any leads. All she knew for sure was that the family that left the LA house was not the family that boarded the plane at LAX.

Beth leaned back in her chair and cleared her mind. She let the case's puzzle pieces appear one by one and float around until they fit. Six minutes later, she sat up. One or more perpetrators had to be on site or watching, to make sure it all went as planned. She grabbed the folder with the transcribed interviews, summaries, and videos. She went over each of them and used a yellow sticky to mark places where she found missing, incomplete, or inconsistent information.

Next, she watched the LAX videos. She ignored the imposters and concentrated on the faces in the background. She ran facial recognition software. If there was a duplication or connection, she'd find it.

By midnight, Beth couldn't see straight. The facial recognition software was still running. There was nothing more she could do except wait. She emailed her boss that she'd be in late the next day and left. She needed sleep.

Beth entered her apartment. Didn't turn on the lights. Went directly to the bedroom. Dropped her clothes on the floor and climbed into bed.

At eight-thirty, Beth woke up with a start. She had figured out a part of the puzzle. When she tried to put it into words, the clue escaped her. She closed her eyes and tried to see what she saw. It didn't happen. She got up, threw on some sweats, and made a cup of coffee.

She'd inherited the small one-bedroom apartment when another agent had been transferred. Furnished it with several pieces from her parents' home and finds in local second-hand stores, her only new purchase was a mattress. The apartment was comfortable. It was home and it was getting cleaned today.

Out came the vacuum and steamer, the duster and dust rags, the cleaning solutions and plastic gloves. Beth had a system. No visual or audio distractions. One room at a time—top to bottom. She straightened, dusted, and wiped. Vacuumed and steamed. After making the bed and putting dirty linens in the washer, she remembered.

Everything in the case appeared to take place in California and China except the New York City based PRAISE Foundation. Ted Donovan managed the award and funded the trip. And yet, there was no evidence of a phone call, email, text, or document that put him or his organization in direct communication with the Meyersons. That didn't make sense. She must have overlooked something.

Beth flew to her office and scanned all the electronic and hardcopies of phone calls and emails for any connection to PRAISE or Donovan. Nothing. She slumped in her chair and threw her ballpoint pen across the room.

"You look like you need some help," said a voice from the doorway.

Beth looked up and smiled. "FBI Special Agent Eric Jerrod. What are you doing here?"

"I'm here to assist." Eric strode into the office and sat down.

"With what?" Beth said. "I'm drowning in a sea of dead ends."

"See, I knew it'd be a good time to team up again," Eric said. "I love a challenge."

"I'm glad," Beth said, "because this is a giant brain teaser."

Eric took notes as Beth filled him in on the case status and her epiphany. "It seems to me that there would be an ongoing 'How're you doing,' or 'Need anything,' or 'How can we help' ribbon of communications between PRAISE and the family. And I find it odd that it's missing. When I have a little more concrete non-evidence, I'll get a warrant to check PRAISE phones and its employee phones."

"Make that 'we,'" Eric said. "I'm reassigned. Desk and computer to arrive forthwith."

"How'd you pull that off?"

"Are you going to interrogate me or put me to work?"

"Work," Beth said. "What I need is research on Theodore Xavier Donovan. Public, FBI, and National Crime." Eric pulled out his tablet and fired it up. "Plus, I've got facial recognition software running on the computer. So far, there have been some hits but none of our movie stars have what it takes to pull this off."

"Consider both done."

"Good. I'll be back in ten."

Twenty minutes later, Beth returned. "Brought you a present," she said and placed a tall cup of coffee on the desk. "Find anything?"

Eric reached over to the printer and handed her documents with one hand, picking up the cup with the other.

Beth pulled up a chair and went through the report, commenting as she read. "I feel sorry for Donovan. He suffered traumatic losses before he even finished high school. Safety Aide in college. Not surprising. Seems like he wanted to protect the girls. PRAISE Foundation. Funding global human rights issues," Beth said. Then her voice changed. "What's this?"

"What's the matter?"

Beth stood up and walked over to Eric. "You're not going to believe this. I know Rachel Allen. She was my college freshman roommate. I hadn't seen her in years until the other day when I met with her on FBI business." Beth reached for the think tank file and gave it to Eric. "Here, take a look at this."

Eric read it and regarded Beth. "You mean these two are together right now?"

"In Lake George. For the month."

"Well, well. Small world."

Beth shot him a look. "You think it's a coincidence?"

Eric said. "These seem to be independent presidential appointments."

"Let's look at this. Out of millions involved in the global problem of human rights, these two happen, by chance, to be on a committee of eight. Right?"

"Well, when you put it that way," Eric said.

"Something's wrong. I can feel it." Beth said. "I have to go to Lake George."

Eric said, "For what? We don't know that he's dangerous or even implicated. You just can't go up there and arrest him. We have to wait until we have probable cause."

Beth stared at Eric, sighed, and said, "You're right."

"Now let's find out more about this guy Donovan."

"And," Beth said, "the White House appointments."

Chapter 29
Lake George, New York

In the early hours before sunrise, Rachel's dream began.

She floated out of bed, down the hall to the balcony overlooking the library. Turning right, she went through an open door into the darkness beyond. A bare bulb, hanging from the ceiling, switched on. She sailed up a circular staircase and hovered in a hallway with six doors, three on each side, all ajar. Beyond each door, a dormered room with a single unmade bed held a chest with three drawers, a small table, a chair, and a hand-sewn doll.

A strong gust of wind blew through the hall, doors slammed shut as the hallway became a twisting, turning, tilting funnel. Like a snowflake, she floated toward the eye. Down. Down. Down.

Daylight streamed through Rachel's bedroom

windows. She felt the light before she saw it. Sitting up, she realized she still wore the clothes from the day before and someone had covered her with a blanket.

She looked around the room, as if seeing it for the first time. A dresser. A small round table and two chairs. A large mirror leaning against the wall. A shelving unit below the window. Rachel stepped closer. Tucked in a corner, almost hidden by the large story books, sat a hand-made Raggedy-Ann-like doll.

Rachel smiled. Her subconscious was working overtime. The clock said six-thirty. She stretched, got out of bed, and into her workout clothes.

She stepped into the hall, acknowledged Jack. "Thanks for the blanket." She'd taken about two steps when Jack came up beside her. "Actually, it was Mr. Donovan. He wanted to make sure you were okay. I never left him alone with you, and I didn't leave your side until he was gone."

"Thanks, Jack. I'll remember to lock my door if I'm ever alone. I plan to hit the treadmill." He nodded and followed.

At the top of the stairs, the smell of coffee permeated the air and distracted Rachel from her mission. She went into the dining area and found coffee, bagels, cold cereal, cheeses, and muffins on the sideboard. She looked at Jack and he shook his head. Passing on the food, she poured a cup of coffee and sat, losing herself in the wintery world outside.

"Good morning."

Rachel jumped and her coffee sloshed over the cup's sides.

"Sorry," Ted said. He grabbed some napkins. "Didn't mean to do damage."

"You startled me," Rachel said, as she tried to contain the spill.

Ted said, "Here, I'll get it." He leaned over and

cleaned up the coffee, took her cup to the kitchen, brought back two cups of coffee, placed them on the table, and sat next to her.

"You must have been exhausted," Ted said. "You never got up for dinner. But I didn't forget you. I checked on you after dessert."

"I heard. And, while I appreciated the blanket, I'd prefer it if you'd wait for an invitation before entering my room again. I've haven't been alone in a strange place for years, and I'll never get to sleep if I think my privacy could be compromised at any time."

"Of course," Ted said and changed the subject. "I must say you look refreshed and... lovely this morning."

Rachel smiled. "If I can find the workout room, I'll be un-lovely in a matter of minutes."

Ted laughed. "It's through the library, under the balcony, and behind the stairs. On your right."

"Excellent." Rachel stood. "I'll be back for breakfast after I've showered and changed."

Ted said, "How about we meet at ten in the library? Will that give you enough time?"

"Works for me."

"Good," Ted said. "And by the way, in case you see any strangers wandering around, General Portman checked in around midnight and Amy Yeager arrived this morning around five. I expect we won't see them until lunchtime, but you never know."

"When do the others arrive?"

"In the next couple of hours, I expect Isabel Upton and Dr. Norman Weisman. This afternoon's arrivals are Quentin Sheffield and James Jefferson."

"Thanks for the heads-up," Rachel said. "See you later."

The workout room was well-equipped with machines and devoid of people. Rachel had her hand on the treadmill when she turned to Jack. "I think I'm going to be okay on my own for a little while. Why don't you and Jay take a break and go down to the village? Enjoy yourselves on me."

Jack agreed and left. As his footsteps faded, Rachel paused. She was alone in this huge home, with four other people, two complete strangers, stashed in second-floor bedrooms. They might appear at any time. Maybe she had been foolish rather than brave to let the boys go. She took her phone out of her pocket. She had her finger poised over J and J's contact number when she remembered Chris. *I can do this.* She put the phone away, got on the treadmill, and began her journey toward independence.

At nine-thirty, Rachel returned to the dining room and ate breakfast. She felt good. Strong. Ready. At ten, holding her second cup of coffee, she walked into the library.

The room was two stories high and featured narrow windows to let in light and maximize wall space. Shelves held books, art, and artifacts. The Adirondack-styled room contained several seating areas accented with cushions and rugs—similar to her bedroom. Family photographs and Native American sculpture graced the tables. Against the library wall and opposite the staircase, sat the magnificent grandfather clock.

In a leather wing chair, Ted typed on his laptop. As soon as he sensed Rachel, he stopped and smiled. "Right on time. Let's go into the study."

He guided her to a door under the upstairs balcony. He flipped open the keypad and entered a code. The door released to reveal General Portman's study.

Ted placed his laptop next to the documents on the desk and said, "Have a seat."

"Only if you leave the door open," Rachel said. "I'm uncomfortable in small enclosed spaces."

"Not a problem," Ted said and they both sat down—he at the desk and she in a visitor's chair. He leaned forward, face serious. "You know he's dead."

Rachel blinked, said nothing, and looked at her hands clasped in her lap.

"The student who raped you is dead."

Rachel raised her eyes to his. "I don't want to talk about it or let it be a part of who I am now, who we are now."

"I thought…."

"No. I've acknowledged the past, but my current goal is to live in the present."

They sat in silence until Ted spoke. "I'm sorry. I didn't intend to upset you. I care for you. I just wanted you to know that he can't hurt you ever again. And I will do everything in my power to make sure no one ever hurts you again."

"Change the subject or I'm leaving."

Ted nodded and leaned back. He opened a folder and retrieved its contents. "Let's get down to business. First, let me know if you have trouble setting up your electronic equipment or accessing the WiFi. Here is your username and password." He handed her a slip of paper. She read it and put it in her pocket.

"Second, I have a favor to ask. Would you mind being the team researcher until my assistant gets here? Of all the team members, you are the most qualified."

"Is that why you made sure the president invited me? To use me?"

"Absolutely not. How could you even suggest that?"

"Well, when I was being considered for the think tank, surely the fact that I rarely go out must have come up. So, was the research a factor?"

"Rachel, you are blowing this way out of proportion," Ted said. "In your isolation, you've underestimated the importance of your work and your incredible mind."

The unexpected compliment embarrassed her. She cast her eyes at the rug, noted its pattern, familiar in a déjà vu sort of way. Returning her gaze to Ted, she said, "Perhaps."

"For sure," Ted said and smiled. He opened another folder and said, "Let's go over the team members."

"First, our host, General Michael P. Portman, retired as of last year, goes back to Desert Storm. He lost hundreds of troops to the machinations of revolutionaries, insurgents, and terrorists. He tried to see the greater good, but each death takes its toll. He wanted the indigenous populations free to live their lives without fear, and yet he had to protect his men. He made the hard decisions even when he got orders with catastrophic consequences. He's known to question authority and present his case for an alternate approach. If the original order stands, he'll execute it."

Rachel said, "A loyal soldier."

"He's got a strong personality, and he's not too fond of Quentin Sheffield."

Ted opened the next folder from the pile. "Quentin Sheffield, former head of Special Forces for Democracy, is a well-paid 'gun for hire' contractor to the United States Armed Forces. His friends call him "Q." For him, a no nonsense guy, the mission is paramount. He executes orders first and asks questions later. Off the job, he's likeable and a good family man."

Rachel said, "In and out. Take no prisoners."

"Right. Quentin's knowledgeable, abrupt, and not to be underestimated. On the other hand, Amy Yeager, our celebrity activist, sees only the orphaned children—starving, dying, or dead. She's smart and believes in negotiation, often depending on public opinion and support to help her sway her opponents. She's persistent and insistent."

Rachel said, "I read somewhere that she's disarming, persuasive, and shrewd—a manipulation trifecta."

"She's nobody's fool. Neither is Dr. Norman Weisman, a Harvard ethics professor. He ponders, in due course, all sides of the issues at hand and holds his conclusions up to an ethical and moral mirror. This may influence our time frame."

"Noted."

"Isabel Upton, former head of Red Cross International, is a straight shooter. She calls them as she sees them. She's furious that tons of supplies funded and transported by the Red Cross sit on docks and warehouses, the needy camped right outside the area. She knows that unfulfilled missions kill donations. Isabel is a compelling force.

"Our final member is James Bristol Jefferson, former chancellor of Yale University. He has extraordinary skills with respect to negotiations with high level donors, administrators, and faculty. He's a tactical genius when it comes to people."

"I'm impressed by President Sandford's choices," Rachel said. "I'm truly honored."

Ted said, "And we're glad to have you. Keep in mind any team solution must pass the closest scrutiny, be self-contained, realistic, doable, and without loopholes." Ted's phone rang. He looked at the caller ID and said, "I hope you don't mind—I have to take this." He raised his hand, palm up, fingers open, toward the door.

Rachel said, "No problem. See you at lunch."

Left on her own, Rachel wandered around the library, checking out the book and art collections. The grandfather clock chimed eleven-thirty. She decided to go to her room, but as she rounded the banister, she saw General Portman, Amy Yeager, Isabel Upton, and Norman Weisman relaxing around the fire. She introduced herself and joined them, choosing to sit on a chair—not ready to share couches or floor pillows with strangers.

They talked about the opportunities the think tank, if successful, would afford the whole spectrum of humanitarian aid. With time and familiarity, they talked of family, travel, hobbies, and interests. The conversation continued through lunch, after which the team members disbursed to check emails and tend to any pressing issues.

Rachel lingered at the table. She had gotten through the team's initial meeting and maintained her personal space with ease. She smiled, toasted her new self with a bottle of water, took a sip of success, and went upstairs.

In her room, door open, Rachel wrote and sent emails to her sister and mother. She wanted to reach out to Chris, but couldn't decide how. Should she apologize for her fears? No. Should she forgive him his unilateral approach to problem solving? No. Could she sidestep both issues? No.

Her phone buzzed and broke her concentration.

J & J Security texted, "*Back. Jay outside your door.*"

Rachel texted, "*Thanks.*"

About to put the phone down, she saw a text from Chris, "*Everything okay?*"

She texted, "*Yes. Comfortable with team members. Expect to send security home.*"

He texted, "*No. Keep.*"

She texted, "*Why?*"

He texted, "*Donovan.*"

She texted, "*MYOB!*" and ended the conversation.

An envelope slid under the door. Rachel retrieved it and read, "You are cordially invited to a Welcome Cocktail Party tonight at five-thirty in the great room. Casual Dress."

She looked at her phone. *Chris opted out of my life. Why is he still trying to control it?*

Chapter 30
Lake George, New York

Rachel arrived downstairs by five-thirty-eight. A trim James Jefferson in a turtleneck and sport jacket and a ripped Quentin Sheffield in camo shirt and pants greeted her, inviting her into their conversation. She smiled and joined them by the fireplace. James said, "May I get you a glass of Chablis?"

Rachel nodded. "Yes, please."

When James left, Quentin stepped closer to her. Too close. She shifted to reclaim her personal space.

"I've read *Communication Strategies*," he said. "I can tell you've never been to a refugee camp or met an insurgent. You'd take a much harder line if you'd smelled what I smelled and seen what I've seen. Your suggested approach…," he paused and looked up as if searching for the appropriate phrase, "lacked a certain practicality."

"Perhaps. I don't believe perpetuating the killing is the answer either." Rachel smiled. "I am looking forward to your take on reasonable alternatives."

"I expect we shall engage in lively discussions."

Rachel noticed Quentin's face harbored artifacts from his tours of duty—a two-inch scar ran from his temple into his hair line and a five-inch scar ran from the base of his neck under his chin to his ear. They added to his rugged appearance.

"Like the scars? I've got lots more." He grinned. "Be happy to show them to you sometime."

Rachel parried the offer. "I'm not *that* interested."

Quentin raised his empty glass and left to get a refill.

"Here you go," James said, returning with her glass of wine. "A toast to the success of our mission."

As if orchestrated, all attention shifted to the staircase. Amy Yeager appeared wearing a beige floor-length T-shirt dress with a deep V neckline. She navigated the staircase with practiced ease. Rachel excused herself from James and approached the actress. "Hello, Miss Yeager, I'm Rachel Allen—a big fan of yours."

The actress said, "Really? I'm surprised, Miss Allen. My films don't have the intellectual depth of your books."

Rachel said, "Perhaps, but your films are far more entertaining."

Ted Donovan entered the room, dressed as usual in a suit and tie. Amy's attention jumped right to him, dismissing Rachel in the process. The actress licked her lips, ran her fingers through her hair, and smoothed her dress over her hips. She glided to his side and latched onto his arm.

"Ted, darling," she said. "I've been dying to see you again. Come. Let's get a drink."

Rachel sipped her wine and watched. Amy, the ingénue, was long gone. She had to be in her mid- to late-forties although she looked at least ten years younger. Amy and Ted made a good match as both were attractive, successful, and confident.

"Amy Yeager knows how to take over a room, doesn't she?" Isabel Upton stood behind Rachel's shoulder. Her hoarse voice whispered, "For Amy, like Shakespeare, 'All the world's a stage.'" She chuckled and moved to Rachel's right. "I've read and enjoyed all your books—although 'enjoy' is probably not the right word considering the topics."

"It's all right," Rachel said. "I'm flattered."

"You're a strong voice for political reason as well as for women," Isabel said. "It's refreshing."

General Michael Portman, sporting a Hawaiian print shirt and khaki pants, approached. Raising his drink in salute, he said, "Good evening, ladies."

Rachel echoed his gesture. "General, your cabin is beautiful."

"Frankly, it's not my doing. I'll convey your appreciation to the missus."

Isabel said, "How long have you lived here?"

"My family has owned the land for generations," the general said. "Frankly, I think we bought it from the Indians."

"It's true." Dr. Norman Weisman said, stepping into the conversation in a cashmere sweater over jeans. "I did the research."

Ted and Amy walked over. He disentangled her from his arm and said, "Have you all met Amy Yeager?" She pouted at his disconnect but perked-up at the mention of her name. She basked in the spotlight as Ted edged closer to Rachel.

At the half-hour chime, as the smell of roast beef, homemade bread, and fresh baked apple pie filled the great room, Ted said, "Dinner's ready."

He turned to Rachel and offered his arm. She took it and they led the group into the dining room.

The linen-covered table set off the cloth napkins and a full complement of dishes, silverware, and glasses. In the center stood a crystal bowl, overflowing with fruit and flanked by silver candlesticks. Place cards sat on each napkin. The ambiance said elegant yet informal.

Ted seated Rachel and whispered in her ear, "I assigned you this seat so I could keep an eye on you."

Before anyone tasted a morsel, Ted rose, glass in hand. "I'd like to welcome you all to Portman Hall. Thank you, General, for opening your home to us. We've a lot of work to accomplish in a short time. I've no doubt that, given the talent, insight, and experience seated here tonight, we'll be successful. I'd like to toast each of you. You answered the call and accepted the responsibility to serve your country." He received a polite applause.

General Portman stood. "While it's my family's tradition to say a prayer before meals, I'll not force that upon you. However, I do ask for a moment of silence in honor of our blessings, for those who have given their lives in service to and for our country, and for guidance in achieving our mission." Heads bowed until the general thanked them and sat down.

After the meal, the group adjourned to the great room. In transit, Rachel took the opportunity to talk to Jack. "I'm surprisingly okay. I'd like to go it alone tonight. If I feel okay in the morning, let's talk about you and Jay going home."

Jack lifted an eyebrow and said, "Are you sure?"

"I'm sure. We'll talk in the morning."

"Okay," Jack said. "Tomorrow."

Rachel stared at his retreating figure, not really

sure at all. With a sigh, she joined her new acquaintances in the great room. Before she had a chance to pick a place to sit, Ted came over with a white towel draped over his forearm and his fingers balancing a tray with one glass.

He said, "This last cordial is for you." Like a well-trained butler, he executed a thirty-degree bow.

Rachel smiled, took the drink, and said, "Thank you, sir."

The tray and Ted disappeared like magic. She walked over to the window and waited until everyone found their conversation niche. Preferring to observe, she chose to sit on an empty loveseat.

By the fire's light, Rachel sipped her drink and thought about dinner. She had caught Ted staring at her throughout the meal. He seemed to know when she looked at him and met her gaze with an endearing half smile. Amy guarded her turf with vigor and made sure these connections were brief.

At the chime of midnight, Rachel glanced at her phone. No message from Chris.

Ted came over. "May I join you?"

She put the phone away and smiled. "Of course."

Just as Ted sat down on her right, Amy appeared out of nowhere and inserted herself into the small space on Rachel's left. Determined to make the two-seater hold three, she forced Rachel to slide closer to Ted. Once seated, Amy leaned toward Ted across Rachel's lap, exposing most of her ample breasts. Ignoring Rachel, Amy said, "Teddy, we…."

In that instant, Rachel hit full panic mode. "Excuse me," she said as she struggled to extricate herself. Amy's lips were inches away from Ted's when Rachel's stomach reversed. Nice wasn't working. So she leaned forward, placing one hand on Ted's knee and the other on Amy's and stood.

The room spun. Her eyes couldn't focus. She tried to take a step but lost her balance and dropped to the floor. The last thing she heard were voices—"Are you okay?" "Let me help you," "Give her some air," before she lost consciousness.

Rachel woke to cold air caressing her face. Wrapped in a Hudson Bay blanket, she was propped up next to an open window. The group stood in a semi-circle around her. She said, "What happened?"

"You fainted," the general said. "How are you feeling?"

"Much better, thank you. I must have been overwhelmed by the combination of a big dinner and the fireplace heat."

"Frankly, that's not uncommon," the general said.

Ted said, "What you need is rest."

"I'm fine," Rachel said. "Really." She reached out with one hand and closed the window, clutching the blanket with the other.

"Let's not take a chance," Ted said. "Come on. Bedtime. I'll walk you up."

Standing on the second step, Ted addressed the group. "I'll be right back."

Rachel said, "Good night. See you all in the morning."

The group responded. "Feel better." "Good night." "See you in the morning."

At her door, Ted lingered, one hand in his pocket playing with his keys.

"They're expecting you downstairs," she said.

"I know," Ted said. He didn't move.

"Go, I'll be fine."

"Are you sure you don't want me to stay?"

"Ted, is everything okay?" Amy stood at the top of the stairs.

Rachel said, "Go. I'll see you in the morning."

Ted started to say something, but changed his mind and turned to Amy, "Yes, I'm coming."

Rachel shut the door, locked it, and shoved a chair under the knob. Within minutes, she was in bed, relaxed, and thinking about the evening.

The people, all at least fifteen years older than she, seemed genuine and nice.

The men were charming. She liked Isabel, smart and quick, if not a bit intrusive. Amy's inside Hollywood stories commanded center stage at dinner, but her Ted-obsession was off-putting.

Ted perplexed her. They had gone out several times after their first meeting and were always accompanied by Jack and Jay. Ted picked quiet intimate restaurants and art galleries where they shared opinions on the art pieces, current events, and food. Ted treated her very well. She could tell he wanted to create a deep connection with her but he didn't reveal much of himself. As a result, she held back. Although the fact that he was fifteen to twenty years older helped to maintain emotional distance. She saw him more as a doting uncle than anything else.

Tonight, Ted attention created some difficulties. She didn't like being in the spotlight or getting hostile energy from Amy.

It feels like he's making a play for me. Taking for granted our time in New York City served to break the ice for a more intimate relationship. She shivered. *That's not happening. Or maybe I'm being too sensitive and misinterpreting his behavior. It's certainly been a while since I've even had to think about this stuff.*

Besides, I'm still connected to Chris.

Not the Chris who walked out. Not the Chris who made unilateral decisions. The Chris who made her laugh. The thoughtful Chris. The Chris who remembered the little things, listened, touched her... and ....

Rachel sat up. *It doesn't matter who was right or wrong. I have to fix this so we can be together.* She picked up her phone and texted. With a great weight lifted from her shoulders, she closed her eyes and waited for his reply.

Her phone screen flashed DRAFT next to "*Chris, I miss you,*" and went dark.

Chapter 31
Federal Plaza, New York City

FBI Special Agents Beth Neilson and Eric Jerrod poured over the life of Theodore Donovan and the PRAISE Foundation via public and police records, insurance claims, and tax filings. Everything seemed in order. They sat back, frustrated.

Beth said, "So, what've we got?"

They swiveled their chairs to look at the large white board covered with notes, time lines, photographs, and a hand-drawn relationship chart.

"Nothing out of California," Eric said. "We ran down all the credit card receipts. They must have paid cash for the limousine service. We have no idea who they used, so we have no vehicle and no driver."

"We checked all the limo services, car dealerships, and rentals. Right?"

"Yep. No record of calls or service regarding the Meyersons within a hundred-mile radius."

"What about car sales?"

"In that same radius, there were three hundred and fifteen used and new transfers. All accounted for. We can go wider but the limo could have been brought into the state anytime between the day the Meyersons accepted the trip and the day they left."

"Do we have the license plates of every vehicle we checked out?" Beth asked. "Because if we do, I'd like them checked against every limo plate entering the greater LA area."

"Are you kidding?" Eric asked.

"Check them against FasTrak. If no matches, then toll area videos. Start from the day the Meyersons disappeared and work backwards to the date when PRAISE notified Imanuela of her award."

"On it." Eric made the call.

Beth got up and paced the room, her eyes never leaving the white board.

Eric said, "LA's on it."

"Eric, we still have no motive," Beth said. "That bothers me."

"I checked Imanuela Meyerson's open cases and any threats she received. All dead ends. I'm not too surprised. Your typical disgruntled killer doesn't create elaborate plans. He or she wants results and quick. I think our perp is atypical—a smart and critical thinker."

"The house sitter's story?"

"Checked out. Talked to her friend at the hospital who confirmed she did refer Ingram to Dr. Meyerson."

"So we're back to Donovan," Beth said. "Mr. Theodore Xavier Donovan."

"Where do we start? So far, he's clean."

"So far."

"You know, if it is him, for an amateur, he's done

a very professional job."

Beth eyes lit up. She slammed her fist on the desktop and ran over to Eric. She took his face in her hands and gave him a quick kiss on the lips. "Eric, you're a genius. Donovan's done it before."

The surprised look on his face morphed into a broad smile. "Does this mean the attraction is mutual or were you going for pure sexual harassment?"

Beth blushed. "I'll only admit that I may have over-reacted."

Eric said, "Guess that means you owe me."

"We'll talk about that after we put Ted Donovan behind bars."

"Whoa," Eric said. "We're a long way from proving he killed the Meyersons, much less being a serial killer. We need some facts before we hang the guy."

"I'm on a roll and you bring up details." Beth threw her hands in the air. "I give in to your wisdom. Let's concentrate on compiling the facts."

Eric smiled. "I'll work on the serial killer aspect, since it was my idea."

"Okay. Okay," Beth crumpled a sheet of paper and threw it at him. "I'll be sure to give you credit in my report."

Eric deflected the missile. "Let me see if I can find similar cases with a common thread." He turned to his computer to search the myriad of databases at his disposal.

"Good," Beth said. "I'll track Donovan's connection with Rachel, starting with the White House." She sat down and got Wendell Waters on the first try. After a few minutes, she hung up. "Eric, Waters said the president picked her." She stared at the folders on her desk and selected "Freedom College." She re-read all the notes. "Eric, you know what? I think Detective Voss was on to something."

She made a call to Voss. She got up, grabbed her coat, and looked at Eric. "Coming?"

Four hours later, at the police station down the block from Freedom College, Beth and Eric sat in an interrogation room with Detective Peter Voss. A thick folder lay on the table between them.

Voss said. "I have my suspicions about Ted Donovan but they are circumstantial and I've had no way, resources, or money to pursue them."

Beth said, "What exactly do you suspect?"

"I think our Mr. Donovan here," he said as he patted the folder, "gets his rocks off beating up perpetrators. Later, if he feels the legal system fails to adequately punish them, he kills them."

Beth and Eric exchanged looks.

"You're serious?" Beth said. "We've found no indications that Ted Donovan is violent."

Voss said, "Take a look." He opened the folder and fanned out pictures of four males—faces and torsos. "They all had to spend days in intensive care."

Beth said, "Donovan did this?"

"Yes. In each case, the man attacked a female student on campus. Donovan, a student safety aide at the time, responded. First on the scene, he made sure the perpetrator did not run away before he attended to the victim."

Eric said, "Was he on duty?"

"Not always on duty but always available."

"Did you say all these rapists are dead?"

"One's still in prison. The other three died within a year of their crime."

Beth said, "And you think Donovan killed them?"

"I know he did. Problem is I can't prove it."

"Tell us about the Rachel Allen case."

Voss leaned forward, arms resting on the table. "After the rape, when I interviewed Donovan, he remained controlled and cool. He didn't even blink when I showed him the perp's pictures. He only reacted when I told him the kid had diplomatic immunity. And by react, I mean he showed minimal interest.

"I'm so sure about Donovan that I tracked the student through Google Reader. Three months later, the boy died. Hit by a bus outside a soccer stadium in Paris."

"Where was Donovan?"

"I'll bet my pension that bastard was in Paris."

Eric said, "Is there any chance we can get copies of these reports?"

"This one is for you," Voss said, as he replaced all the pictures and papers in the folder. "Get him."

On the way back to New York City, Beth and Eric stopped at the Allen residence and interviewed Rachel's parents.

"Mr. Donovan? He's a very nice man. He spent the whole night at the hospital until he could see Rachel for a few minutes. He gave us his card and left. Other than calling a few times after we got home, I haven't spoken to him since. However, he did save Rachel's life. We'll always be grateful to him."

After the short interview, Helene and Harry transformed the empty dining table into a smorgasbord of deli delights in fewer than five minutes. They invited Beth and Eric to join them. "You can't leave here hungry," Helene protested. "What would the neighbors think?"

An hour and a half later back in New York City,

the agents parked near their office. Beth said, "Here, take the Donovan folder. I need some air."

Eric said, "Okay," and took off.

Beth walked east for several blocks. The FDR Drive resonated with traffic as she crossed the pedestrian bridge. In the small park by the East River, she sat down on a bench and huddled inside her coat. She watched the river as it flowed toward the Atlantic, slowed by the ice and slush on its salty, dark gray-green surface. A tugboat pulled a barge. The wake, a ribbon of cleared water, disappeared in the current.

Beth concentrated on the river's movement to calm her mind and clarify the situation. On one hand, she wanted Rachel out of that Lake George camp, but on the other, she had no actual cause or proof. If Donovan kidnapped the Meyersons, she wanted to make sure she had an airtight case. If not, she didn't want to create a false panic. Besides, Rachel did have protection of sorts, as Eric had pointed out. There were two soldiers up there with her.

Beth returned to Federal Plaza and headed upstairs to her office. She wasn't at all certain that waiting was in Rachel's best interest.

Chapter 32
White House, Washington D.C.

President Franklin Taylor Sandford's day took a turn for the worse. Tawandian President Adebowale Okoro dominated the news, manipulating the media with a vengeance. He had let the reporters slog through the refugees' slums and film the tent-like housing, crammed full of sick and starving families, and hordes of flies attracted by the unsanitary conditions. The White House email was full of outrage.

Sandford had his people working around the clock to come up with a plan that didn't bankrupt the country, would satisfy corporate backers, and would appease Okoro. The global commotion dropped his approval ratings like a rock. Worse, it diverted his attention from pressing issues in the States.

The intercom announced, "Mr. Waters, Mr. President."

"Wendell," the president said, as Waters entered. "You're early for our meeting."

"Sorry, Mr. President, I just got a call from the FBI. They wanted to know how you chose the Human Rights Think Tank members."

"Strange. Did they give you a reason?"

"No. Just said it came up as part of the investigation into the Meyerson disappearance," Waters said as he handed the president a piece of paper with the team members' names.

President Sandford looked at the list. "I remember. They supported my election either directly or indirectly. Ted Donovan, through PRAISE, is a major player in funding human rights advocacy groups and Rachel Allen...."

"She's the writer," Waters said.

"Right. Read her book. An obvious choice."

"So, to be clear, you picked them all?"

Sandford raised his eyebrows.

Waters said, "Sorry, Sir. Just want to give the FBI a definitive answer."

"Tell them, 'yes.'"

"Thank you, Mr. President. I'll see you at later at our two o'clock meeting."

Sandford nodded. Alone, he looked at the list again, crumpled the paper, and threw it in the trash.

By mid-afternoon, no major country had agreed to Okoro's terms. Ignored, the Tawandian halted all aid to the refugees, holding them hostage. The world had underestimated the tenacious, ruthless, egomaniacal Okoro.

The U.S. companies rejected Okoro's plan and started dismantling their operations in Tawanda. Sandford ordered the immediate evacuation of U.S. citizens.

Over the intercom, Nancy said, "Secretary of State

Uriah Henderson, Mr. President."

Henderson entered holding a folder. "I've got the draft of your speech on the response to Okoro, Mr. President." He handed the folder to Sandford. "Let me know when it's ready." Henderson left.

Sandford reviewed the document. He made a few revisions in the intro and the ending, but kept the main message as written. Before returning it to Henderson, he read the key statements aloud.

"The United States does not, and will not, succumb to blackmail. We are withdrawing all our financial and corporate interests from Tawanda. We ask the United Nations and the African Union to take the leadership role with respect to President Adebowale Okoro's abuse of his people and all matters involving Tawanda. In addition, I am directing the United States State Department to impose travel restrictions across the board with the exception of humanitarian organizations."

Satisfied, he called Henderson to the Oval Office and handed him the revised draft.

"Thank you, Sir. I'll be back in fifteen minutes so you can practice before going before the cameras at six."

"Good. This is not a speech I give lightly. It seems like a no-brainer, but there could be dire consequences."

"I hope not, Mr. President. I hope not."

At ten o'clock that evening, Sandford was still in the Oval Office. He sat in his desk chair facing the windows and the night sky beyond. He nursed a glass of single malt Scotch, neat, filled more than half way. The speech had gone well. The feedback from other world leaders echoed his approach. Only a united front could end this stalemate.

Sandford finished the last of his drink in one gulp and set it down. He turned off his desk lamp, stood, stretched, and sighed.

Before he crossed the threshold, his private cell phone rang. He checked the caller ID—Philip Vanderhagen, one of his most influential financial supporters. The man appeared to be the spokesman for a powerful cartel that influenced world-wide eco-political events. Considered a myth, this clandestine group cloaked itself in anonymity. To refuse them meant, at best, political or economic suicide.

Sandford had to take the call. "Hello."

"Good evening, Franklin," Vanderhagen said in a cheery voice. "How the hell are you?"

"Tired," Sandford said. "It's been a long day and a hectic week."

Vanderhagen said, "I know. I heard your speech this evening. Anything I can do to take the pressure off?"

Sandford paused. The men had met years ago at a political fundraiser when Sandford ran for city council. Over time, their relationship developed. Vanderhagen donated to his election campaigns and socialized when it served his purpose. Over drinks, they'd talk politics. Sandford shared his goals, problems, and strategies. Vanderhagen, a good listener, offered differing points of view for discussion and consideration. In the end, Sandford accepted with Vanderhagen's not so subtle advice.

It was Vanderhagen who suggested Sandford consider running for president. When Sandford agreed, consultants and cash flowed into election headquarters. Professionals honed his positions, philosophy, and goals. More cash came in. He worked with advisors and emerged as a forceful, engaging, and inspiring speaker. He amassed the largest campaign chest in recent memory. Empowered by his supporters and funded by Vanderhagen and his friends, Franklin Taylor Sandford ascended to the top of the political landscape.

"Thank you for your offer, Philip. I'll call if I need anything. I promise."

Sandford had his thumb over the "End Call" button when he heard Vanderhagen still talking. Bringing the phone back to his ear, he listened.

"Franklin, I'm having dinner with a few friends," Vanderhagen said. "Your name came up in conversation. I've heard you've proposed aggressive policies to get the US back on solid financial footing."

"That's true. It's in keeping with my administration's overall strategy to bring our ratings up to optimum levels."

"Which I wholly support, as you know."

"Your influence has certainly made a difference."

Vanderhagen paused and cleared his throat.

Sandford, in Pavlovian response, tightened the grip on his phone and clenched his jaw while the vein in his temple distended.

Vanderhagen continued, unaware of his tell. "A situation is developing that may derail our plans. It needs your immediate attention."

"A situation?" In truth, it was the last thing Sandford needed on his plate. He spent his whole day dealing with situations. Phone pressed to his ear, he walked over to the bar. He took a new glass, poured two fingers, and took a sip. He hoped for a last minute reprieve. It didn't come.

"My friends and I have considerable assets in Tawanda. Adebowale Okoro's plan to nationalize all mining operations is a direct threat to us. We believe you have the power and resources to implement the necessary action to avert this financial disaster."

"Philip, I can assure you my team and I spent all week developing strategies for dealing with Okoro. I'm as concerned as you are."

"I'm not talking politics," Vanderhagen said. "This is personal. Our operations face foreclosure. If we take a financial hit, it will affect those who depend on us—people like yourself. Okoro must be stopped… permanently."

Sandford took another sip and began to perspire. "I don't see how I can help."

Vanderhagen said, "My public position within the industry demands that I not be linked to any solution. That's why, Franklin, I turn to you. You are now the most powerful man in the world. If anyone can do this, you can."

"Philip, trust me. I have explored all our options and implemented what's within my power—short of declaring war."

Vanderhagen switched to an ingratiating tone. "Franklin, haven't we become close friends? Think of our family barbecues, fishing expeditions, and fundraising bashes."

"Yes, Philip, we have," Sandford said. He snatched a tissue from the box on the table and wiped the perspiration out of his eyes.

"Franklin, listen to me. I'm asking, as your friend and financial backer, that you take a more direct approach—like a '*bin Laden.*'"

Sandford gasped. "What? Are you kidding?"

"I never kid about business," Vanderhagen said. "If you need a reliable agent, contact the young man you met at the political fundraiser I organized at the Philadelphia Museum when you were a councilman. He seduces individuals to abandon their misguided activities in problematic situations. I believe you needed help with a violent drug dealer. Didn't he disappear a few days later?"

Rivulets of sweat streamed down the side of Sandford's face and neck faster than he could wipe them away. Under his jacket, his shirt was drenched. Still, his voice remained steady. "Philip, I had nothing to do with that."

"In fact you did. You set the ball in motion—gave the directive. All you have to do is repeat the process."

"What? You can't mean I...." Sandford couldn't speak the words.

"Please take care of this seduction as soon as possible," Vanderhagen said,

"Good talking with you. We'll get together soon." The line went dead.

Sandford looked at the phone in his hand and threw it at a pillow. He took off his jacket and tie, and unbuttoned his shirt's top three buttons. He got up and went over to his desk. Sitting down, he searched through his electronic Rolodex, indexed by contact name, context, and association.

He typed in the keywords, "vanderhagen, museum, Philadelphia," into the search bar. As he scrolled through the results, the young man Vanderhagen had mentioned started to take form— friendly, yet cool and distant. They had a brief conversation about making communities safer and influencing people who rule through terror and intimidation. The guy couched his concepts in psychological mumbo jumbo with an intensity that touched on madness.

The search engine finished. "Theodore X. Donovan."

Sandford pitched forward in his chair, terror

obliterating the liquor's effect. He jumped to his feet with such force that his chair jettisoned backward into the wall. "No way! No Fucking way!"

Sandford reached into his wastebasket and grabbed the crumpled piece of paper and flattened it on the desk. There it was. Theodore X. Donovan, the PRAISE Foundation CEO. The man worked for him at this very moment.

Sandford grabbed his phone and called Wendell Waters.

Chapter 33
Lake George, New York

All the team members had retired for the evening except Ted. He sat in the study working on his computer. He set up a time line for the think tank, key strategic points, and tomorrow's agenda. When he finished, he closed the computer. While he aligned all the items on the desk, his phone rang. The caller ID said "White House." He took the call.

"Hi, Ted, this is Wendell Waters."

"Mr. Waters, what can I do for you?"

"Just checking in. How are things going up there?"

"Everything's fine, sir."

"The deliberations?"

"We're formally starting tomorrow."

"How's the team working out?"

"Good. Why? Did you expect problems?"

"No. Just curious. The president asked," Waters said. "He also mentioned that as a councilman he first met you at a museum fundraiser in Philadelphia a while back. Is that true?"

"A Philadelphia Museum fundraiser? Let me think." Ted said. "Hmmm. Yes. I believe it is."

"Did you have a hand in his district's revitalization?"

"I wouldn't go that far. The councilman had a concern which I verified."

"You did an investigation?"

"More like an observation. By chance, I did meet the problematic individual. We talked. He shared his goals and dreams with me. I encouraged him to redirect his energies and offered an incentive. Not a big deal."

"Where is he now?"

"Gone."

"Can he be reached?"

"No."

"Were the police ever involved?"

"In what?"

Waters paused. "We have another similar situation."

"I'm listening."

"If you and your team use Tawanda as one of your case studies, you'd encounter gross human rights violations. It's urgent that Adebowale Okoro be seduced into modifying his current policies."

"Seduced?"

"Exactly."

"Time frame?"

"Yesterday." The phone went dead.

Ted leaned back in his chair and studied the phone for a few minutes. Then he

he reached under the desk for his brief case, selected one of several throwaway phones, and made a call.

Under his breath, he said, "Thank God for Lucy."

Chapter 34
Harrison, New York

The modern-style Kilmer home, constructed of glass, wood, and concrete, sat on five secluded acres, less than ten minutes from the Westchester Airport. Lucy stood by her bedroom's massive sliding glass doors and gazed at the garden beyond. She stood still as a statue in a long silk nightgown, arms folded beneath her breasts, her cell phone in one hand.

In this elegant house, in this life, Lucy didn't have to compromise—bow to the whim of parents, or others, who had neither the intellect nor good sense to bring up a child of her ilk. Geniuses like her needed parental commitment—not excuses, the best—not seconds, attention—not disregard.

Her phone's ringtone broke the silence and she answered.

"Ted, just going to call you."

"We have a…. Why?

"After all these years, we may have cracked Vanderhagen's server."

"About time."

"As soon as I get data, I'll send it to you."

"Good. Now focus. High priority seduction."

"Excellent."

"Texting."

Lucy received the text, "*Adebowale Okoro, President, Tawanda, Africa.*"

She texted, "*Are you serious? The man is well-guarded and hasn't left his compound in years.*"

Ted said, "I need an executable plan in less than four hours."

"Not much time."

"Lucy, make it happen. Call me when everything is in place. We do not execute the seduction until I get confirmation and give you the okay. Understood?"

"Understood. I'll get back to you."

She sent a quick text, "*Tawanda, Africa,*" and waited.

The phone buzzed. The text message said, "*Contact established.*"

Lucy moved with grace and speed into her closet, the size of a small store. She put on a silk T-shirt and yoga pants, and went down the hall to her office.

The high bare windows spanned the entire outer wall. The interior walls were light gray, accented by brushed chrome, gray suede, and a cherry hardwood floor. Monitors hung on the walls. A secure server, with power and international linkage, insured untraceable transmissions.

Lucy controlled everything from her desk. She could watch in real time as agents put up visuals from their various locations. This was the nerve center of her whole operation.

Sitting down at her command station, she put on her ear bud, logged in, and set up a new operation folder. Her keystrokes were sharp and quick. Her eyes took in all the screens at once and formed a picture of the whole operation. With adrenaline pumping, Lucy's senses sharpened like a cheetah stalking prey—focused and tense, as it moved through the high grass, sensitive to the slightest wind change, before its lethal charge.

Chapter 35
Lake George, New York

Rachel woke with a start, checked her phone, and frowned. Chris hadn't answered her text. *Oh well. I tried.* She puffed her pillow and drew the covers around her. Safe and warm, she slept. And dreamed.

Voices in the distance. Words indecipherable. Her body levitated above the bed. A tornado-like funnel swept her to the cabin's rooftop widows' walk—a small landing surrounded by a picket fence. Immune to the frigid air, Rachel marveled at the clear moonlit sky sparkling with stars.

The unexpected shove surprised her. She recovered her balance and pivoted to face her attacker. No one. A stronger shove. Her skin turned clammy. She turned in jerky movements, trying to identify her attacker. A hard push. She reeled backward and hit the railing hard. She twisted and grabbed it for support. It came away in her hand. She fell—plummeting through space, like sleet through wind. "Nooooooo…."

Rachel awoke with a start. She sat up—heart pounding and mouth dry. She snapped on the light and got her bearings. She went to the bathroom, drank a glass of water, and washed her face.

Feeling better, she returned to the bedroom and walked to the window. She opened it and stuck her head out. The frigid air made her shiver. She leaned out and craned her neck so she could see the sky. It mirrored her dream.

Rachel withdrew and shut the window. Beyond the silence of her room, she heard muted conversation—this time for real. She glanced at the digital clock. One-thirty-seven.

It seemed odd at first, but plausible given the team's international connections. Rachel ignored the temptation to investigate and went to bed. Fifteen minutes later, unable to sleep, she decided to see who was still up. Maybe they'd share a cup of hot cocoa, her favorite soporific—even better with a quarter-shot of vodka or the coffee-flavored Kahlua.

She put on her robe and slippers, moved the chair, and unlocked the door. The hallway was empty. She edged toward the balcony overlooking the library. With ten feet to go, she recognized the person talking. It was Ted.

Rachel reached the end hallway, about three feet from the banister. Ted's voice, like his footfalls, ranged from audible to indistinct as he paced back and forth, in and out of the study, on and off the library rug.

Rachel tried not to listen—bad manners and all, and failed.

"Yes….Good….and the seduction? You have the

timing down? Good….Any flags yet? Uh-uh….Is that true for all? Good…. We'll begin the prep for that one….Not sure. Anything else? … *Her* name is Rachel. Don't forget it…. Good. We'll talk soon."

"What's going on?" A woman's groggy, annoyed voice called out. "It's the middle of the night." Amy Yeager appeared. Her mauve silk robe, more open than closed, revealed her black faux-fur-trimmed nightgown and matching "fuck me" slippers. "Am I missing something?"

Rachel said, "Uh, no. I don't think so."

Below, the pacing stopped for a moment and started again. Ted went into the study and closed the door. Rachel felt ridiculous for being out in the hall in the first place, and more than a little frumpy in her long flannel nightgown, fleece robe, and thermal scuffs.

Amy said, "Then what are you doing out here?"

Rachel said, "I heard something downstairs and wanted to make sure everything was okay." She spoke so fast she doubted her coherence.

"And is it?" Amy said. She sauntered over to the railing and looked over.

Rachel said, "Is what?"

"Is everything okay?" Amy said, turning her head toward Rachel as she leaned on the railing. "I don't hear anything."

Rachel forced a smile and said, "All's quiet. No problems here."

The study door opened and Ted stepped out, still wearing his suit and tie. He looked up. "Hi, Amy. Can't sleep?"

Amy leaned over the railing, revealing the back of her thighs to Rachel and, Rachel figured, her breasts to Ted. "Teddy, how come you're up so late?"

Ted said, "Working. You?"

Amy took a furtive sideways glance at Rachel, who was inching backwards toward her bedroom. To Ted, she said, "Heard your voice. Want some company?"

"Not tonight," Ted said. "Have to finish tying up loose ends for tomorrow."

Amy let out a low moan. "Teddy, I'm soooo disappointed, but I'd be more than happy to wait up for you."

Ted said, "Get some sleep, Amy. I'll see you in the morning."

Rachel had reached her bedroom door when she heard the study door shut.

Amy turned. "Wait." She walked toward Rachel, the silk robe billowing behind her. "I want to talk to you."

"Let's talk in the morning." Rachel said as she stepped inside the room. "I'm exhausted."

"No." Amy said, putting her hand on door. "I want to say what I have to say right now."

Amy stepped closer to Rachel. So close that Rachel smelled the remnants of her perfume and observed paper-thin lines that swirled around her eyes and cut into her lips.

"Teddy's mine," Amy said. She backed up a step. "At least while we're holed up in this godforsaken place." Without waiting for a response, Amy pirouetted and headed back to her room.

Rachel shut her door and heard another open. "What's going on?"

Amy said, "Nothing. Go back to sleep, Quentin."

Locked in, chair in place, and wide awake, Rachel lay in bed. She closed her eyes, to rest if not sleep, in darkness and opened them in sunlight.

Chapter 36
Lake George, New York

After her workout, Rachel headed upstairs to shower. The study door was open. She veered off course to see if Ted was there. He was, absorbed in work on his laptop.

"Good morning, Ted," Rachel said, standing in the doorway. "You're up early."

Ted's head jerked up.

She said, "Do you have a minute?"

He beamed at her and closed his laptop. "For you, always."

Rachel entered the study and sat down. "I overheard you on the phone last night."

Ted's smile faded, his eyes narrowed and his chin lifted as his face hardened. Rachel sensed his negative energy and tried to put him at ease. She leaned forward. "Ted, I'm so, so sorry. It was an accident. I heard voices and went into the hall to investigate. I had no idea it was you."

Ted remained silent and impassive although the throbbing vein in his temple changed tempo from a jitterbug to a waltz. Her apology seemed to be working. Rachel leaned back in her chair. "I assure you I wasn't spying. It even took me a minute or two to recognize your voice. Seconds later I heard my name."

Ted's head dropped, his chin resting on his chest.

"What? What is it? What's the matter?"

He lifted his head. "Rachel, I'm sorry you heard that." He paused.

She held her breath.

Ted said, "I was talking to… my… psychiatrist…. No one knows."

Rachel sighed with relief. "Well, don't worry. Your secret is safe with me. I've been working with one on and off since my attack."

"I guess we both have issues."

"We do," Rachel said in agreement. "But why were you talking about me?"

Ted stood and walked around the desk. He put his hand under her chin and lifted it gently until he looked into her eyes. His voice was deep and low. His face as soft as she'd ever seen it.

"Rachel, you have changed my life. Awakened my senses. Given me hope."

Before she could respond, he surprised her with a light kiss. "And because I never thought I'd feel like this again, I had to talk to someone." His eyes searched hers as he leaned in for another kiss.

Rachel put her hands on his chest and stepped back. "Ted. I'm flattered and touched. You're an amazing, accomplished man. While I consider you a close friend, I don't have *that* kind of feeling for you.

Besides, we've talked. You know I'm not interested in a relationship right now."

Ted's face darkened. "It's the landlord, right? He's standing in our way."

Rachel fear-flight response tingled and she sought immediate relief. "No. Not true." His eyebrows lifted. She took a step closer and softened her voice. "He walked out on me, remember?"

Ted mood lightened. "Say no more. We'll work this out."

"Ted, there's nothing to work out."

"Not a problem." Ted returned to the desk, sat down, straightened his pen and notepaper, opened his laptop, and began working as if she were invisible.

Rachel didn't move for a second, uncomfortable with the instant disconnect. Then she headed upstairs to get ready for breakfast.

Ted called out. "Wait."

She paused and leaned over the banister. "What?"

"Come back," he said. "I've got a job for you."

She entered the study. Ted waved her over to the side of his chair. He said, "I want you to see something." She complied and looked at the laptop monitor. "This is our agenda for today. I'd like you to do me a favor and create a case study to keep our team discussions focused."

"Good idea," Rachel said. "Specifics always help."

Ted talked as he typed and touched the screen to make his point. "Here are the countries currently in turmoil. Any one of them would work."

Rachel leaned forward so she could read the list—Columbia, Afghanistan, Somalia, Yemen, Nigeria, Sudan, Tawanda, Palestine, Central African Republic. "That's true."

"So… hmmm…." Ted paused, tapped his fingers

on the arm of his chair and then stroked his chin. "So, how about... Tawanda?"

Rachel said, "Good choice. Okoro wants to nationalize all foreign interests.

In fact, he's halted all aid to his people until his demands are met. It's today's headline."

She left Ted and walked to the stairs where she met Jack and Jay. Jay said, "What's your pleasure?"

Rachel said, "I think I can take it from here. You guys can head home."

Chapter 37
Gramercy Avenue, New York City

Christopher Gregory crossed the checkerboard tiled floor in front of Nikolai's desk.

Nikolai said, "So, tell me. What is your problem?"

Chris stopped. "What do you mean?"

"You know what I mean. I usually don't see you for days or weeks at a time. But today, this is the fifth time I have seen you and it is not even noon."

Chris said, "You're counting?"

Nikolai shrugged. "Okay, maybe it is six times.

"Not true. I'm swamped. Got to go." Chris stormed out, banging the door behind him.

Eight minutes later, Chris shuffled through the doorway and slumped in a chair.

Without looking at Nikolai, Chris said, "Of course, you're right. She's gone. A two-second text conversation and that's it."

"By 'she,' you mean Rachel, right? The woman you dumped."

Chris shook his head. "I thought she'd never leave her apartment."

"You made it easy. Ummm… what is that called?"

Chris looked at Nikolai, "What are you? My shrink?"

"I am just saying," Nikolai said, raising his hands in a defensive motion. Then he snapped his fingers and pointed at Chris. "Enabling, that is the word, is it not?"

"Point made. I thought she'd always be here no matter what."

Nikolai mumbled as he shifted back to work.

"What did you say?"

"I said, so you could date other women and still have her?"

"Are you kidding me?" Chris said in a voice tinged with anger. "That's a cheap shot. You know me better than that."

"Do not shoot *this* messenger," Nikolai said, pointing to his chest. "I am just saying what I am seeing."

"It's not that simple."

Nikolai leaned back in his chair and turned to Chris. "I see that."

"What should I do?"

"Whatever gets you out of here," Nikolai said. "My boss is tough and I have a ton of work to do."

"That's cold," Chris said, getting to his feet. "And I'm not *that* tough."

"You're right," Nikolai said. "I love it here." He paused. "Now go and let me work."

Chris returned to his office on the third floor. He tried to work but couldn't sit still. Pacing didn't calm him either.

The red alarm flashed and beeped. Chris flew down to the second floor. The techs were all over the intrusion. Chris turned the alert off and watched the monitor.

"Red Fox gained entry," one tech said. "Happen to hit us as we engaged the update. The chances of that happening are astronomical."

"We were onto him within seconds," another said. "Stopped him before he could download a file."

Chris said, "Did he get anything?"

"Name of server—maybe."

"No data?"

"All encrypted."

Chris said, "Any info on the hacker?"

"Same as before. Always hammering at our system from new and old vantage points," a tech said. "This is the first time he got past us."

Chris said, "Change the server name and password and fix the problem."

"Already done," another tech said. "We're testing now and will implement in all systems."

"We've alerted all users to change their passwords to regain access."

"If the hacker got into our space, we can identify him. Who's working on that?"

"I am," said a voice behind him. "I'll get the information to you as soon as I have it."

Chris said, "Okay. Good job everyone."

He left the tech room and was climbing the stairs to the third floor when his business phone rang. He answered. "ICU Security."

"Christopher Gregory?"

"Yes. May I help you?"

"FBI Special Agent Elizabeth Neilson."

Chris knew the name and tried to control his frustration. "Aren't you the agent who convinced

Rachel Allen to go to Lake George?"

"I am," Beth said, keeping her tone even. "However, Rachel made her own decision to go."

"You're right," Chris said. "I'm sorry. You caught me at a bad moment. What can I do for you?"

"Rachel mentioned that you are in charge of the DoD security system for General Michael Portman's home in Lake George. Do you have access?"

"I do. In fact, the DoD knows that I'm doing tests at that site over the next several weeks."

"How long does the system hold the recorded data before erasing it?"

Chris knew but he sat down and checked. "Technically, nothing is erased. We hold data for five years before turning it over to DoD archives. The current archive schedule is every quarter and this quarter began in January."

"I'd like some more specific information on the overall system. Mind if I come up? I'm downstairs."

Chris alerted Nikolai, who let Beth up.

She arrived on the third floor with two cups of coffee.

"Have a seat, Agent Neilson."

"Call me Beth. We're both friends of Rachel's."

"Okay, Beth. What do you need?"

Beth took a sip of coffee and chose her words. "I'm not at liberty to discuss the case I'm working on," she said. "However, there may be some pertinent information on the Lake George security videos for the past week. May I view them?"

Chris said, "Where's your warrant? Remember, I work for the DoD."

"I don't have one. I don't want anyone aware of our interest. No electronic footprints."

"Well," Chris said, scratching his head. "As it turns out, I am about to do a full system review. If you like, you can stay here and wait. When it's done, I'll let you know if there is a glitch in any module. How's that?"

Beth looked puzzled. "Um, I don't think you...."

Chris handed her his tablet before she could finish. "Patience." A few taps at his computer and the output showed up on his monitor and the tablet. Beth saw everything.

Chris clenched his jaw and gripped the arms of his chair every time Rachel and Donovan were recorded together. When the last image left the screen, Beth walked over to Chris. "How are you doing? You seem... tense."

"I'm fine," Chris said. "Let's just say I'm not a Ted Donovan fan."

"Do you know him?"

"Of him," Chris said. "When Rachel started to see him, I did an anonymous background check. Something about him doesn't ring true."

"I agree," Beth said. "May I see your findings?"

Chris got up and grabbed his tablet. A few quick finger taps and strokes brought a document on screen. He handed the tablet to Beth, and she read the information with no visible reaction. He said, "You don't look surprised."

"I'm not. I've seen most of this before. Is this document on the internet or just in your personal files?"

"Personal."

"Good. Please keep it that way." She produced a thumb drive from her purse and held it out to Chris. "May I have a copy?"

With the information in hand, she said, "Let's go back to the surveillance. Can you trace Donovan's phone calls?"

While Chris searched for the data, Beth paced.

"No. He used a throwaway. His calls are untraceable," Chris said, swiveling his chair to face her. From Beth's perplexed look, he knew there was a problem. "Why, what did you hear?"

"Not sure. Something's off."

"Want to review it again?"

"Do you mind?"

After two more viewings, Beth said, "I have to sleep on it." She took out a business card and put it on the desk. Call me if you see or hear anything, and I mean *anything*, out of the ordinary."

"Is Rachel in danger?"

"I think she's fine. Donovan seems genuinely fond of her."

After Beth left, Chris jumped on the mission. He went through the videos again and isolated the sections with Donovan either alone or with Rachel. His impulse control plummeted to zero, and he texted Rachel. *Call me.*

While he waited, he tested all security sub-systems at the Lake George facility—electric, gas and water; network including broadband, wireless, hotspots and users; environmental including heating, cooling, circulation and air filters; and emergency including security cameras, shortwave radio, access and egress, doors, windows, fire exits, and the sprinkler system. All systems go.

Chris pushed back from the table and checked his phone. No text. He called her.

Rachel answered. Before he could say a word, she said, "How come you didn't call last night?"

"Was I supposed to?"

"I sent you a text."

Chris checked his text messages. "Didn't get it. What'd it say?"

"Doesn't matter. How come you're calling?

"I…." Chris swallowed.

"What? I'm in a kind of a rush. Preparing for a presentation."

This was not the right time for an apology. "Just wanted to let you know all the camp systems are in top working order."

"Good. Thanks."

"Rachel, what…."

"Oops. Have to go. The meeting is starting. Let's talk later."

Chris looked at his phone—CALL ENDED.

He took the phone and banged it against his head. "I'm so fucking stupid!"

To redirect his energies, he brought up the video on Donovan's phone call—the one that bothered Beth and studied every movement, word, and intonation.

"Come on, Donovan, you son-of-a bitch. Tell me what you're up to."

Chapter 38
Gramercy Avenue, New York City –
Federal Plaza, New York City

Outside 215 Gramercy, Beth sat in her car to call Eric Jerrod. "Start checking out Philadelphia Museum fundraisers that Sandford attended as a councilman. I want the attendee lists. Also, see if there were any problems within his constituency. If yes, who, what, where, and when. I'm headed back now."

"Sure. Anything else?"

Beth heard the sarcasm in his voice and laughed. "No, Agent Jerrod, not at this particular minute. I'm headed back to help."

On any normal drive through New York City, Beth's aggressive driving rivaled top cab drivers. She knew how to make the lights, snake in and out of traffic, and what avenues and streets carried the lightest traffic. Today was different.

Today, Beth drove with the traffic. Stopping and starting. Waiting for buses to pull out, double parked trucks to move, and jay-walkers to cross. On automatic pilot, she digested the security video's images.

She called Eric. "Why would Wendell Waters want to use Donovan as an international mediator?"

"Is this a trick question?"

"I wish. See if Donovan does work abroad. I want to know how he fits into the international scene."

Eric said. "Got it. And, Beth, do me a favor—stop thinking and get back here. There's enough work for ten people as it is."

"Sorry. Just calling as things occur to me. I'm almost there."

Outside the office door, she called Eric and heard his phone ring.

"Beth, not another thing," Eric said, and happened to glance at the doorway. "Not funny." He turned his phone off.

Beth chuckled. "Sorry. Couldn't help myself. Get any hits yet?"

"Sure," Eric said. "It's only been thirty minutes and I've wrapped up the whole case."

"That would be nice."

"You'll be happy to know I've started calling the twelve major museums in Philadelphia. I'm getting lists of fundraiser events Sandford attended and an attendee list for each. It's going to take some time. If we don't hear by the end of today, I'll call them back in the morning. I've done half and working on the rest."

"And Donovan's international credentials?"

"You're just in time."

"You've got it?"

"No, you're just in time to do it," Eric said. "But

first, you might want to look at this."

Eric handed Beth a print out. "This is a current list, meaning last two years, of missing persons with similar circumstances. I queried the FBI's National Incident Based Reporting System and the National Missing and Unidentified Persons System for the past two years on 'kidnapping/abduction,' figuring 'missing' reports would be included. I also searched on 'reported incidents with no identified perpetrator,' 'suspected murder with no bodies,' and 'deaths ruled accidental after coroner's inquiry.' What you are looking at is a subset of 'multiple disappearances with more than one parameter in common.'"

Beth read the list.

> Two years ago
>> September—DC, Charles Hubner, wife Elissa and daughter
>> December—CA, Esteban (aka El Jefe) Suarez and girlfriend, Carmela Perez
>
> Last year
>> June—TX, Louis Mendoza, wife Maria, son and daughter
>> July—VT, Rep. John DeSalle, wife Mary DeSalle, and three boys

"Oh my God," she said. "I must have all these in my case load. I never imagined they were linked."

"Very interesting reading," Eric said, and handed her the case summaries.

> • Charles Hubner, a lobbyist, lived in Washington, D.C. He represented the insurance industry and fought against the single-payer option. His power, backed by his corporate clients, intimidated legislators and created huge rifts between parties that kept critical legislation in committee. While on vacation in Florida, he and his family rented a

boat for an afternoon of fishing and partying. They, and their boat, remain missing to date.

• Esteban Suarez was a leader of a gang in Los Angeles, California. He and his crew were responsible for over twenty killings, including rival gang members, onlookers, and store owners. The police couldn't touch him until a gang member snitched. Suarez went down for torching three businesses, the owners of which had banded together to stop Suarez's mandated weekly payoffs. By the trial date, no witnesses agreed to testify. Free, Suarez and his girlfriend took off for a vacation in Hawaii. No one has seen or heard from either of them since.

• Louis Mendoza, a lawyer, born in Mexico, raised in San Antonio, Texas, was an advocate for migrant workers. He worked to reform immigration policies and created a sponsor program so that workers and their families could gain access to the United States for their sponsor's seasonal work. After several seasons, they would be eligible to apply for citizenship. He wanted to eradicate exploitation by traffickers in human cargo and border killings and/or detention by border patrols. His approach threatened to expose the shadow economy perpetrated by American agriculture. He took his family to Washington, D.C., so they could see the sites while he spoke to several legislative committees. After D.C., he and his family went to spend the Labor Day week in Colonial Williamsburg, Virginia. They never checked in or returned home.

• Congressman John DeSalle, a former

Navy pilot, was up for re-election in his home state of Vermont. He sat on the Energy and Commerce Committee and advocated banning Hydraulic Fracturing. Based on the current concoction of injected chemicals, there were just too many reports of poisoned water destroying land around the operation. Gas companies targeted him for being Anti-American, against fuel self-sufficiency and anti-job development. On the other hand, conservationists and the communities targeted for drilling called DeSalle a hero. One weekend, he flew his family up to Lake Champlain. Air traffic controllers confirmed DeSalle's takeoff. There is no record of his landing—anywhere.

When she looked up, Eric said, "The Meyersons are the next name on that list."

"Good work."

"It's not finished yet. We need to figure out what these cases have in common."

They had something within the hour. Their small sampling showed two out of five cases contained PRAISE award winners. Beth wanted to shut the foundation down but Eric's cooler, analytical head prevailed. "We need more."

In time, other similarities became obvious.

"All those missing were away from home when they disappeared," Beth said. "Their family, friends, and neighbors knew the what, where, and why of the trip. No secrets. Nothing clandestine."

"Interesting," Eric said. "Look at these lead times—no second thoughts."

"They made their minds up—just like that." Beth snapped her fingers. Why would they drop everything and leave?"

"Why would you?"

"Winning the Powerball lottery."

"No. Really?"

"I've always wanted to own a ranch," Beth said. "Horses mainly, with a few alpacas thrown in. And maybe a few llamas to police the herds."

"What if I gave it to you?"

"I'm out of here before you finish the sentence."

"I think that's what happened here," Eric said. "Look at these last few things they all have in common. Quick decisions, no stress, happy, and gone within days."

Beth said. "I bet that if Ted Donovan's connected to at least two, he knows about the other three."

"I agree."

"Let's do this." Beth returned to her computer. After working for less than twenty seconds, she turned to Eric. "By the time we're done with Mr. Theodore Xavier Donovan, we're going to know him better than he knows himself."

Chapter 39
Lake George, New York

Rachel entered the conference area which Ted set up in a corner of the main room.

He said, "Ah, here's Rachel with our case study. I want you to know that I gave her the assignment this morning, so I expect we'll be looking at an overview and some historical background." He looked at Rachel. "Right?"

Rachel, now standing by Ted's side, nodded. "My tablet is connected to our WiFi, so you'll be able to follow me on the big monitor. Also, I've sent each of you an email with all the referenced websites in case you want to refer to them later." She looked at Ted. "Lights, please." He turned off the lights and took a seat.

"During the presentation," Rachel said, "feel free to ask questions or comment if you feel it's pertinent.

As you view the images and websites, I'll do a voice over with my condensed version."

"In 2000, Adebowale Okoro, a Menanandu tribal prince, following the Democratic Republic of the Congo's (DRC) revised laws, sent in his annual application to affirm his people's nomadic status. In the capital city of Kinshasa, a clerk declared the application invalid because a tribesman owned a house through a bequest of dead relative. Since nomadic status prohibits real property ownership, the clerk stamped the application, "DENIED.""

Democratic Republic of the Congo, Africa, 2000

"It is of no use," Adebowale Okoro said from his hammock.

"You must try again," Opeyemi Okoro said, standing in their mud hut's doorway with her broom—a sturdy limb with dried grasses bound and wound on one end.

"My energy is gone," he said. "My bones are tired and my head aches." He adjusted his body in the worn fabric hammock so he faced away from her stare. It did not help. Her eyes burned into his back.

"Get up and get going," she said. Her broom swept the fabric under his butt and startled him. Arching away from her swipes, the hammock tipped and he fell to the ground.

"Opeyemi, no. I cannot. I am not well." He held his arms up, defending himself from the incessant sweeping. She did not stop so he rolled away. It did not help. She came after him.

"I am the daughter of the Menanandu warrior chief. Therefore, you are his appointed prince."

"I am broken."

"You will fix yourself when you stand up for your

people. Take cousin Kwanh Uba and go to Kinshasa. You must get the necessary papers and return our heritage and freedom to our people." She walked back to the mud house.

Adebowale made no effort to move and closed his eyes. When he opened them, Opeyemi stood over him. "Get up. It is time."

He obeyed. Eyes downcast, he shook his head. "This is the errand of a fool."

"You must try." She held a cloth bag in her outstretched arm. "Take this food and change of clothes with you," she said. "Go now. It will be a long journey."

"And if I choose not to?"

Opeyemi erect, chin high, arms at her side, said, "I will renounce you, curse you, and the tribe will cast you out. You will forever be banished and alone. I will take another husband. Our tribe will scatter to the winds, and we will be no more." She looked at her husband. "Adebowlae, do not let this happen."

Without uttering a word, he took the parcel and began his journey.

Three months later, Adebowale Okoro trudged up the dirt path to his home.

"Welcome, my husband," Opeyemi said, coming up behind him.

Adebowale turned. She carried river-washed clothing in a basket. He said, "I am glad to be home, but my news is not good."

"Let us go inside. We will talk over tea."

Adebowale looked around. "Where is everyone?"

"The Harvest Festival begins next week, and we are preparing," she said over her shoulder. "Our children are with my parents."

Inside, Opeyemi put her basket on a chair and hung the kettle over the fire. She made a plate of manioc bread and corn pudding. She placed a cup of tea by his setting. "Here, eat. There will be more at dinner."

Adebowale ate while she drank her tea.

When he had finished, she said, "Tell me."

"There is nothing to be done. After three weeks of working our way through the maze of governmental offices, we could find no one who would help us. 'The law is the law. Permission to roam the lands of our people denied.' Again and again."

"The Menanandu count on you to fix this outrage."

"There is nothing more to be done."

"We must put together a plan," she said. "We must not let our people know you are defeated."

"Did I not just tell you there is nothing to be done?"

"You will soon be chief. Act like one." Opeyemi stood up and paced the dirt floor. "I will not let the government rob our people of their rights."

"Opeyemi, no one cares but us. Let it be."

"Rest," she said. "I need to think."

She still sat at the table when Adebowale awoke. Papers were scattered around. A pencil rocked between her fingers, the eraser drumming on the table. In two strides, he was by her side. He said, "What is all this?"

Opeyemi said, "It is a list of the tribes that surround us and a rough map of their lands. The combined parcel is large—more than enough land for their animals and ours." She looked at him. "You have the gift of persuasion. You must create alliances so that we may share the land...as we did in the past."

Adebowale waved his hand over the table. "They would kill us if they could."

"We will die anyway," she said. "Can you not see that? You are dying before my eyes. Soon all will follow." Tears filled her eyes and ran down her cheeks. Opeyemi wiped them away. "It is time you led your people to prosperity. It is our birthright and our future. You cannot, must not, fail."

Opeyemi rose and retrieved his ceremonial staff from under the bed. She thrust it into his hand and said, "Take Kwanh Uba and select three others. You must be wise. Emphasize our common interests and ancestral bond. Gain their trust. Unify the tribes. Our lives, our future, and our freedom are in your hands."

Rachel stopped reading and looked up. "Adebowale Okoro negotiated the treaty, the Menanandu's fortunes grew, and Okoro's people thrived. On September 14, 2003, a DRC patrol happened upon a tribal herd and asked the herder, Kwanh Uba, for his papers, which of course he did not have. Instead, he offered a copy of the tribal agreements, but the patrol leader brushed it aside. Out of the brush, tribesmen appeared and surrounded the patrol. The patrol leader withdrew his men. He promised to return with reinforcements and arrest documents.

"On October 15, 2003, twenty DRC soldiers, armed with guns and official papers, arrived to demand the Menanandu return to their village. They were met by Adebowale Okoro and a hundred men representing the newly created Tribal Federation of Tawanda.

"This would be the last peaceful, albeit tense, meeting between the soldiers and the tribes."

After the long victory celebration and most satisfying sex, Adebowale and Opeyemi whispered in the darkness.

He said, "The coming weeks and months will be difficult. Our resources will be strained."

"We must create new alliances beyond our borders," she said. "We need money to buy weapons, ammunition, and supplies."

The silence between them lengthened and she nudged him.He said, "I am awake."

She flipped onto her back and stared at the ceiling. "What about gold?"

"Gold comes from the foreigners' mines. They will never part with it."

"African resources should serve Africans. Perhaps a tax for doing business within the Tribal Federation of Tawanda borders."

He scooped her up in his arms and whispered in her ear, "Brilliant."

"By January 22, 2004, the revolution was in full swing," Rachel said. "Okoro declared independence for the new state, Tawanda, and unfurled its flag. He offered men in the region the option of fighting or exile.

"By February 16, 2004, Tawandian forces exacted their first gold tax.

"On March 5, the first shipments of supplies arrived. Okoro's men received weapons, ammunition, trucks and jeeps, dried food, medical field packs, hospital supplies and equipment, uniforms, tents, and communication equipment.

"Adebowale Okoro thrived on the activity and

power. With Kwanh Uba as his trusted aide, he's the self-appointed undisputed ruler of the fledgling African country.

"By May 12, Tawanda and DRC forces were in a life or death struggle. Many border villages collapsed. Refugees filled the roadways going out of Tawanda or into its new capital, Damir.

"In 2005, the war still raged. The blood of men, women, and children soaked the earth, infused the air, and seeped into the water."

"Are we ready?" Okoro sat at the large oval table in the council room. He looked from advisor to advisor for a dissenting reaction. As there were none, he said, "Good. Let us begin. Finance Report."

An advisor, three chairs down on the left, said, "Currently, the taxes from foreign holdings are stable at ten million dollars per month. One tenth goes to support leadership staff and civilian population issues. One tenth is invested. And the rest supports our leadership, government, and army food, medical services, clothing, weapons, and ammunition."

Okoro's new cell phone vibrated in his pocket. The caller ID showed "Opeyemi." He excused himself from the meeting. "I better take this."

He went into his private study and came face to face with Opeyemi. Standing tall and rigid by his desk, she wore a long dress and matching head scarf in a traditional colorful liputa print.

Before he could say anything, she said, "You have ignored my calls."

"I have been busy."

"Too busy to care for your people?"

"I command a war—a war you wanted, if I remember correctly."

"Adebowale, you were to bring our people honor and freedom. Instead, you have brought them war and misery. They are refugees in their own land."

"As I have said to you countless times in the past, I do not have the resources to feed my army and the people. I will not stand here and debate this with you again. I have an advisor meeting to run." He turned to leave.

"Adebowale Okoro, do not turn away from me."

Her tone made him pause. He turned back. He took a step toward her and said, "Say what you came to say and be done with it."

"If you do not find a way to serve the needs of your people, Adebowale, you will have no people left to serve you. There is a circle of shanties over a mile wide circling Damir, starting seven blocks from we stand. The people are war refugees. There are no services, waste disposal, food, or medical help. Black marketers buy anything and everything people are willing to sell, including themselves and their children."

He said, "They do, we all do, what is necessary."

"Adebowale, you do not remember you were once the disenfranchised. You led us into rebellion against insensitive government leadership. Our children once worshiped you and your ideals. But now, today, you are indistinguishable from your enemy. Your people suffer and your children despise you."

"Enough," he said. "Sacrifices must be made." With a dismissive wave of his hand, he turned and stormed out.

Opeyemi stood still as a statue as her eyes filled with tears.

Three hours later, Kwanh Uba entered the

president's office. Okoro sat at his desk.

"Mr. President, an urgent message."

"Read it."

"With great sorrow, we report that enemy mortar shells decimated the home of President Adebowale Okoro. Immediate and heroic emergency operations failed to rescue Opeyemi Okoro and her three children. All died from injuries suffered at the blast site."

Okoro did not move or respond. He did not show sorrow or remorse.

Kwanh said, "Mr. President, I know this news is most shocking. What can I do for you?"

Okoro stood. He walked over to the window and stared at the city before him. His voice hollow, he repeated his last words to his wife. "Sacrifices must be made."

Rachel said, "Today, the war is still in progress. The refugee situation continues to deteriorate. Earlier this morning, Okoro asked, via a press conference, to address the United Nations. He wants the UN to recognize Tawanda as a member organization and take the lead in stopping the DRC attacks."

The team erupted with excitement. Their "new baby" had just taken a major step in the world arena. The situation added spark and immediacy to their mission. Without ceremony, Ted pushed his chair back and got to his feet. Conversation ended as the team waited for his assessment and direction.

"Interesting," Ted said, as if Rachel had announced the weather report. He looked over at the dining area. "Lunch is ready. Go and enjoy. I'll join you later." With that, he disappeared around the corner.

Rachel watched him leave and then looked at the group. No one had moved. Since she was the only one left standing, she said, "I'm sure everything is okay. Let's eat. I'm starved."

She was wrong.

Chapter 40
Lake George, New York

Okoro's request to speak at the United Nations gave Ted an idea. He went to the study, closed the door, and called Lucy. "Progress?"

She said, "Good."

He said, "Morning headline?"

She said, "Perfect. By the way, we found the server's owner."

He said, "Excellent. Eliminate."

Ted hung up. Their verbal shorthand saved time and minimized electronic eavesdropping. Lucy would put a plan together with a backup in case they'd have to abort. His excitement and anticipation energized him. He didn't want to, couldn't spend the afternoon in session. He needed action. He wanted Rachel.

The team was still at lunch when Ted took his seat at the table.

Rachel noticed the slight flush in his cheeks and his elevated energy, dissipated through drumming fingers, or tapping toes, or both. Plus, he was chattier than normal all through lunch. During dessert, he addressed the group.

"So," Ted said. "Are you ready to get down to work?" He looked into the eyes of each person. Then he motioned with his hands for them to lean in. He dropped his voice to a conspiratorial level. "Or would you like to take a break and go down to the village for the afternoon?"

The team exploded in unison, "Take a break!" Ted held up a forefinger, left the room, and came back with a handful of brochures. "Here are maps of Lake George and The Winter Festival event listings. Decide what you'd like to do. I'll arrange for two limos at the front door by one-thirty."

Rachel had a brochure and unfolded it out of curiosity. James Jefferson, on her left, leaned over with his arm around the back of her chair, and Isabel Upton on her right, put her elbow on the arm of Rachel's chair and leaned in. They started to explore the map with their fingers. James took out a pen and circled the areas they deemed most interesting.

Imprisoned, Rachel's breathing accelerated. She rubbed her hands on her thighs. Her body heated with anxiety and perspired to cool down. "Excuse me," she said, and pushed her chair away from the table. "I'll be right back." She escaped to the powder room, shut the door, and splashed her face with water. She felt better sooner than she expected.

For extra measure, she opened the window, sat down on the closed toilet seat cover, and leaned back. Several cleansing deep breaths later, she returned to the dining room. Only Ted remained.

Rachel said, "Are you waiting for me?"

"Of course. I didn't want you to think you'd been deserted."

"You're a good friend, Ted. I'll see you in a few minutes." She left the area to go upstairs.

At the appointed time, the team assembled at the front door. Rachel stopped halfway down the stairs. Ted saw her. "Come on, Rachel. We're leaving."

"Sorry, I'm not going. I've got some personal things to take care of. Have a great time. And take notes. I want to hear all about the village when you get back."

Amy looped her hand around Ted's arm. "No problem," she said. "We'll miss you."

Rachel waved. "Enjoy yourselves. See you all later."

In her room, she heard car doors opening and closing. *Alone at last.* She left the door open and got comfortable. She kicked off her shoes, grabbed her phone and tablet, propped the bed pillows against the headboard, and snuggled against them.

When she checked her phone for text messages, she saw—DRAFT attached to her text to Chris. She'd never sent it. He must think she's crazy.

A knock made her jump. Ted, wearing a double breasted overcoat, stood in her doorway. He had her coat over his arm. Rachel scrambled off the bed. "What are you still doing here?"

He stepped into the room. "I saved the second limo for us. I've packed a thermos of hot chocolate, a fresh baked stash of chocolate chip cookies, a chilled bottle of champagne, and a fur throw. Our afternoon will be warm, cozy, and romantic. I promise you'll love it."

The man personified Prince Charming— handsome and suave, yet innocent and disarming. He held an open hand. "Come on, Rachel. Please."

Rachel shook her head. "You've gone to a lot of trouble but I can't."

"Don't say no." He removed her coat from his arm and held it up for her to put on. "Come on. For me," he said. "For us."

"Ted," Rachel said, backing away. "There *is* no us."

He ignored her and stepped behind her. He maneuvered the coat so her arms slipped into the sleeves and caressed her as he brought it up, slowly until the coat rested on her shoulders. Rachel didn't move.

Ted's hand slid from her back to her shoulder as he moved around to face her. He placed both hands on the shawl collar and adjusted it, from behind her neck down to the first button—his thumbs following, touching her jaw, exerting light pressure as he began to engage the button. *Oh my God.*

"Ted, stop. Enough." Rachel jerked away and shrugged her shoulders. The coat dropped into a puddle on the floor. "I'm not going. I want you to leave."

"Rachel, I want to be with you. I love you."

"Don't."

"Perhaps it is too soon," Ted said. "I know we both have transient people in our lives. You have that landlord and I have Amy. They're both meaningless. Our lives are intertwined—fated to be together."

"You're wrong."

"Rachel, no one could possibly love you like I do."

She walked to the door and put her hand on the knob. "Ted, there is no 'us.' Go join the others. I'll see you at dinner."

As he left, he said, "Don't worry. We'll figure this out."

She went downstairs, hung up her coat, and

watched him drive away in the limo. Rachel made a vodka tonic and brought it up to her room, securing the door with lock and chair—in case.

Drink in hand, she relaxed on the bed. She thought about Ted. Any feelings she might have had for him were gone. Chris, however, was a different story. She wanted him more than ever—but how? Her eyelids grew heavy. She put her drink on the nightstand and dozed off.

She woke to the sound of laughter and conversation. The clock said five—an hour before dinner. Rachel sat up and took a sip of her drink. The fizz had fizzled, but she didn't care. She took another sip and checked her phone. Her "*Chris, I miss you*" text still said DRAFT. Annoyed, she punched SEND and made sure it received a time stamp.

She waited for a few minutes for a response. When none appeared, she got up and dressed for dinner. Before leaving the room, expecting nothing, she checked her phone again. *A text from Chris.* After a flash of fear and insecurity, she tapped the screen. In letters that seemed to fill the room, she read, "*I miss you too. Let's talk.*"

Rachel called.

Chapter 41
Lake George, New York

Rachel glowed after her conversation with Chris. She couldn't stop smiling. Her pre-set alarm sounded—dinner time.

She jumped up, went to the mirror, fixed her hair, tucked and smoothed her clothes, and applied lipstick. Nothing more was necessary because her excitement did the rest. Ready, Rachel floated down the hall and skipped down the stairs like a teenager on her first date.

Amy Yeager noticed the shift in Rachel's demeanor. She frowned and tossed her hair as she leaned into Ted, slipping her hand around his arm. Ted saw Rachel and gave her a skeptical raised eyebrow before re-engaging with Amy.

General Portman and Quentin Sheffield were sitting in two side chairs separated by a chessboard.

They must have sensed a change in the room's energy because they looked up. Both gave her twisted grins before returning to their game.

"Rachel, you missed a lovely afternoon in town," Isabel Upton said. Then she leaned in, gave a little hip bump, and whispered, "How'd it go with Ted?" Without waiting for a response and for all to hear, she said, "The village looked like a fairyland all decked out for its Winter Festival."

Rachel glanced at Ted. Ignoring Isabel's whisper, she said, "I'm glad you had a good time."

Isabel whispered again. "Guess you two had your own good time."

Rachel, offended, stepped back. "I beg your pardon?"

"Oh, I know it's none of my business," Isabel said. "But you have the look that comes from... you know."

"I don't know."

Turning toward the wall, away from the others, and leaning close to Rachel, Isabel said in a low whisper, "Sex."

Rachel said, "That's a pretty big presumptuous assumption."

"By me *and* Amy," Isabel said, directing Rachel's gaze to Amy. "If looks could kill." Isabel sipped her drink.

Rachel said, "Well, you're both way out of line and wrong." She spun and headed to the bar for a drink. Vodka tonic in hand, she took a seat on a couch.

"May I join you?" James said, and sat down without waiting for an answer. "Impressive presentation this morning."

"Thank you."

He patted her knee and let his hand rest there.

"Yes, good work. You made the Tawanda situation come alive for all of us."

"Please don't," Rachel said as she removed his hand. The man sat back and sipped his drink without offering an apology. After a few moments of silence, she got up to find another seat.

The huge house seemed to shrink before her eyes. There were no obvious isolated places to sit. Her eyes scanned the room, back and forth, faster and faster as the panic built. Nowhere to go. People closing in. Perspiration. No air. *Oh no. Not now. Not here.* She struggled to remain upright as the room started to spin. She put her hand out hoping to find an anchor. She did—the back of a chair.

Rachel steadied herself and repeated her new mantra—*Breathe. Relax. Think of Chris.* Like magic, her panic subsided. *This time faster than the last.* The realization made her smile.

Yvonne appeared. "Dinner is served."

Rachel felt an arm encircle her waist. It belonged to Ted. She removed it. He offered his elbow. "May I escort you to dinner?"

"Yes, of course." Rachel put her right hand in the crook of his left elbow. He patted her hand with his. After he sat her at the table, he took the empty seat next to Amy.

Rachel put her napkin on her lap, looked around the table. She wanted to be with Chris. *This is going to be a long night.*

Chapter 42
Federal Plaza, New York City

Beth Neilson, after a day of sifting through information, slammed her hand down on her desk. Eric Jerrod jumped.

She said, "I know what's wrong in the security footage. Donovan and Waters knew they were being taped. They talked in code."

"C'mon Beth. We're not talking terrorists here. Why would they care?"

"Eric, I'm telling you something's up and Ted Donovan's part of it. I can't prove it but I know it."

"Okay, let's run with your assumption that Donovan and Waters are planning a secret event. How are they even connected outside the think tank?"

Beth said. "Donovan goes to Europe several times a year. That's a fact. If he's attending conferences or mediating situations, it's private or under the radar. No press."

"Maybe that's the answer. He works for the private sector, and Waters needs a negotiation handled outside the White House."

"Plausible," Beth said. "Maybe it's not a negotiation. Maybe Waters needs someone beaten half to death or killed?"

"So you've gone over to Detective Voss's theory? We still have no proof Donovan's killed anyone."

"You're right," Beth said. "I'm just tired after a day with no luck."

"Well, maybe that's changing."

"Why? What have you got?

Eric said, "I just got an email from The Philadelphia Museum of Art."

"And?"

"I'm reading. I'm reading," Eric said. "They were able to find a fundraiser from 1990 that Sandford attended as a councilman. The guest list's attached."

"The museum people are good."

"It doesn't hurt that the Director of the FBI sits on their board," Eric said with a big smile on his face.

Beth took the list, found and highlighted "Sandford" and "Donovan."

Beth said, "Okay. Now we have to find out what was going on in Sandford's district and how it changed after they met."

"I'm on it," Eric said.

Beth's phone rang. "Special Agent Neilson."

"Beth, it's Chris. Chris Gregory."

"Hey, Chris. What's going on?"

"I've been going over the security footage that we viewed, and I think I've got something."

"What do you mean?"

"Remember when you said there was something going on, but you couldn't figure it out?"

"Yes."

"Well, I think… "

"Wait!" Beth stopped him. "Not over the phone. I'm coming over."

She hung up and looked at Eric. "Are you up for a ride?"

"You go. I'll stay here. Follow up on this lead," Eric said. "I'll call you when I have something."

"Ditto."

Chapter 43
Los Angeles, California

The wet, foggy night turned chilly. At the end of his shift, Homicide Detective Victor Zabinsky sat at his desk. He straightened folders, made notes, and returned critical emails. Done, he stood, pushed in his chair, and put on his raincoat. The phone rang. He paused for a split-second and looked at the door. He sighed before he answered and cursed when he hung up.

Fifteen minutes later he stood on an LA backstreet, filled with ex-bar patrons and police, and decorated with lights and yellow tape. Zabinsky wanted to be home with a beer and a sandwich, watching the Lakers. Instead, he ducked under the tape, showed his ID, and found the officer in charge. "Let's walk and talk."

The officer led him through the commotion and

exhaust fumes outside, into the crime scene's noxious air inside. "Two drunken big boys were doing stupid beer bottle tricks and taking pictures of each other. One followed the other into the men's room and came out laughing.

"The subject of the picture, our perp, was not laughing. Enraged, he demanded to see the picture. The photographer, our victim, gave a phone to the perp. When he couldn't turn it on, our victim got the giggles. Our perp decided to shut him with a roundhouse to his jaw and a left to the side of his face. Our victim flew off the barstool and cracked his head on the edge of a table. That blow shut him up permanently. We have incident videos from four other patrons."

Zabinsky left the others and wandered around the crime scene, taking in the details. He approached the crime scene investigation unit. "Got anything?"

"Victim died from the impact with the table," the Assistant Coroner said, standing up. He reached toward one of his staff who gave him a bunch of plastic bags. "These things came from the vic's pockets—his wallet, ID, and cell phone. His other cell phone is in this bag. We got it off the bar. He must have been too drunk to realize that he gave the perp the wrong cell phone."

"Get everyone's statements and phones. I want them all checked for videos and pictures," Zabinsky said, taking charge.

The CSI tech interrupted. "I'm way ahead of you. I've got one of my people setting up a computer station by the door. We can download each phone before anyone leaves."

Two other detectives from the squad arrived. For the next two hours, they interviewed bartenders and patrons while the computer tech downloaded phone images and videos, and kept track of which download belonged to whom.

When the room emptied of non-essential persons, the CSI tech held up a plastic bag to Zabinsky. "This phone, the victim's second phone, is dead. It's unlikely any pertinent images are on it. Do you want us to download it anyway?"

"Yes," Zabinsky said. "We don't know when it died."

The computer tech opened the phone and took out the data card. He put it in his card reader, downloaded the images, and brought them up on the monitor. Zabinsky watched the slide show. No images pertained to the bar fight. They were all taken outside in the California sunshine.

"Stop," Zabinsky said, pointing. "Go back. Slowly. There. That one. Stop. Zoom in. Good." He stared at the monitor. "I know that place." He stroked his chin as he searched his memory. He snapped his fingers and said, "Got it."

He grabbed his phone and punched in a number. While he waited for the connection, he asked the computer tech to email him the last six images from the phone card—ASAP.

Eric Jerrod took the call as soon as he saw the caller ID.

"Zabinsky," he said, happy to hear from his friend. He pushed away from his desk and leaned back in his chair. "How's it going? Miss our early morning jogs."

"I'm so touched I've got a present for you."

"You're a sweetheart."

"I got pictures of your missing Meyerson family," Zabinsky said.

Eric snapped straight. "Tell me what you've got."

"I'm sending them to you right now," Zabinsky said. "The story is we had a fight in a bar. Found an extra phone with dead battery—extra, in that no one claimed it. Our on-sight tech downloaded its pictures."

Eric saw the email arrive, clicked on the attachment, and said, "Got them."

Zabinsky said, "Remember this place? It's the Meyerson neighborhood, and I'm guessing the pictures show them leaving home for their vacation."

Eric reviewed the pictures—the limousine, the driver, the family getting into the limo, the family seated inside the vehicle, and a shot through the rear window of a woman standing and waving. "Where did you say you got these?"

"We took the phone off a dead guy in a biker bar," Zabinsky said. "No idea where he got it or how."

"What did his friends say?"

"Friend," Zabinsky said. "Only one. And when I interviewed him the poor guy still couldn't believe that he killed his best friend and, in a twist of fate, his cousin. He cried the whole time, answering questions through dripping snot, wads of tissue, gulps of coffee, and coughing spells. After sitting through all that shit, I still got nothing."

"You got a lot," Eric said. "This is our first tangible lead. The woman is not the house sitter so we may have our perp. Thanks, Buddy. I owe you big time."

Eric hung up the phone. He sent the woman's image to the facial recognition program. As soon as the processing started, he called Beth.

Beth took the call in Chris Gregory's apartment. "Send me the picture, and call me when you have a hit."

Chris said, "You've got a picture?"

"Maybe. Possibly one of the Meyerson abductors."

"Is it Donovan?"

"No. A woman. Eric, an agent working on this with me, is running a facial scan as we speak. So, let's get down to business. What did you find?"

"I'm not sure." Chris said. "Here." Chris picked up two sheets of paper and handed her one. "This is a print-out of Donovan's conversation. First, I found the conversation stilted. They must have known about the video and audio surveillance. If nothing was up, the conversation should've been normal. I think they were trying to hide something."

"I agree. I'm also finding it is very strange that Waters would try to persuade Donovan, an apparent novice in international negotiations, to do anything."

Chris bolted upright. "That's it. That's the key." He started pacing.

"Donovan?"

"No, your use of the word 'persuade.' That particular word is not in the text. Waters used 'seduce.'"

"Same thing, right?"

Chris said, "Maybe. But, it bothers me. It's an odd choice. It reminds me of 'ordinance,' a sanitized version of 'bomb.'"

"You think...." Beth sat straight as the idea exploded in her brain.

"Whoa. I'm just saying there may be another way to look at these conversations. I didn't want to jump to any conclusions. I figured you'd know what to do."

Beth said, "You're right. There is no proof that what they're saying isn't what they mean. On the other hand, we could be listening to a murder plot."

Chris dropped into his chair. "You know, while I do care about international affairs, what bothers me more is that Rachel's up there with Donovan. If he's a killer, I want her out of there…and now."

"Me too," Beth said, "but, despite what we suspect, we don't have any concrete evidence. I can't just go up there and arrest the man."

Beth stood and put her coat on. She folded the written conversation and put it in her purse. "I'm going back to my office to see if I can confirm or deny our suspicions. Will you continue monitoring communications in and out of Lake George? Let me know as soon as you find out anything—that is, if you do."

"Of course, no problem. I'll call you from Lake George. I'm going up tomorrow."

Beth stopped and turned. "I can't stop you, but it's not a good idea."

"It's not a good idea to leave Rachel alone with that nut job."

"If you want to go get Rachel, fine. But you leave Donovan to me. I don't want either of you getting hurt. Understood?"

Chris nodded, "Don't worry."

Chapter 44
Lake George, New York

After dinner, the team sat around the table, talking, waiting for Yvonne to serve warm pie a la mode. Nickel-sized snowflakes shimmered in the cabin's exterior lights.

Quentin said, "Looks like we're getting a nor'easter."

"Not technically," Norman said, more to himself than the others who had grown used to his obsession with details. "There are a number of particulars that would have to be in place. First, it would have to come up from the south. Second, it needs to have a low pressure area whose center of rotation is off the East Coast. Finally, the winds need to come from the northeast."

Rachel watched the snowfall's density change. The wind picked up. The flakes, now smaller, swirled like oceanic waves. Visibility dropped and the woodland backdrop vanished in the white out.

"Lots of snow," Isabel said to no one in particular. "Do you think we'll be snowed in?"

"No," Ted said. "The grounds-keeper will clear the driveway, paths, and landings every four to six inches. Lake George people are used to this kind of weather."

"Good," said James. "I have the flyer with the listings for tomorrow's Winter Festival. It looks like a lot of fun."

"Let me see," Ted said and held out his hand. James gave it to him. After he scanned it, he said, "How about we have a round table discussion after breakfast, around ten, eat lunch around 11:30, and take off for the village at one?"

Nodding heads confirmed the schedule.

As the group lingered over coffee, Ted said, "So, now that you've had time to think about Rachel's presentation, what's the consensus about Tawanda?"

The general said, "Frankly, I'm not sure I know what you mean."

Ted elaborated. "Is Okoro a hero or tyrant? Is he out of his depth or a world leader? Is he smart or brazen?"

James said, "Maybe both or neither. Maybe he's emulating *The Mouse That Roared*. And if that's true, I don't know what that makes him."

Amy said, "Oh, I love that movie. Peter Sellers was great in the lead. Came out around 1959-1960, I believe. Grand Fenwick, a tiny country facing bankruptcy, decides to declare war against the United States. The country's intention is to lose so it can get 'defeated nation' status and foreign aid. A good plan except for the fact that they won."

Quentin said, "Don't be ridiculous. Okoro went

from lazy oaf to inhuman dictator. The man should be sanctioned."

Isabel said, "Are you proposing we assassinate him?"

Quentin nodded and drew his forefinger across his throat.

The general said, "Frankly, I support your thinking but deplore your methods. On the other hand, it's better to know your enemy than face one you don't."

Amy said, "So, what do you think the Tawandian people dying in the streets would say? The babies starving to death? The women and children being bought and sold in the sex-slave trade? Who do you think they'd agree with?"

"Amy's right," Norman said. "We're here to come up with a solution to address the needs of the people as well as the country. Once we do that, if we do that, then we've got to sell it to Sandford, who'll have to convince Okoro."

Quentin said, "Good luck. That son-of-a-bitch Okoro is running with the bit in his teeth. He plans to win at any cost. I've seen it before. Nothing or nobody's going to change his mind."

Isabel said, "Sure, it's going to be hard to find a workable solution from that point of view. Perhaps we can offer a trade—ideology for goods."

Rachel said, "That's a win-win. If we can figure out Okoro's key tangible need, we can offer a trade for humanitarian relief."

Isabel got up and returned to the table with pen and paper. "Okay. I'm ready. Let's brainstorm on what Okoro wants or needs most for the war or otherwise? I'll take any ideas."

Quentin said, "Weapons. Bet he'd take an atomic bomb if we offered." He chuckled.

Isabel said, "Medical supplies."

James said, "Food for the army."

Amy said, "Food for his starving people."

"Frankly, that's not happening," the general said. "He takes everything that enters the country. Nothing gets past him. His army patrols the ports, the airstrips, and the roads. And nothing gets to his people living in the squalid refugee camps."

Norman said, "There must be a way to divert his attention so he can address the crisis under his nose. Every person has his price."

Amy said, "I agree. The man's an egomaniac and believes his own bullshit. If we play into that, there might be a chance of success."

"You're right," Rachel said. "We tap into his vanity and give him the recognition he craves, like the United Nations invitation, in exchange for refugee humanitarian services."

"Frankly, we have no legal standing if he doesn't hold up his end," the general said. "Just because he says he agrees, doesn't mean he'll do it."

James said, "There's another problem. The UN can't just invite him. Okoro must agree to meet certain conditions."

Norman said, "That's true. I quote, in part, 'to reaffirm faith in fundamental human rights, in the dignity and worth of the human person, in the equal rights of men and women and of nations large and small.' However, let's remember the UN does not have an enforcement arm."

James said, "All that's well and good, but we have to take a step back. We can't come up with a plan that involves the UN because we don't represent them."

Isabel said, "Other kinds of recognition may be just as enticing. What about a heads-of-state dinner at the White House. Or a US tour...."

Amy finished her sentence, "...of Hollywood. I bet he'd love to mingle with the stars."

"Munitions plants," Quentin said. "The man will salivate over our weaponry."

"Frankly, I think he'd prefer our military training facilities," the general said. "A firsthand look at how to train an effective fighting force."

Ted said, "Good ideas. Isabel, did you get them all?" Isabel nodded. He continued. "Now we have to flesh out the process. Remember, whatever we set up for Tawanda, we hope will address similar situations all over the world."

"Yes, you're right," Isabel said. "We need to set up guidelines to make it easy to buy into our program."

James said, "Our program. I like that." He picked up a pen and reached for a napkin and scribbled on it. Crossed out some words and added others. He looked up and smiled. He held the napkin in his hand and read. "An international Big Brother program for wayward dictators."

No one said anything.

James blushed and laughed. "Okay, okay. I agree it needs some refining." He looked around the table. "I'll work on it."

Rachel said, "Yes, do. I think you're on to something."

Norman said, "We also have to figure out the best way to get to Okoro. I know the president can talk with him. However, he may feel less threatened if we can reach him through his advisors and major supporters. That way he may be more amenable to agreement conditions, whatever they may be."

Amy said, "Let's find out whom he admires. The people on his list may be willing to visit Tawandian refugee camps under the UN banner and make time to meet with Okoro." She ended with a toss of her hair followed by a coy tilt of her head as she covered Ted's hand with her own and looked into his eyes. "Maybe we could go with them."

Ted removed his hand and patted hers as he said, "Great start. We've still got a lot of work ahead of us." Then he looked at his watch. "It's getting late. Let's continue the discussion in the morning."

The general announced, "Brandy in the great room by the fire. Who knows what additional ideas will emerge."

Chapter 45
Lake George, New York

Rachel got into bed around midnight. She texted Chris, "*Thinking of you.*" As she reached over to turn out the light, someone knocked at her door. "Who is it?"

Another knock.

"One minute." Rachel got out of bed, stuck her feet in her slippers, and put on her robe. With her belt half knotted, she put her hand on the knob and said, "Who is it?"

"Ted."

She moved the chair, flipped the lock, and opened the door less than the width of her body. Ted stood there, sans jacket and tie, grinning like a school boy and leaning on the door jamb. His shirt was open at the collar, sleeves rolled up to his elbows. Rachel's eyes widened in surprise. *This can't be good.*

"Ted, it's late for a visit." Ted straightened and laughed. She detected a slight wobble of his head and the smell of liquor. She closed the door a little more and leaned against it with her body. "Go to bed. We'll talk in the morning."

Ted's body stiffened and then relaxed. He put his hand on the door. "Let's talk now."

Rachel's gut wrenched and sent a sour taste to her mouth. Her whole body tensed. "No. Tomorrow." She pushed the door shut. It didn't close.

Ted had his foot in the door and his hand on the doorknob. His face peered through the narrow opening. "I'm sorry, Rachel. It can't wait. Please. It's important."

"Whatever it is, it can wait." she said. "Go away."

He didn't move. Instead, he lowered his chin which made his eyes larger. He stuck out his lower lip to look even more pathetic. It was a spot-on desperate puppy impression.

She almost laughed. "Not working. Go away."

"Look, Rachel. I just want to give you a present and then I'll go. I promise."

Rachel released her pressure on the door, letting it move only as much as necessary for Ted to remove his foot. "Tomorrow, Ted. Move your foot."

Ted reached for a chain around his neck and lifted it over his head. With great care, he hung it on the fingers of his left hand. He held it up so she could see the dangling silver heart charm, three-quarters of an inch long.

"What's that?"

"It's Brenda's necklace. She was wearing it when she died."

"Really?" Appalled, Rachel tried to keep her voice even. "It's lovely."

"It's inscribed." He held the heart higher so she

could see the writing, "With All My Love, Ted." He had tears in his eyes. He looked at her. "I want you to have it."

"No, I can't. You know I can't."

"You have to. I mean, you must. Brenda wants you to have it."

"You're drunk. Go to bed."

He didn't move. "I was sitting in my room, doing my usual end of day routine—having a Scotch and watching the news before bedtime. Except tonight Brenda appeared. She looked beautiful in a white dress with ribbons in her hair. She sat down next to me. She told me she still loved me, but the time had come for me to move on. I swear, Rachel, she was as close to me as you are now. I gulped down the rest of my drink, reached for the bottle, and poured another."

"Ted, you were dreaming."

"I know this sounds crazy, but she was as real as you or I. She said she had met you and approved. Don't you see? I have—we have—her blessing. Then, she leaned over and kissed me, a kiss so light I hardly felt it at all." He touched his lips. "I drank the Scotch in one gulp. And had another. I sat with her until she disappeared."

Rachel tried to shut the door. It didn't move. *Where're Jack and Jay when I need them?* She saw her phone on the bedside table, out of reach. To get it, she'd have to let Ted in and that was a bad idea. "Please, Ted. For me. Go back to your room."

He reacted like he understood the words but not what they meant. His face muscles were slack and his eyes vacant as he looked from Rachel to the ceiling and back again. The shift of focus caused him to sway ever so slightly. Then, to her relief, Ted put the necklace back on and said, "Okay." His body shifted.

He removed his foot and took a step toward his room.

Rachel shoved the door closed, leaned against it until the latch clicked, and took a deep breath. She grabbed the chair to wedge it under the knob. Before she could get it into position, it was knocked out of her hands. Ted Donovan stood in her room, back against the door.

With one hand, he locked it. As she opened her mouth to scream, he blocked it with a tongued kiss. Then he buried her face in his chest as he hugged her and said, "Rachel, my love, I just can't leave. This is our time, our moment."

Fuck! Where's Chris—and his fucking security system?

Rachel tucked and twisted until her head was free. "Ted, you're drunk. You don't want to do this." She said the words in awkward spurts. Hyperventilation made it hard to talk. She wiggled and shifted to create enough space to free her pinned arms. At the same time, she scanned the room, looking for a weapon.

His mind must have wandered because he eased his grip. Rachel took the opportunity to shove him away. She stepped back, but not far enough. He grabbed her and moved with her. As she struggled to break his hold, they did an awkward dance around the room, bumping into walls, dressers, and the overturned chair.

Where is everyone. Can't they hear this racket? Where's Chris? The police?

Without intention, she backed into a triangular cage—her back against the door, her side against the armoire, and her escape blocked by Ted. *Shit.*

He said, "Come on, Rachel. No more foreplay." Leaning in, he gave her a probing prolonged alcoholic kiss. He withdrew. Fingered her hair. Licked her ear. Caressed her cheek. Whispered, "Forget about Mr. Landlord Christopher Gregory." He entered her again with another forceful kiss, withdrew, and said, "You must feel it. Our destinies are intertwined."

Rachel gasped, fighting hyperventilation and struggling for leverage on a physical and emotional level. "Ted, stop. You're not a rapist. You're a hero."

"What?" He took a small step back. "What are you talking about? I'm not a rapist."

"If that's true," Rachel said, her arms taut against him, "be my hero, again. Leave now."

"Your hero," Ted said. With vacant eyes, he took another step back and released her.

Rachel lunged for the lamp on the bedside table. She grabbed it and jerked it free from the wall. Holding it with both shaking hands, poised over her shoulder, she got ready to swing for a home run and send his head to the outfield. "Ted. Go."

Ted looked at her. "What are you doing?"

"Leave." Rachel, balanced, stood her ground.

"I'd never hurt you." He took a step toward her.

"Stop. Don't come any closer." Rachel shifted her weight so she could put as much force as possible into her swing.

"What's wrong?" He opened his arms and invited her in. "I love you. I'll take care of you." She didn't move, but he did. At that exact moment, Rachel's fear morphed into rage.

She swung the lamp with all her might. Ted blocked it, snatched it out of her hands, and threw it on the floor. His face twisted with fury. He lunged for her. She brought her knee into his scrotum as hard as she could.

Ted yelped-grunted in surprise and hit the floor in a fetal position.

Rachel kicked him hard, in his side, with the heel of her foot. He arched his back and gasped. She threw the door open so hard that it bounced off the wall.

"Get out!"

Ted didn't move.

"I mean it, Ted. Get out now or I'll kick your nuts like a soccer ball, wake the whole damn cabin, and call the police."

Ted groaned, rolled to his hands and knees, and raised his head. Eyes wild and teeth bared, he flew straight at her, arms outstretched, curled fingers splayed.

With a sensei's instinct, her training took over. Rachel's body flexed, muscles ready, position assumed. Her left arm broke his momentum, and the heel of her right hand delivered an upward blow right under, and up into, his nose. Stunned, he reeled backwards and fell against the dresser, hands covering his face.

"Jesus Christ, Rachel," Ted said through his fingers. "I'm bleeding. I think you broke my nose."

"Get out of here before I break something else."

When he didn't move, she yanked his arm and flung him into the hallway. He lost his balance and hit the far wall with a thud. Rachel slammed the door closed, leaned on it, locked it, and blocked it with the chair.

Ted looked up and down the hallway to see if anyone was up. He heard some movement, handles turning. He ran for his room, using his shirt sleeve to cover his nose, bleeding like a son-of-a-bitch.

"Ted is that you? Are you okay?"

"Fine," Ted said. "Everything's okay."

He staggered to his room, applied first aid, and washed up. He disguised his nose's swelling with a Band-Aid and concocted a story for breakfast.

Before going to bed, he texted Lucy. "*Excise landlord.*"

Lucy texted back. *"In process. Landlord owns server."*
Ted smiled and texted, *"Perfect."*

Rachel slid down the door's face to the floor and stayed there. When she felt her legs would hold her, she got up, stripped, and stepped into the shower. She let hot water purify her body and steam clear her head. After a while, she soaped up the wash puff and became engrossed in the cleansing process—until she heard a noise.

She stood still and listened. Nothing. She went back to her shower. She heard it again. Only this time she laughed. The noise was her. She was humming Queen's *We are the Champions*. She lifted her chin and squared her shoulders as the water rinsed away the past and prepared her for the future.

Rachel stepped out of the shower and wrapped her body in the extra plush towels. She took her time drying herself, enjoying the sensation of the deep soft pile against her skin. She was still humming as she slid under the covers, ready to welcome a good night's sleep when her phone rang. The caller ID showed "Chris."

"Want me to call the police?" Chris asked before she could say hello. "I took a break when you went to bed. I just saw what happened on the security video. I must say you've got one terrific right cross."

Rachel laughed. "It was a good shot, wasn't it?"

"That's not funny, Rachel," Chris said. "It's time to leave the cabin and come home."

"C'mon. You don't mean that. Ted was drunk. He won't try to seduce me again."

"You knew?"

"Knew what?"

"That he would try to seduce you?"

Rachel noticed a change in his voice. "Yessss," she said, choosing her next words with care. "I overheard him on the phone talking to his therapist. Didn't you? You're the one watching the security tapes."

"Nope. Must have missed it. Lots of footage. Sorry. Can't remember everything."

'I'll let that big lie pass," Rachel said, in a soft throaty whisper. "You know why? I can't remember everything either. I might need a 'stages' refresher course. Are you up for it?"

"Don't mess with me right now. I'm coming up to get you."

Rachel licked her lips before answering. "I'm all yours," she said and ended the call. Exhausted, she fell into a deep sleep.

Later that night, she entered a dream state. A noise above her. In the attic. Footfalls. She went down the hall toward the balcony and through the last door on her right. Inside, the light was on illuminating a staircase, which she climbed.

At the top, she entered a room filled with sunlight. Bright new painted toys sat on shelves and a rag doll lay on the bed. Soft purple lilacs graced the walls, pink polka dotted fabric made up the ruffle-bordered curtains, and a pink-purple-white plaid quilt covered the bed.

Rachel heard the sound of laughter and smelled wild flowers after a rain. She walked into the room expecting to see a happy child playing with her toys. Instead, with each step the colors faded to sepia and then to charcoal gray. The sweet air soured with decay's pungent odor, and darkness cloaked the light.

She stood in the void. A cool breeze caressed her face and a droplet fell on her cheek. Rachel wiped it away. The residue was sticky. It smelled of blood. Death. She tried to back away. Hands grabbed her feet. She fell, kicking, struggling.

Rachel's eyes flew open. It took her a moment to realize she was in bed, safe and sound. As she straightened the covers, her hand did not glide across the sheet—it stuck to it. She touched her cheek. *Eew. No way!*

She ran to the bathroom and turned on the light. The mirror confirmed a reddish smear on her face and hand. She must have scratched her face. She washed and looked for the telltale mark. She didn't find it.

She checked the time. *Three o'clock.* Wide awake, Rachel went downstairs to scrounge for some ice cream and maybe a book to read. A half hour later, armed with two naked scoops of vanilla and the "History of Portman's Landing," she sat in bed, savoring the smooth ice cream while she read.

The book contained the cabin's architectural drawing. It included the floor plan, heating and cooling systems, electric wiring, and descriptions, of materials—stone, wood, pylons, iron, and glass. In addition, it had an extensive visual record of the land preparation and the building's metamorphosis. It all made her head spin and her eyes tired. Tomorrow she'd read some more and talk to General Portman.

She fell asleep with the book next to her and the light on.

Chapter 46
Damir, Tawanda, Africa

In the Tawandian presidential office, Adebowale Okoro sat at his desk going over options for his next public address. He paused to check his email and opened this one from the unfamiliar PRAISE Foundation.

Date: Saturday, February 11, 2017
Time: 2:00 AM Eastern Standard Time
       9:00 AM Central Africa Time
To: President Adebowale Okoro, Damir, Tawanda, Africa
From: The PRAISE Foundation, New York City, NY, USA
    The PRAISE Foundation has been following your plight since the first injustices were inflicted upon your people by the Democratic Republic of the Congo. Based on your accomplishments to date, our Board of Directors is pleased to announce that you have earned the PRAISE Foundation Humanitarian Award (PFHA).
    Each PFHA is tailored to fit the objectives and goals of each recipient. To that end, in view of your

wish to speak to the United Nations, the PRAISE Foundation has gone to extraordinary lengths to arrange a special presentation session with UN officials. From that point on, it will be up to you to convince these officials to allow you to speak in an open session.

In addition, the PRAISE Foundation, in recognition of Tawanda's critical financial situation, will assume all the costs associated with your trip. We will provide first class round trip transportation to the United States, including lodging and food for you and your entourage.

If you choose to accept this award, your private plane will leave Tawanda at midnight tonight and arrive in New York City on Sunday, February 12, 2017. This will give you all day Monday to prepare for your meeting at the UN on Tuesday morning at 8 AM.

In closing, please let us know your decision by 4:00 PM your time.

Okoro read the email three times and printed it. He went on-line and searched for more information on the PRAISE Foundation. He skipped the Public Relations drivel and focused on the Board of Directors. If the list was real, the board members were powerful individuals with connections that made the foundation's offer plausible.

Glancing at his watch, he had four-and-a-half hours to decide. It was what he wanted, but it was more back-door than official. Still, it got his attention and excitement. He paced the room—hands and jaw clenching and releasing in sync. Out loud he said, "Opeyemi, it is in times like this that I miss your wise counsel. Tell me what to do."

He waited, draped in the ever-present shroud of

her anger and disappointment. The silence pierced him like her avenging dagger. He hung his head then shrugged off the moment, made a decision, and punched a number into his phone. When it rang, he ended the call. Five minutes later he heard the knock at his door and said, "Come in."

The door opened and Kwanh Uba appeared. "Yes, Mr. President?"

"Do you have time for a walk?"

Kwanh looked surprised until he saw Okoro put a finger to his lips and look around the room. "Yes, of course."

They left the building, under guard, and walked in the Presidential Gardens, beyond their protectors' earshot.

Adebowale said, "I have been offered the chance to speak before the United Nations."

"That is good news. What you wanted, yes?"

"It is by private arrangement through a highly visible American foundation. But I am concerned. It is a clandestine operation—no press. No unusual preparations that might alert others to my absence. If our enemies find out, I shudder at the consequences. I hesitate to leave under these conditions."

"Yet the offer is just what you need at this time."

"True. I have checked this PRAISE Foundation. It has much money and powerful supporters. Still I wonder why, if I deserve this opportunity, it does not come from the United Nations directly? And why I cannot have full press coverage."

"Perhaps, my cousin, in secrecy you will not have to admit failure, should you be denied. Although if you bring an entourage, it will surely come out that something is happening."

"Failure is not an option—thus my conundrum. Is it right to refuse this offer and wait for another? Do I take this chance to make Tawanda a world power or wait for the next?"

"Tell me Cousin, what is the root of your indecision?"

"It is happening too fast. If I accept, I must leave tonight. Here is the email." Okoro handed the printout to Kwanh. "What do you think?"

"Call PRAISE and I will listen." Kwanh pulled out his personal phone and handed it to Okoro. "Best not to use one of your own phones."

Okoro nodded and called. After a brief courtesy exchange, he said, "What is the plan for tonight if I accept?"

Lucy, as the PRAISE official, said, "I have arranged for a Boeing Executive Jet Series IV 747 number FL05472 to meet you at midnight at a private airstrip on the outskirts of Damir," Lucy said. "When you arrive in New York, you will be met by our driver escorts and brought to the Millennium UN Plaza Hotel under the name of Kamau Ekwensi. On Tuesday, you will meet with Henry Hillsople, UN Membership Coordinator, and his committee. You may choose the day of your return flight. I suggest Friday so you have time to see the city. How does that sound?"

Okoro looked at Kwanh, who was scribbling down the information. Kwanh looked up and shrugged.

"I congratulate PRAISE. The arrangements are very thorough."

"If you are unhappy with any phase," she said, "I will be happy to make the appropriate adjustments. All I need at this point is your acceptance and an entourage count, so I can order onboard supplies and confirm the number of reserved rooms with the hotel."

"I understand. I will call later with my answer."

After the call, the men stared at Kwanh's list.

"The answer may be in the details," Kwanh said. "Here, check this information before you decide." He placed the list in Okoro's hands. "While I cannot make the decision easier, I would be honored to stay behind and safeguard your presidency and the country."

Okoro smiled and put his arm around Kwanh's shoulders. "You are my cousin, best friend, and wise counsel. You have alleviated my worst fear. I will do as you advise. May it happen that this lowly shepherd will bring our country to the international stage as a world power."

Back in his office, Okoro checked the plane and the hotel reservations. PRAISE had three hotel suites reserved for his exclusive use, Sunday through Friday. Henry Hillsople's aide de camp, Mr. John Smith, verified their Tuesday meeting.

Date: Saturday, February 11, 2017
Time: 8:00 AM EST; 3:00 PM CAT;
From: President Adebowale Okoro, Damir, Tawanda, Africa
To: The PRAISE Foundation, New York City, NY, USA

I thank the Board of Directors of the PRAISE Foundation for the PRAISE Foundation Humanitarian Award. I am humbled and grateful for the opportunity presented and, with much gratitude regarding their effort on behalf of Tawanda, I accept.

I will forward information regarding the Tawandian entourage by 4:00 PM CAT.

Lucy Kilmer smiled when she got Okoro's

acceptance. This seduction would be the best ever. Okoro and his entourage would board the corporate jet under the cover of darkness at a small airstrip used by black market enterprises. Okoro would occupy the executive suite with a presidential desk and private galley.

The other passengers would be in the main body. Their amenities would include an open bar, head phones, movies, TV, and abundant Tawandian and American cuisine.

After the party, sated by food, exhausted by excitement, all passengers would be relaxed. By midnight, they'd enter the final stages of their lives: sleep, unconsciousness, and death.

Lucy went over the plan several more times to make sure she had everything covered. Satisfied, she drafted a statement in Okoro's name to be emailed to all major news agencies Sunday morning as soon as the plane was confirmed missing. It would bounce off several servers and appear to be sent from Tawanda.

Date: Sunday, February 11, 2017
Time: 8:00 AM EST
1: 00 AM CAT
To: Kwanh Uba and the Tawandian People

For Tawanda to take its place in the United Nations, a consortium of world powers, we must enact changes from within. In my absence, and under the leadership of my trusted aide, Kwanh Uba, the following directives are to be instituted immediately:

1. Release all remaining supplies in our warehouses to the army, Red Cross, and other authorized agencies for dissemination to the people of Tawanda—this includes purchased and donated food, clothing, and medical supplies;

2. Release funds earmarked for the rebuilding of housing and schools for the Tawandian people as soon as the supplies are distributed;

3. Set up election and balloting procedures so Tawandians can determine their own future through a democratic process; and

4. Create the University of Damir to take the lead in educating and preparing our young people to take their rightful place in the local and global spheres of government, economics, and finance.

I will be working behind the scenes to maximize the impact of our people and their achievements. I am proud to be the Father of Tawanda. However, the time has come for the Tawandian people to take charge of Tawanda's global ascension.

Your Loyal Servant,
Adebowale Okoro

Next, Lucy itemized the remaining operation's procedures.

• Transfer the contents of Okoro's Swiss bank account, estimated at over fifty million dollars, to the Relief Fund at the Tawanda National Bank upon confirmation the new government distributed the existing supplies.

• Remove all electronic traces of event from all passenger phones and computers as well as documentation and governmental papers related to trip.

• Clean any electronic footprints related to, or pointed at, the PRAISE Foundation from all Tawandian government servers and phones.

• Sweep and clean the Damir Airport data of an unidentified plane or PRAISE Foundation's identification codes.

• Clean the Millennium UN Plaza Hotel records of

any references to PRAISE or phone numbers connected with the foundation or the reservation.

• Remove electronic footprint of all phone calls to the United Nations.

Pushing her chair away from her desk, she sighed, stood, and stretched. It had been a long day that had gone well. She'd go over everything many times before the morning trying to find and mitigate anomalies. All lessons learned would become a part of her *modus operandi*, insuring positive outcomes for all future seductions.

After a final check with her team assured her the seduction was good to go, Lucy sent a text to Ted. *"Ready. Confirm."*

She sent another to her in-house assistant, *"Come."* He arrived within minutes. She said, "I'd like a massage before my bath."

"My pleasure," he answered.

"Good. Go. I'll be right in."

After he left, she checked all her equipment, backed-up the day's work, and shut everything down. Right now, all she needed was her phone—and a text from Ted.

Chapter 47
Gramercy Avenue, New York City

Chris Gregory, plagued by images of Rachel and Donovan, lay awake all night.

At six, he got up and showered. When Nikolai arrived at seven, they'd set up the day's schedule and Chris could leave by eight. He picked up his phone and booked transportation to Lake George. He'd be with Rachel, at the cabin, by noon.

He packed his electronic gear in his messenger bag. He planned to monitor the security videos during the ride up, and back, if necessary. At six-forty-five, he decided to go downstairs, have a cup of coffee, clear his mind with a game of Evil Sudoku, and wait.

Just before seven, Nikolai barged through the lobby door, his face grim. He ran to the concierge desk and activated his computer. If he noticed Chris, he didn't acknowledge him.

Chris watched for a couple of seconds and then said, "What's going on?"

Nikolai kept his eyes on the monitor. "I cannot talk now." He typed as if possessed.

Chris jumped to his feet and put his coffee down with such force, it sloshed over the cup's edge. At Nikolai's side in two strides, he peered at the screen. "This is serious stuff. How can I help?"

"This morning, I saw a man—an unrepentant murderer of thousands—on the street. I am finding out if that is even possible. His name is Dragomir Ekmečić (Ech-me-chi-ch), a Bosnian Serb. He led one of many soldiers' groups that marched on Srebrenica, July 11, 1995. They massacred over eight thousand men and boys, and raped the women."

"My God."

"I thought he was dead." Nikolai kept typing—searching the internet as he spoke.

Chris used his tablet. He copied the man's name and started his own search. "Nikolai, were you in Bosnia?"

"Yes. Horrific. All sides did terrible things. I fought with the underdog and defended the innocents when I could."

"Does he know you? Did he see you?"

"I think he followed me, but I cannot be sure and I do not know why. I saw him walk into Alfie's." Nikolai turned a second monitor on and the security screens popped up. "We can watch."

Chris said, "Got it. Here's Ekmečić's picture." Nikolai stared, speechless. "Is that the guy?"

Nikolai said, "Older now. I will walk across the street to make a positive ID." He opened the desk's bottom drawer and pulled out a locked metal box. He opened it with a key and removed a gun. He checked the cartridge for shells. Satisfied, he snapped it into place and tucked the gun into the back of his pants. His jacket camouflaged the bulge.

Chris watched. "Be careful."

Nikolai said, "I am betting he does not know who I am and does not suspect I know who he is. The gun is just a precaution."

He pulled a second gun from the box, made sure it was loaded and ready to fire. He handed this one to Chris. "Take it." Chris shook his head. Nikolai lowered his chin revealing eyes dark colored with concern. He glared at Chris.

"No time to argue. Take the gun. Sit at the desk and rest it in your lap, pointed at the door. If I am right, we may both be in grave danger. If you have to shoot, do it. Don't think." Nikolai shoved the gun into his hand. "Go on instinct. You'll be fine."

Chris took the gun and sat down on chair's edge, muscles taut. Working the cameras with his free hand, he watched Nikolai walk across the street. At Alfie's, Nikolai had his hand on the door when a man stepped out and bumped him. Nikolai released the door and turned toward Chris. The man was directly behind him. They crossed the street together, Nikolai's eyes darting back and forth. It was Ekmečić.

Chris hit the silent alarm and locked down the building. The techs on the second floor got the emergency notice on their monitors. They grabbed the drives and fled down the back stairs to the secure basement room.

When the two men reached the front door, Nikolai knocked. Chris activated the outside speaker, "Hi. Locked out?" as he positioned his finger on the trigger.

Nikolai said, "Yes. I must have left my key on the desk."

Chris entered the four digit "duress" release code.

The door opened without a problem and sent a signal to the monitoring company. Chris stopped checking the street when the men entered. Now it was all about saving Nikolai.

Ekmečić shoved Nikolai toward the coffee counter with such force that Nikolai grunted and fell to the ground.

Chris started to rise to help his friend.

"Sit down."

Chris looked at Ekmečić and saw the man's gun aimed at him.

"Get Christopher Gregory down here or I kill you both before I start tearing this place apart." The man's eyes darted between his two hostages.

Chris's look of surprise was real. The man must have an old picture of him when he had long hair, scraggly beard, and glasses. Speechless and open-mouthed, he looked at Nikolai.

Nikolai sat up, back against the counter base, and said to Chris, "Your boss, stupid." To Ekmečić he said, "My sister's idiot son."

The gunman reached into his pocket and pulled out his cell phone, glanced at it and put it back.

He motioned for Nikolai to get up and move toward the desk. When Nikolai was standing next to Chris, the gunman smiled and pointed the gun at Chris. "You are Christopher Gregory, no?"

Chris's hand tightened on the hidden gun and his finger sat on the trigger as he shifted his gaze from the man's gun to the man's eyes.

"Mr. Donovan says stay out of his business and out of Paris."

Chris squeezed the trigger and ducked as soon as the word Donovan registered. The gunman took the first shot in the groin.

In sync with Chris, Nikolai hit the floor and pulled

out his gun, getting off one shot to Ekmečić's chest just as his gun with its silencer burped a missile at Chris's head. The kill shot missed its target.

Nikolai released his second shot a fraction of a second before Ekmečić fired one at him. The hit man took one between the eyes.

Silence.

"You okay?"

"You?"

"A scratch," Nikolai said, holding his upper arm. "I'm fine. Just a flesh wound."

Chris got up and went to Nikolai's side. "Let me see."

Police rushed in, pulled Chris away, and made room for a medic to assess Nikolai.

Outside, Chris let another medic check him over until he saw Nikolai seated on the ambulance bumper. He brushed the medic away and ran over to his friend. "Can't be too bad. You're sitting and talking."

"A few stitches and I will be as good as new."

A detective arrived to hear Nikolai's pronouncement and said, "This other guy, not so lucky. A bullet between the eyes. Good shooting. Anyone care to enlighten me?"

Chris said, "It's all on our security tapes, which I'll email you."

"Humor me," the detective said. "Tell me what happened."

After they recounted the morning's events, the detective looked at Chris. "Can you tell me why would anyone want to kill you?"

After exchanging glances with Nikolai, Chris said, "I have no idea. I'm a tech guy. My company is located on the upper floors of this building." Chris pulled out his phone. "In fact, my guys are waiting in the basement." He tapped in the "all clear" code and released the basement security door.

"Let me through. FBI. Let me through." Beth came charging toward the ambulance. "I'm Special Agent Elizabeth Neilson. This man is working with me." She nodded at Chris.

The EMT interrupted and nodded toward Nikolai. "We need to take this man to the hospital. You can continue questioning him there."

After the truck left, Beth turned to the detective. "Thank you for your fast response. Mr. Gregory is consulting on a classified FBI case. His search on Dragomir Ekmečić set off all kinds of government alarms. I'll take it from here."

The detective said, "I don't think so. I've got a New York City murder here, and it's my neck if I don't follow-up."

Beth nodded and made a call. After a few words, she handed the phone to the detective. He listened, nodded, shrugged his shoulders, and gave the phone back. "Okay, Special Agent Neilsen. Homeland Security says the case is all yours. We'll help anyway we can."

"Please maintain the integrity of the area until my team arrives." The detective nodded and moved away.

Turning to Chris, Beth said, "What happened? And no bullshit. I want the truth."

"I'll tell you all about it on the way to Lake George. My driver will be here any minute."

"Oh, no, you don't. You stay here. I'm going...."

"Donovan tried to kill me. I'm getting Rachel out of there just as fast as I can."

"Can you do your tech wizardry on the way?"

"Absolutely."

"Okay. Get your stuff. We're going by helicopter."

On the ride to the helipad, Beth said, "Chris, it could be dangerous. Promise you'll stay in the helicopter when we land?"

He held up two fingers to his temple. "I promise."

Chapter 48
Lake George, New York

In the study, Saturday morning at nine-thirty, Ted received Lucy's text. *"Primary ready. Confirm. Secondary failed. Advise."*

Ted hit the desk with his fist. Christopher Gregory had to be dealt with—and soon. But first things first. He needed White House confirmation for the Okoro seduction activation. Donovan picked up the phone and made the call.

"Wendell Waters, please," Ted said to the White House operator. "This is Theodore Donovan at the Lake George Human Rights Think Tank."

"Hello, Mr. Donovan. This is Mr. Waters's secretary. He's unavailable until noon today."

"Noon will be fine. Please ask him to call me."

Next, he texted Lucy, *"Primary. Stand by."*

Then, he snapped three pencils into quarters and two pens in half. He sent all evidence of his self-indulgence into the round file.

Ted stood, ran his fingers through his hair, shot his sleeves, straightened his tie, and buffed his shoes on the back of his pants leg. One last shrug to set his jacket and he was ready to join the others.

Rachel finished her workout. On her way upstairs, she passed the study. She neither stopped nor looked for Ted. Four feet away from the staircase, Ted called her name. She ignored him.

Her foot was on the first step and her hand held the banister by the time he reached her. He covered her hand with his. "Rachel, please. Can we talk?"

She looked at him with cold eyes, arched eyebrows, thin lips, and raised chin. "Ted Donovan, you have very serious control issues. Remove your hand this instant."

"I'm sorry," Ted said, leaving his hand in place. "I don't know what got into me."

She heard manipulative pleading in his voice. She deflected. "I don't know or care." She flipped her hand into the air to break contact with him and hissed, "Knowing my history, how could you?"

"Let me explain."

"No. I don't want to hear. You attacked me, violated my trust."

"You've got it all wrong. Please listen."

She shook her head. "From now on, for the team's sake, we only interact as professionals, only on the main floor, and only in groups of three or more people."

"Rachel, you can't be serious. We're meant to be together."

She stared him. "Professionals. Main floor. People. That's it. Period."

Chapter 49
New York City

On the way to the helipad, Chris tried to ignore Beth's kamikaze inspired driving as he gave her the Lake George updates. "Donovan tried to force Rachel to have sex with him."

"What? Wait." Beth turned to look at him. "Why are you so calm?"

Chris pointed to the road. She gave him a wicked smile and returned her gaze to the traffic war.

He said, "I'm not calm. I'm racing upstate with you to bring her home."

"Is she okay?"

"Rachel fought him off and gave him a bloody nose. I'm telling you," he switched to an imitation of Marlon Brando, *On the Waterfront*, 'she *could-a* been a contender.'"

"I called her as soon as I saw the footage. She said

she was fine. Still, I was just about to leave and go for her when the shooting interrupted my plans."

Beth said, "What do you think Donovan's message meant?"

"Business might mean Rachel, but Paris is an international security problem. Hackers have targeted our Paris servers for almost six years. Yesterday, they broke in for less than a second. Long enough to identify my company as the owner. I had no idea Donovan was behind it until this morning."

"He wanted to kill you for owning a server?"

"I don't think so. It doesn't make sense. Maybe he thinks I know what's on the server."

"Do you?"

"No. The data's encrypted as per the client's request."

"Still," Beth said, "I think the data has something to do with PRAISE winners gone missing. And he thinks you know what it is."

"You've got to be kidding."

"I never kid about murder." Beth paused. "Eric and I did some background on Donovan's conversation with Waters. We think the person being targeted for seduction is Adebowale Okoro, President of Tawanda. Please keep a close watch on what's going on today. My gut says whatever's happening is happening soon."

Chapter 50
New York City ‑ Lake George, New York

Beth paced the helicopter pad, eyes skyward, as she spoke with the head of the New York FBI Field Office. Chis stood where she placed him, his duffle bag of electronic gear slung over his shoulder.

Her conversation ended as the helicopter came into view. Another call—Eric. She said, "Tell me we have something."

"We may have a picture of one of the kidnappers," he said.

"Send it."

The helicopter landed. Beth got in the passenger seat and Chris slid in the back. "Here're the coordinates," she said to the pilot.

"Landing?"

"Understand the backyard is large enough for a stealth bomber."

"That'll do."

She turned her attention back to her phone. "Eric?"

"Still here. What do you think?"

"I've never seen her before. You?"

"Running her pic through recognition software. Will call as soon as I have something."

"Okay. Later." Beth put on her 'copter head phones. "Chris?"

He said, "I'm reviewing current video feeds."

His tablet glowed with the video—the grounds-keeper clearing the snow from the night's storm, followed by people walking or jogging the trails. Inside cameras showed Rachel going and returning from her morning workout, ignoring Donovan until he stopped her. She conversed with him for less than a minute and went upstairs to change.

Chris switched to study the feed. The timer said nine-thirty. Ted worked on his computer. Stopped, picked up his phone, tapped it, read the screen, and slammed his fist on the desk. Then he returned to his phone, tapped it several times, and called Wendell Waters. From his response, he expected a return call around noon.

Chris scrolled the video back to when Ted read the text image and paused. The video camera's angle hid the phone screen. Frustrated, Chris studied the still image. He put on the headphones and reported to Beth.

She said, "So, you can't read the texts. And you know Waters is calling Donovan around noon."

"Right. Not... enough... info...." Chris stared at his monitor.

"What is it?"

"I see Donovan's phone screen reflected in the window," Chris said. "I'm going to enhance it."

"Tell me when you've got it."

A few minutes later, Beth interrupted him. "Can you cut the land line and cell phone service at the cabin?"

Chris looked up at her. "Sure. No problem."

"Would that include all electronic communication devices?"

"It does now."

"Kill everything right after the Wendell Waters call. And if you're not sure which one that is, just make it after Ted's next phone call or text."

Chris said, "I could do it now."

"No. We need to verify Donovan's connection to the White House."

Chris nodded and got the electronic block ready. As a precaution, he made sure no one inside the cabin could tamper with the security settings. That done, he returned to working on the reflected phone images. Mid-process, he texted Rachel, "*Call.*"

Seconds later, his phone rang. He took off his headphones to keep the call private.

Rachel said, "Hi, Chris. What's going on?"

He said, "Busy but need some help. Around noon, I'm cutting off all cabin communications. Now if I were Donovan and couldn't get service in the cabin, I'd go outside. Maybe even walk down to the village."

"Sounds logical."

"That's where you come in. Don't let Donovan leave the cabin to make a phone call or text."

"I don't know if I can do that, Chris. We're not on the best of terms at the moment."

"Perhaps this will motivate you. Beth thinks Donovan may have ordered a hit on me because of you. She thinks he may be a player in a plot to kill Tawandian President Okoro."

"Ted tried to kill you? When? Are you all right?"

"I'm fine. Nikolai's the real hero. He saved my life, took a bullet, and killed the assassin. And get this—the man was a mass murderer during the Bosnian war. Lucky for us that Nikolai recognized him."

"Wow. Sounds like a rough morning. I'm so glad you're both okay."

"Me, too. You can thank Beth when you see her. She arrived right after the police and took over. Impressive. She's not a woman you'd want to mess with."

"Wait. Did you say, Ted wants to kill President Okoro?"

"That's not a for-sure. But we don't want to take any chances."

"Son-of-a-bitch."

"Rachel, what do you know?"

"Can't talk. Gotta go. Will keep Ted inside. Don't worry."

"Rachel?"

Chris looked at his phone. She'd ended their conversation. On his tablet, the reflected image became clear. It was the receiver's phone number and the texts: *"Primary ready. Confirm. Secondary failed. Advise."* Followed by, *"Primary. Stand by."* He sent the image to Beth and put on his 'copter head phones.

She looked at the message and said to Chris, "Good work. I'm forwarding this to Eric."

He said, "I'm guessing I was the 'secondary target.'"

Beth said, "I think you're right. I'll ask Donovan when I see him."

"Uh, Beth." Chris stopped and looked away.

"What?" She let the silence last a few seconds. "Come on, Chris. Tell me."

He swallowed the lump in his throat and looked at

Beth. "I asked Rachel to keep an eye on Donovan and keep him in the cabin when the communications go down. If he even makes it half-way down the driveway, he'll find phone service. Rachel said she'd do her best."

Beth jerked around in her seat—jaw clenched, brow furrowed, eyes dark and narrow. "You're not authorized to do that, Chris—to put civilians in danger."

He said, "If this call is that important, Donovan's going to run. Rachel's the only one I trust to stop him."

"You better hope we get there in time."

"I'm counting on it."

Beth's phone rang again. She turned away from Chris to take the call. "What's up, Eric?"

"Hold on. Patching in the Director of the FBI.... Go ahead, Sir," Eric said.

"Special Agent Neilson?"

"Yes, Sir. I'm here."

"I've spoken to the head of the New York office. I understand you are investigating Theodore Donovan and the PRAISE Foundation. Is that correct?"

"Yes, Sir."

"Intelligence information has reached my desk that President Adebowale Okoro has been invited to speak with United Nations representatives via the PRAISE Foundation. However, that information cannot be corroborated by the UN at this time. Furthermore, we understand President Okoro is planning to leave Tawanda under a cloak of secrecy. Until we have intel that Okoro is in jeopardy, we can't warn him without putting our informant at risk."

"I'm on my way to talk to Donovan, right now."

"Keep me informed. Agent Jerrod?"

"Yes, Sir."

The director said, "I'm forwarding email copies from our secure server," and hung up.

"Eric, are you still there?"

"Yes. Opening the emails," Eric said. "Okoro's supposed to leave at midnight over there, five o'clock here."

"Not much time," Beth said. "Did you identify the Meyerson limo lady? It's likely she's the other end of Donovan's texts."

"Working on it," Eric said.

Beth hung up and turned to Chris. "Any word from Waters?"

"Not yet. Donovan keeps looking at his phone but no calls or texts."

"Tell me when you kill the cabin's communications."

Below the helicopter, the landscape changed from colorless winter gray to a dusted snow-white as the pilot followed the Hudson River North. Her phone rang—Eric.

"Beth, found her. The facial recognition software took me to the driver's license of one Lucy Kilmer. Kilmer was definitely involved with the Meyerson disappearance."

Beth said, "I bet Donovan's using her to bring down Okoro."

He said, "I've asked for an emergency warrant for a pick-up and search."

She said. "Don't wait. Take a team and get to her ASAP while the warrant is in process. You'll have it by the time you arrive."

She called the Director of the FBI with an update and a request to authorize agents from the Albany FBI Field Office for immediate back-up at the cabin. When she hung up, she said, "Donovan is not going to kill again on my watch."

Chapter 51
White House, Washington D.C.

Even though it was Saturday, President Sandford followed his usual routine—at his desk in the oval office by six-thirty. The call came in on his private phone at nine.

"Good morning, Franklin," Philip Vanderhagen said. "What's the status of our little problem?"

"I have a bigger one. Unverified emails inviting Okoro to the United Nations via PRAISE have been secreted out of Tawanda," President Sandford said.

"How does that impact our goal?"

"I can't take the chance of blowback to the White House or me."

"Nonsense," Vanderhagen said. "Honor our conversation, Franklin. If you fail, you might see the end of your first term, but I guarantee you won't see a second."

The phone went dead, and the president's hands went cold and clammy. Without his permission or decision, Sandford's fate now lay in tandem with Okoro's and not with his pending bold revitalization of United States internal economic policy.

Sandford's phone alarm sounded. Adas Israel Congregation had invited him to join the visiting Israeli Prime Minister as their guests at this morning's Shabbat Service. He had to go. Offending the prime minister would be political suicide. The service ran from 9:30 to noon. After lunch, back at the White House, he and the prime minister would meet for a private conversation. He invited Wendell Waters to accompany him as the first lady and their children were skiing in Vale, Colorado.

A knock on the door. "Mr. President, are you ready?"

"Come in, Wendell. Any word on Okoro?"

"Donovan is waiting to hear from me. I need to let him know if we're going to do this or not."

"I'll let you know before noon."

At the synagogue, the president and the Israeli prime minister sat on the bimah, a raised platform in front of the congregation. As noon approached, Sandford had to act. Smiling, as if he were responding to someone wishing him well, the president nodded to random worshipers and then to Waters, who responded in kind to confirm. Sandford held Wendell's gaze for a second. The deed was done.

At the rabbi's signal, everyone rose for the final blessings and prayers. Few noticed Wendell Waters slip out. No one heard him make the call.

Chapter 52
Lake George, New York

Ted sent someone to kill Chris! And now he's going to kill the President of Tawanda. Who does he think he is? How dare he use me to do his research. That son-of-a-bitch made me an accomplice. Bastard.

A furious Rachel showered and dressed. She was ready to confront him at breakfast and let everyone know about Ted, except that she had no facts. Besides that, she still had to work with him when the communication systems went down. Retribution would have to wait.

As soon as her hand gripped the door knob, her knuckles went white. She knew she couldn't go downstairs. Angry, frustrated, and tense, Rachel stepped back, took a few quick breaths, and rotated her shoulders. She rolled her head around, trying to loosen her muscles. Still tight, she sat cross-legged on the bed, cleared her head, and did her deep breathing exercise.

She had to let the anger go to keep her promise to Chris and restrain Donovan from going outside.

She felt her body change, relaxing with each breath deeper than the last. She fell backward—head on her pillow, and opened her eyes. Now she was ready to face the day.

In the hallway, she took a right toward the balcony instead of a left toward the staircase. She wanted to see if the child's bedroom of her dream existed. She opened the door by the balcony. In place of a staircase to a third floor was a large storage area filled with boxes, sports equipment, household objects, and clothing bags. The far wall backed onto her bedroom wall. The space was finished—walls painted white, wood floor covered in protective paper. It didn't look as if it had ever been lived in, much less like a child's decorated room.

Rachel returned to her bedroom to get her tablet for the meeting. Something had changed. Someone had been there. A rag doll with a red tear on its cheek lay on the floor. Fearing that other things might have been disturbed or taken, she scanned the room. All seemed fine.

She picked up the doll unable to recall if the red tear had been there before or not. Rachel started to put the doll back but changed her mind. She carried it to her bed and leaned it against the pillows. With her phone's camera, Rachel took a picture of the whole rag doll and a close-up of the tear.

Voices emanating from the dining-room reminded her people were waiting. She put her phone away, picked up her tablet, and grabbed *The History of Portman's Landing*. Downstairs, she returned the book to its place on the library shelf and went to the breakfast area.

"Good morning, Rachel," Isabel Upton said. "We

had quite a storm last night. Looks like almost a foot of snow."

"I think you're right," Rachel said, surveying the landscape through the windows. She plated a hard-boiled egg, a bagel, and cream cheese. Then she filled a mug with coffee. She brought it all to the table and sat across from Isabel. "You're up early."

Isabel said, "The grounds-keeper plowed us out around six. I've already taken my morning walk."

"Me too," General Portman said. He sat down next to Rachel. "Frankly, I enjoyed getting out into the brisk air."

"Good morning," the women chorused.

"General, I have a question for you," Rachel said. "Does this cabin have a third floor?"

General Portman said, "No. We opted to double the main floor's height instead. Why?"

"Dreams," Rachel said. "Since I've been here, I've been dreaming. The last one placed me in a child's room on the third floor."

"Strange," the general said. He bit into a cheese Danish and took a sip of coffee.

"I also dreamt about a doll," Rachel said. "And this morning I found this." She showed him the images on her phone.

"An old rag doll." the general said. "Frankly, I haven't seen one in years."

Rachel said, "You've seen it before?"

"Yes," the general said. "It's quite a story. One I'd like to forget."

Rachel said, "Would you please tell me? Perhaps it would make sense of my dreams."

The general nodded and Rachel tapped her phone's microphone icon—RECORD.

The general said, "This house is built on the site of an old Mohawk Indian village where the communal longhouse used to be. I wanted to honor the tribe. Although it's been close to two centuries since the Indians lived here as a tribal unit, the families continue to live and work in the area. Many took up the building trades, and a few worked on this project. They brought their families here and lived in the house while they worked on it. I'm sure the doll belonged to one of the children."

"Do the families still live around here? I'd love to talk to someone about the meaning of my dreams."

The color drained from the general's face. He covered by dabbing his mouth with a napkin. He held out his hand for Rachel's phone. "Let me see that picture again." She hit PAUSE and brought up the picture. He stared at the image for a few seconds and gave the phone back. She switched back to RECORD. "Frankly, that looks like a gift I bought for a little Indian girl."

Rachel said, "Can you remember her name? Maybe I could return it to her."

"Frankly, that's impossible," General Portman said. "You see, she died over twenty years ago—several months after work started on the house. It was such a shame. Beautiful girl. About four, as I remember. Black plaited hair. Big brown eyes. Flawless skin. She reminded me of a prancing fawn as she played with the other children. Alone, she walked with a cat's grace. A tease if ever I've seen one."

Rachel's stomach clenched into a tight knot. *Pedophile?*

The general continued. "Sadly, she ran ahead of me. I shouted out to her. I told her to stay away from the slippery rocks crossing the mountain stream. Despite my warning, she must have lost her footing and fallen. We found her in the stone quarry on the far side of our stairway down to the lake.

"Frankly, she was way off limits and she refused to listen to me." General Portman paused.

Rachel said, "That must have been horrible for you."

"Yes," General Portman said. He pushed his chair a few more inches away from the table and settled back, crossed his legs, and folded his hands on his stomach. "Frankly, it's quite a story."

Rachel's eyes never left his. "Tell me about it."

"My family and I were in Lake George that summer with my aide-de-camp and several soldiers. I made it a point to visit the building site every day and monitor the crew. When I could, I enjoyed solitary walks through the woods. That fateful day, I saw the child playing sticks and stones when I remembered a doll we had left over from our Christmas gifts.

"I retrieved it from the store room and brought it out to the little girl. She didn't want to take it, so I asked her if she'd like to take a walk with me and the doll. She agreed. We were having a great time when she ran away from me. I called to her, but she never turned around. I lost sight of her as she scrambled over rocks and disappeared in the underbrush.

"I figured she knew this area better than I did, so I didn't worry about her safety. I was almost home when I heard her scream. In a panic, I shouted to my aide-de-camp to get help and ran back into the woods. I remember tripping over a root and hitting my head. Three soldiers caught up to me. I must have looked terrible because one decided I needed to go back to the house. I ordered the other two to continue searching until they found the poor dear and then to bring her body home."

Body? How did he know she was dead? Unless... unless he killed her.

General Portman shook his head and rubbed his

eyes. "It was a terrible accident. I helped out where I could. I even gave all the workers the rest of the day off as well as the next. For the funeral. I, myself, couldn't make it. You know, called to Washington."

Bastard.

Isabel said, "That must have been awful."

Rachel turned to the woman with hard eyes and a subtle shake of her head.

Isabel didn't miss a beat and changed the subject. "It reminds me of a Red Cross mission to Zimbabwe...."

Rachel hit END RECORD and listened to Isabel, grateful the conversation's focus changed. She sipped her coffee and took a bite of her bagel. More team members joined them. She looked up and smiled. Out of the corner of her eye, she saw Yvonne staring at her.

As their eyes met, Yvonne tilted her head toward the far kitchen entrance. Rachel micro-nodded in return. As she pushed her chair away from the table, her phone rang. It was Chris. Rachel excused herself with, "I have to take this," and went into the library.

"Just a reminder," Chris said. "Be careful, Rachel. Nothing's worth your getting hurt. I'd blame myself for getting you into this in the first place. Beth is furious with me."

"You're with Beth? Where exactly?"

"We're in a helicopter on our way up to Lake George. Until we get there, it's you I'm worried about."

"Don't worry. I can take care of myself," Rachel said. "By the way, I need a favor." She saw Yvonne walking toward her. "Wait. I'll call you right back."

"Excuse me," Yvonne said. "May I see the picture you showed General Portman?"

"Sure," Rachel said, bringing it up on her phone.

Yvonne took one look and her eyes filled with tears. Rachel put her arm around the young woman with an ease that surprised her. "Take your time."

"Her name was Aponi," Yvonne said. "It means 'butterfly.' Aponi Hill. She was my sister. She died the summer of 1995. Right after the general gave her this doll. Rachel, the Mohawks are sure-footed. I don't believe Aponi slipped."

"I'm so sorry for your loss," Rachel said. "If it helps, I don't believe she slipped either."

Yvonne looked at Rachel. "You're the first."

"Don't get your hopes up," Rachel said, removing her hand from Yvonne's shoulder. "It was a long time ago. For now, what can you tell me about the doll?"

"I thought we buried it with Aponi."

"You never saw it up in my room?"

"No," Yvonne said. "If I had, I would have brought it home."

"That's so strange," Rachel said and told Yvonne about her dreams.

Yvonne said, "Aponi's spirit is reaching out to you to make this right."

"I'm not sure what I can do, but if your family remembers anything about the day Aponi died, let me know."

"I will. I'll ask tonight."

"Good," Rachel said. "Let's keep this between us for the moment."

Yvonne nodded. She brought her hand to her heart before returning to the kitchen.

Rachel emailed Chris with an attachment—the audio file of the general's story. She asked him to research the 1995 Aponi Hill incident at Portman's Landing and do a thorough background check on Portman ASAP. She finished her message with, "If he killed one child, odds are there were more."

She tapped SEND and called Chris. "I just sent you an email. It is self-explanatory. Please call me when you know something."

"Will do," he said. "Stay in one piece until I get there."

"I love you too."

Chapter 53
Lake George, New York

Ted appeared in the dining room at ten o'clock with a little more bounce in his step than usual, sporting a Band-Aid across the bridge of his nose.

"Good morning," he said, rubbing his hands together. "It's going to be a very productive day. I can feel it." Ted's enthusiasm, a change from his usual calm and reserved manner, caused everyone to sit straighter in their seats.

Norman Weisman said, "Been hitting the caffeine?"

Ted said, "I admit to having one cup too many. I've been up for a while. To calm down, I used the exercise room, jogged outside, and took a long shower."

"Do any self-flagellation with willow branches?" Amy Yeager said. "I ask because it seems one hit you in the face."

Ted touched his nose and laughed. "No. No willow branches. Just a low hung birch branch, practically invisible against the snow. Caught me by surprise during my morning run."

Amy leaned forward, stretched her arm toward him, and purred, "Come to my room later. I've got make-up that'll cover it."

Ted smiled and said, "Thank you." He sat down, fingering his tie and smoothing it down his chest. "Now, what's up? Everybody ready to work?" He glanced at his phone.

Rachel checked hers. It was ten-twenty.

Amy said, "Do we have to? It seems a shame to waste such a beautiful day indoors."

Ted said, "Must keep our focus. There will be many beautiful days."

Quentin Sheffield said, "We've signed on for up to six weeks. Seems we can accommodate the lady without too much debate." He patted Amy's hand.

Amy said, "If we go down to the village now, we can eat lunch whenever we get hungry. That'll give Yvonne a break."

James Jefferson said, "If we stay and work, we might get out of here in two weeks instead of six. I could use the extra time myself."

Amy got up and slithered behind James, putting her arm out and letting it slide across his neck and shoulder as she bent over and said, "What's a little hour or two?"

James nodded, muted by the nearness of her cleavage. Amy straightened and walked over to Ted. She sat on the edge of his chair, forcing him to encircle her waist with his dislodged arm. "See. James agrees. Come on, Teddy. Let's go."

Isabel pursed her lips at Amy's antics. "Each working session gets us closer to our goal," she said.

"So I vote for getting some work done first."

"Frankly, Ted," the general said, "the wheels of bureaucracy are famous for moving as slow as a well-fed lion in the midday sun. I don't think a couple of hours will make any difference at all."

Someone's phone rang and eight hands moved at the same time. Amy said, "It's mine. I'll be right back."

"I agree with Isabel," Rachel said. "Let's go over her list from last night and create a work plan."

With Amy and her cleavage out of sight, the men agreed. When she got back, Amy pursed her lips in disappointment, sighed, and joined the discussion.

A phone rang at eleven forty-five. Ted, like the others, grabbed for his phone. "It's the wife," the general said. He excused himself. "I'll be right back."

At noon, another phone went off. This time, Ted stood up and said, "That's mine. Let's break for now." He put the phone to his ear and strode out of the room. Rachel heard him go into the study and close the door.

The dining room cleared and Rachel went into the library. She selected a book on North American birds and sat down near the window that overlooked the landing across from the study. If Ted decided to go outside, he'd have to pass her.

She opened the book, and it self-selected a color-plate spread on northeast winter birds. The grandfather clock measured time in syncopated measures. Tick. Tock. Tick. Tock.

The study door opened with a bang. Ted emerged waving his phone around. He mumbled under his breath. Rachel ignored his histrionics and focused on her book.

"Rachel." Ted sprinted to her side with his hand out. "Got your phone? Mine's stopped working."

Rachel looked up. "Sure." She reached into her pocket with deliberate and excessive care, ignoring Ted's right hand signaling "hurry up, give it to me" while his left played with the keys in his pocket.

When he saw her phone, Ted snatched it out of her hand and held it at eye level. "No bars. This isn't working either." He tossed it back to her without looking.

Rachel, twisting to the right, caught it before it crashed to the floor. "Happens all the time."

Ted said, "Not to me, it doesn't."

Rachel shrugged. "Don't worry. Signal's probably overloaded from so many people accessing it at one time. I'm sure it'll be back up any time now." She glanced at him to see if he questioned her assertion because she had no idea if it could be true or not. If he thought her wrong, he didn't say anything.

"Not good enough," Ted said. "I've got to make a call right now. Have to find a signal." Ted checked his phone again. "Maybe upstairs."

Tick. Tock.

Ted vaulted the stairs, taking them two at a time. He vanished into the hallway and reappeared at the balcony and held his phone above his head. He grimaced in disappointment and disappeared. Seconds later, he flew down the stairs, turned to the study and paused in front of her. "Nothing. This is ridiculous. This place has an electronics system that rivals the White House... and no phone service!" He ran into the study.

Tick. Tock.

He dropped into his desk chair and started banging on the computer keyboard, his efforts punctuated with grunts, groans, and curses. In a voice filled with frustration, Ted called out. "Yvonne! The computer's down. So's my tablet. What's going on? What happened to the WiFi?"

Yvonne appeared in the kitchen doorway. "Mr. Donovan, did you call me?"

Ted got out of his chair and walked into the library. "I need a working phone, computer, or tablet."

Yvonne looked confused. "Is there a problem?"

"Yes, of course there's a problem. I can't get a signal."

Yvonne said, "I'm so sorry, Mr. Donovan. I had no idea. Could it be a fuse?"

Ted said, "Could be anything. Where's the electrical panel?"

"I know," Yvonne said and ran into the kitchen.

Tick. Tock.

She returned with a flashlight. "I'll go check."

"Never mind," Ted said, taking the flashlight out of her hands and turning it on. "Where is it? The panel. Exactly."

She pointed to a door and stepped out of his way. Ted breezed past her, jerked the door open, and stared at her. "Well?"

Yvonne said, "Down the stairs and to the right. In the corner by the workbench."

Ted reached the basement before she finished her sentence. Rachel and Yvonne looked at each other and shrugged in unison. They went to the doorway to listen for any sounds of progress.

Tick. Tock.

Ted cursed at the disarray. He bumped into boxes, tripped over stuff. At one point, they heard glass shatter.

Yvonne reached inside the doorframe and searched for a switch. "Found it." A dim light went on. "Is that better, Mr. Donovan?"

Rachel called out, "Can you see it?"

"I'm in hoarder hell!" Ted's booming voice rasped, hoarse from the dust. After few more grunts, he said, "Got it."

The basement went silent.

Tick. Tock.

Without warning, the sound of falling boxes, kicked cardboard, and broken glass filled the air. The first stomp on the bottom step alerted all that Ted was not a happy camper.

"He's coming," Yvonne said. "I'll be right back." She turned and went into the kitchen.

Disheveled and covered with cobwebs, packing peanuts, and dust, Ted came up the stairs like a charging buffalo—heaving, panting, eyes wild and wide. "The fuse panel's fine and still no bars."

Tick. Tock.

"Mr. Donovan," Yvonne had returned with a glass of water in her hand. "Perhaps you'd like a drink."

As he reached for the glass, Ted caught sight of his disarray in a branch-framed mirror. He brushed off his clothes, shrugged his shoulders to set his jacket, straightened his tie, shot his cuffs, and ran his fingers through his hair. Then he stepped into the powder room. Leaving the door ajar, he washed his face and hands—twice.

Done, he walked over to Yvonne, accepted the glass of water, drank it all, and handed it back to her. "The DoD configures rockets that hit outhouses in the Afghanistan mountain caves, but it can't keep an internet connection working in a Lake George cabin. What's that about?"

Tick. Tock.

Rachel said, "Ted, I'm not sure why you're so upset. It's only been a few minutes."

He snapped his fingers. "The world can change like that." He strode toward the living room.

"Okay, okay," Rachel said. "Let's see." She stared at her phone. "How about taking out the phone battery and rebooting?"

Ted turned. "Worth a try." He took off his phone's cover and pulled out the battery. He looked at Rachel. "Hey, you too. Maybe one will work."

Rachel fiddled with her phone, feigning difficulty with removing the cover. Ted, meanwhile, reinserted his battery and started his phone. When he realized Rachel didn't even have the cover off, he ripped her phone out of her hand. He did the hard reboot for her. In less than a minute both phones lit up but neither had bars.

The grandfather clock chimed the half hour. It was twelve-thirty.

Tick. Tock.

"Dammit," Ted said.

Rachel hit her forehead with her hand. "Duh! We are so stupid. Just use the land line."

Ted's face looked puzzled as if he had forgotten such a thing ever existed. With a quick turn, he said to Yvonne, "Land line!"

Yvonne jumped to attention. "Right." She disappeared for a few seconds and returned. Shaking her head, she said, "It's dead."

Rachel said, "I have another idea."

"No." Ted marched toward the front door.

"Wait. Let's try rebooting the modem. Sometimes just unplugging, waiting thirty seconds, and re-plugging will do it. Other times, you need to depress the recessed REBOOT button with the end of a paper clip."

Ted did an about face and brushed past her. "Why didn't you say so before?" He raced to the study, slamming the door after him.

Yvonne disappeared and Rachel ambled over to

the library. She sat down, opened the bird book, and placed it in her lap. Her eyes were downcast but her ears strained to hear the approach of a helicopter. *Where were they? She couldn't keep this up for much longer.*

Tick. Tock.

Ted bounded out of the study, held on to the bannister as he swung into a hard left toward the front door. "Dammit!"

Rachel jumped out of the chair and sprinted to grab hold of Ted's arm. "Wait! Don't go outside. The phone won't operate when it's so cold."

He looked at her as if she had lost her mind. "Ridiculous." He unhooked her hand. "Move."

She persisted. "Well, not the phone exactly, but cold fingers don't register on the touch screen." Rachel tugged on his arm. "Come by the fire. The phone will come on by itself in a minute or so. It's the world-wide Internet for God's sake. It's never out for long."

Ted yanked his arm out of her grip and pushed her away. He grabbed a jacket, opened the massive front door, and stepped outside. "I need service now."

Rachel ran to the doorway and stood on the threshold. "What are you doing?"

As he put the jacket on, he said, "Heading toward the village." His voice trailed off as he walked down the driveway, holding his phone up and looking for bars.

Rachel watched Ted leave, immobilized by fear and her promise to Chris.

Tick. Tock.

Chapter 54
Harrison, New York

Lucy Kilmer sat in front of her monitors waiting for the 'GO' signal from Ted Donovan. Her phone showed eleven fifty-seven—almost noon. The plane was three hours away from its destination and the crew had its orders. They were to fly to the private airstrip in Tawanda and pick up the passengers. On their return flight, after gassing those onboard, they were to jettison the bodies into the North Sea.

At the moment the plane left Tawanda, her tech people were to erase any reference to PRAISE or the trip from Okoro's phones, computers, and servers.

A low slow steady beeping caught her attention. She engaged the early warning security video feed which covered a ten-mile radius around her house. On Route 684 north, she observed a car chase. It amused her when smart-ass drivers self-destructed when challenged by police. She decided to watch as she waited for Donovan's signal.

The live video showed three black SUV's racing up the highway. No police in sight. They turned at the Westchester Airport Exit. The beeps increased in frequency and volume. Lucy reduced the surveillance cameras' range from ten to five miles out. The SUV's were on a direct course for her house.

She threw her tablet and thumb drive into her travel pouch. After one last look around, she pressed the pre-programmed key combination to secure the data. The system activated the sequential back-up to a password-secure off-site location, formatted the drives, and filled them with music files. Then she disengaged her security system, pulled out a pocket knife, and severed the video cable.

Lucy grabbed the pouch at her feet and ran into the bedroom. She threw on a jacket, shouldered her purse, pouch, and emergency backpack, and exited through the sliding doors. After sliding down the backstairs railing, she raced into and through the shadows cast by the shrubs encircling the pond. Halfway around, she jumped the locked gate and snuck into the pyracantha-vine-encrusted shed that sat under the weeping boughs of an old pine tree.

She entered the four digit code and the garage door opened. She slid into a white SUV, standard issue for this town, and dumped her bags and backpack on the passenger seat. Lucy drove down the short driveway, closing the shed door behind her. In no apparent hurry, she turned into the street—just another busy mom taking care of business.

Camouflaged in town traffic, Lucy relaxed. She wondered how the authorities had found her. She glanced at the car clock—twelve-fifteen. "C'mon, Ted. Call."

To minimize detection and be ready to initiate the seduction, Lucy parked at the local shopping center. She became one of many shoppers sitting in a car and using electronics. She checked her phone—charged and working. She set it to ring and vibrate to make sure she didn't miss Ted's call, leaned back, and waited, playing solitaire on her tablet.

Special Agent Eric Jerrod knocked on the door of Lucy Kilmer's house. The young man who answered the door looked like a Chippendale dancer. Eric showed his ID and asked to talk with Mrs. Kilmer. The young man stepped to the intercom, tapped it, and waited.

"She doesn't seem to be answering," he said. "One moment, I'll go get her."

Eric showed him the search warrant on his phone. "We'll go with you."

As soon as Eric verified her absence, the FBI team went to work. They tore the place apart scouring for evidence of her involvement with the Meyerson disappearance and possible Okoro assassination.

Eric remained in the center hall and called Beth. "Lucy Kilmer's not here. I'm checking with operations to see if they can track the burner phone. Maybe she's still using it. Will also put out a warrant for her arrest."

"Stay on it. I'll be on the ground in five to seven minutes."

Beth ended the call and looked at the pilot. "Right?"

"Yes ma'am. I'm doing my best. The head wind is slowing us down."

Her phone rang. The FBI agents were on their

way. Making good time considering the road conditions.

"Can't you make this thing go faster?" Beth said. She feared for Rachel's life and wanted to be there already.

The pilot said, "Not if you want to make it in one piece, Ma'am."

From the rear seat, Chris said, "Ted's running around trying to get a signal. He's going to bolt any minute."

Beth made a decision and called the Lake George Police Department. She needed them to make sure Ted didn't leave Portman's Landing.

"Desk sergeant, Lake George Police Department."

"Sergeant, this is FBI Special Agent Elizabeth Neilson. I need three cruisers up at Portman's Landing to stop one Theodore Donovan from exiting the premises."

"Are you talking about Mr. Donovan, General Portman's friend?"

"Yes. Theodore Donovan. I need him restrained."

"Ma'am. We've been working with him over the past several months. I think you've got the wrong guy. Besides, we're in storm emergency mode. All our guys are tied up."

Beth paused. She had to raise the stakes or lives might be lost. "Sergeant. I'm on my way by helicopter. This is an FBI Federal Terrorist Operation. We are at emergency level *DEFCON One*. I need you and your men at Portman's Landing ASAP. Got that?"

Beth said this outright lie with such conviction that the pilot jumped which made the helicopter quiver. She heard an audible gulp from the sergeant. This time got the response she wanted. He said, "Yes, ma'am. Right away."

As soon as the called ended, she heard Chris giving her a play-by-play.

"Donovan's about fifty feet from the house. He hears something." Chris increased the volume. "Sirens. I'm switching to the gate cams." He paused. "Police cars are streaking past Fort William Henry."

Beth interrupted. "Chris, Donovan's our guy. He's dangerous. Tell Rachel to back off."

"I can't. Communications are off. Rachel is stuck in the doorway. If we're lucky, she'll stay put."

Chapter 55
Lake George, New York

The helicopter entered the Lake George regional air space. Beth saw the Northway and Route 9. Plows and snow blowers were digging out from last night's storm. Main roads were passable. She could now see police cars weaving around the lake. She pointed and the pilot nodded. He flew over and beyond them.

Beth's phone rang. "Eric, tell me you have Kilmer."

"Can't. Not yet. We tracked her phone to a nearby shopping center, and it hasn't moved. She may be sitting and waiting for Donovan's signal. We don't know what she's driving, but all our agents have her picture. If she's in disguise, we may not get her on the first pass. And you?"

"I'm almost on the ground. Police are at the front gates. Let me know when you have Kilmer." Beth ended the call.

As the chopper descended, eight people got out of two black SUVs and joined the police. After a quick debriefing, agents breached the gates. Donovan was moving toward the lakeside staircase.

Beth unclipped her seat belt, checked her gun, and prepared to jump.

Chris packed his gear, unclipped his seat belt, cross-shouldered his pouch. No way would he stay put and risk losing Rachel again.

Chapter 56
Lake George, New York

Rachel stood in the doorway, tears in her eyes, watching Ted walk down the driveway. She had failed Chris. Donovan was outside.

She wiped her eyes. She still had a chance to redeem herself. All she had to do was stop Ted from making the call.

Arms crossed to ward off the cold, Rachel called out to Ted. "Come inside. You'll freeze out there."

He ignored her and kept checking his phone as he hurried toward the gates.

Rachel shivered. She reached into the coat closet and grabbed a heavy woolen Irish fisherman's sweater, put it on, and went outside. Ted was running toward her. Every few steps he checked behind him or above him.

Rachel said, "What's the matter?"

"Police."

"How can I help?"

Ted said, "Leave me alone." He rushed past her, following the path leading into the woods.

"Shit!" Rachel muttered and ran after Ted. Catching up to him, she latched on to his elbow and stopped him. "Ted, please come inside. It's freezing."

"No," he said, tearing free from her grip and trotting toward the landing.

Rachel stayed with him. "What's so important?"

"None of your business."

"Tell me," she said. "What can I do?"

"Go away."

Ted started to run. Rachel stayed with him. "Ted, are you in trouble?"

The wind whipped his words into the air. She heard something about PRAISE. They passed the library windows. Rachel caught a glimpse of Isabel and Amy watching them.

Ted's words were incoherent. They came in spurts—work…communities… safe….

Sirens were louder now. The helicopter's thwump thwump was much closer.

At the landing, Ted did an about face. In a white cloud of breath, he said, "…in Brenda's honor," and grabbed her upper arms and pushed her away—hard. "Get out of here, Rachel."

Rachel faltered. The snowy path was slippery. She reeled backward into a stand of birch trees and somehow managed not to fall. Regaining her balance, Rachel went back to the landing to face Ted.

Ted stood above the stairs, his back to her, sweeping his phone side to side. "Come on. Come on."

Rachel gauged the rhythm of his movement and lunged for the phone. Her timing was perfect. As soon as her hand closed over the phone, she used the railing to stop her forward momentum and pushed against it to send her into reverse. Taking advantage of Ted's surprise and hesitation, she made a run for the cabin as the helicopter landed.

A froth of icy wind and snow slammed into her body and sent her backwards into Ted's waiting arms. He encircled her like a python, tightening his hold, pulling her close. His head snaked around her neck, teeth bared. When his mouth reached her ear, he said, "Phone. Now."

Despite the searing turbulence and the excruciating pressure exerted by Ted, Rachel didn't give up or give in. She struggled until Ted's strength advantage took its toll. In one last effort, she heaved her body against his hoping to knock him off balance long enough to throw the phone into the woods. He read her mind and caught her arm in mid-air.

With the constriction released, Rachel gasped for air and found new energy. She fought back—tumbling, twisting, kicking, jerking, pushing, as she staved off the inevitable. Out of ideas, she fell to the landing. She brought the phone to her breast, covered it with both hands, and curled up to protect it.

Sirens pulsated. Strobe lights painted the snow. Help was close. But where? *Where was Beth? Chris?*

Ted dropped on top of her, inserted his hand over her shoulder and plunged it down, into her chest. Rachel tucked in her chin and, when his wrist was in range, bit him—hard.

Ted jerked his hand out with a yelp. "That's it." He rolled her over and delivered a furious open-handed slap to her face. Rachel's body relaxed and Ted got his phone. He pushed her away, stood up, and checked for a signal.

Rachel's eyes watered as she reeled from the combination of the winter's numbing cold and the slap's stinging heat. Determination overcame pain. She jumped to her feet and confronted Ted. "Stop. I know everything."

Ted looked at her, eyes narrow. "Liar."

Rachel took a step closer, her hand outstretched. "Phone."

Ted shook his head. "No. This seduction must happen."

"Seduction? What are you talking about?"

"You know nothing."

Rachel inched closer, emphasizing each word. "So, Mr. Theodore Donovan, seducing me was a lie? The shrink, a lie? You used me."

"No," Ted said. "I love you."

She lowered her chin, stared into his eyes, and said, "Is that why you tried to have Chris killed?"

Ted raised his chin and looked down at her, his mouth tight and jaw muscles flexed.

Rachel edged a little closer, softened her voice. "Maybe I over-reacted, Ted. Let's start over."

"Stay back," Ted said, glancing at his phone.

"Why? So you can assassinate Okoro?"

Ted's eyes widened then narrowed, his brows furrowed, and nostrils flared. He reached behind his back, retrieved his Chiappa Rhino Snub-Nose .357 Mag, and pointed it at her.

Rachel saw the gun. To her surprise, she wasn't afraid. "Really? You're going to kill me? The woman you love?"

Ted straightened his arm and aimed the gun between her eyes.

In the face of imminent death, Rachel became hyper-vigilant—sirens silent, turbulence gone, air clear, and clouds parted. Her body crouched and tensed, eyes focused on the weapon. A shaft of sunlight glinted off the gun's barrel.

Danger. Danger.

This time, the first time since her rape, Rachel didn't panic—she focused.

"FBI! Drop the gun."

Thank God. Beth.

Donovan didn't move.

"Donovan!"

Chris.

"You want me, Christopher Gregory, not her."

Donovan's eyes shifted.

Not Chris!

In that split second, Rachel executed a drop kick to Ted's solar plexus. His gun went off and the phone flew into the air as he did a back-dive over the staircase.

She hit the deck hard as the woods echoed with a sickening crack, like heavy snow snapping a thick tree branch, followed by a cushioned thump.

"Rachel!" Chris rushed to her side, knelt down and started to look for a bullet wound. "Are you all right? Did you get hit?"

"No. I'm okay." She threw her arms around Chris' neck. He returned the hug and kissed her.

Beth stood behind them and punched Chris on his shoulder. "You promised to stay in the 'copter, remember? I could've lost two civilians. Apparently you're not too interested in saving my career, are you?"

Chris turned his head to look at her and said, "I'm sorry. But I...I just couldn't...do nothing." He got to his feet and helped Rachel up. Beth didn't hang around to watch.

Rachel brushed the snow off her butt and said, "Where's Beth?"

"Down here," Beth said. "I'm with Donovan."

Rachel went to the landing's edge and saw Beth

kneeling beside Ted, checking the pulse point in his neck. "Is he okay?"

Beth looked up and shook her head. "He's dead."

Rachel's legs buckled. Chris caught her but not before she spotted the phone caught in the railing. She picked it up and looked at the screen. "Beth, I found Ted's phone. It's working."

While Beth climbed the stairs to the landing, Rachel tapped RECENT CALLS. None. When she tapped TEXT, she gasped.

Beth said, "What's the matter?"

Rachel handed her Ted's phone. "We're too late."

The text said, "*Go.*"

Chapter 57
Lake George, New York

While agents outside the cabin took care of Donovan's body, Beth, followed by Rachel, hand-in-hand with Chris, went inside. Chris stopped at the basement door. "I'm going downstairs to reboot the system and do a manual check to insure everything's up and running."

Beth continued into the library. Rachel watched Chris until he disappeared and then she joined Beth.

The room vibrated, like Madison Square Garden when the New York Knicks scored. The sound level was through the roof as the team members bombarded Beth with questions.

Beth calmed them down and asked them to be seated. With all eyes on her, she said, "Why didn't anyone go out and help?"

"We didn't know there was a problem."

"I was trying to reach my agent."

"It wasn't our business."

"Frankly, until we saw Ted pull a gun, we thought it was a lovers' quarrel."

"Yes, and then you came."

"And we saw the police. What could we do?"

"Right. All we could do was watch."

Beth nodded to each response.

"So," Isabel Upton said, "if it wasn't personal, what was it?"

That opened another floodgate of questions. The team wanted to know everything. What happened? How was Ted? What were they really talking about? They fired questions at her like the seasoned White House Press Corps, each one demanding to be heard and answered.

Beth put two fingers in her mouth and let loose an ear-splitting whistle. In the ensuing silence, she said, "Please sit down. I will tell you what I can and answer any questions I can. But first, please give your statements, one at a time, to my colleagues."

Her phone buzzed. She glanced at the caller ID and answered. "Hold on. I'm going to a private area."

She signaled to an agent from the Albany Field Office. "I have to take this. Please manage our witnesses. You know the drill. Then, please collect all of Donovan's things—clothes, notes, and electronics and put them in the helicopter. I'll take everything back to New York for processing. Okay?" The agent nodded and took off.

Beth put the phone to her ear, walked into the study, and closed the door. "Hey, Eric. What's happening?

"We've got Kilmer's car and phone, but she's in the wind."

"Put her picture out and get agents over to the

local and regional airports, train and bus stations."

"Way ahead of you. Already done. I've put her on Most Wanted and sent alerts to all media—standard and social, and all transportation hubs—planes, trains, cars, trucks, and all Canadian and Mexican border crossings—by car or on foot."

"Sounds like you're firing on all cylinders. Continue to take the lead on that. I've got to address the deadline when Okoro thinks he is taking off for the United Nations. See you in a couple of hours." Beth paused. "Eric—good job."

"Thanks. We'll celebrate tonight."

"You bet," Beth said. She ended the call and paced the small study. She had to notify the White House, but she didn't want to embarrass the president. She heard a knock and looked up. "Come in."

"I just gave my statement," Rachel said, standing in the doorway. "How's it going in here?"

"Thinking about my next move."

"This has really turned into a mess," Rachel said. "Wish I could help."

"You've already...." Beth stopped mid-sentence and motioned for Rachel to enter the study and close the door. "When I brought you the invitation to this meeting, didn't you say you knew Wendell Waters?"

Rachel nodded. "I met him at a book signing in D.C."

Beth handed her the phone. "I'd like you to call him. Don't give anything away while you're speaking to his secretary. If she balks, tell her you're calling for Ted Donovan. Waters will definitely take that call. Once he's on the line, tell him what just happened. Be calm and brief. Then give me the phone."

"Could you be a little more specific?"

"Tell him Ted got a call around noon, phone service stopped, he panicked, ran outside, tripped, and broke his neck. So sad. Got hold of his phone. He sent a 'Go" text. His last call was from you. FBI here. Thought you should know before the press."

"I can do that."

"Rachel, keep it simple then give me the phone," Beth said. "Wait. Before you call, talk to Chris. See if he can make your phone secure."

Rachel's phone buzzed and she read the text message, *"Done."* She looked around for a camera, smiled, and waved to Chris.

Over the next hour, Beth spoke to Wendell Waters, explained why she was involved and that the seduction of Okoro was in progress. He assured her he would handle the Tawandian president. And, they agreed, as far as the press was concerned, Beth was in Lake George to talk to PRAISE CEO Theodore Donovan to clarify information for Meyerson case. The accidental death of the international philanthropist is a great loss to humanitarian efforts around the world.

After the phone call, Beth returned to the library and spoke to the team as agreed. "No big secrets. Rachel and Ted were arguing over protocol, process, and overstepping boundaries. She threatened to present her concerns to you. That's when he pulled the gun and slipped. An accident. I came up because I wanted to speak to Mr. Donovan regarding the Imanuela Meyerson disappearance. She was a PRAISE Foundation awardee."

Beth evaded all questions poking holes in her story, assuring the team of full disclosure once all the loose ends were tied up. In the end, tired of the impasse, the team voted to adjourn and go home. The FBI had several SUVs on site and offered rides to the

Albany International Airport or the Amtrak Albany-Rensselaer train station.

By four o'clock, the only ones left in the library were Rachel and Chris, standing next to her luggage. Beth came in and said, "Chris, do you have information for me?"

"In your email, as promised."

Rachel said. "What's going on?"

Yvonne raced into the library holding her computer and spoke to Beth. "My family is ready, just like you asked."

"What's going on here?" General Portman stared at them as he walked downstairs. Then he addressed Yvonne without waiting for a response. "Shut that thing down. We've got to get this house closed up."

Beth stepped forward. "First, General Portman, you're under arrest for the murder of Aponi Hill."

General Portman stood erect, proud, and angry. "Don't be ridiculous. Whatever you've heard is the product of twenty-year-old hearsay and foggy memories. Case closed."

"Sir," Beth said. "Are you aware that there was an autopsy? That Aponi Hill was sexually assaulted?"

General Portman said, "As a decorated military man, I do not get involved in civilian matters as I am not subject to local or civilian law."

Chris said, "You're right. I found similar cases at all your postings and you were never charged."

"Frankly, that's ridiculous."

Beth said, "Well, sir, it's time you stood trial." She cuffed him, handed him over to the Albany FBI team, and said, "Read him his rights and treat him with the respect he deserves."

Beth, Rachel, Chris, and Yvonne watched the general leave. Excited voices emanated from the computer. Yvonne took the computer into the kitchen and returned. "Thank you, from me and my family." She gave Rachel a hug.

Rachel said, "Here." She picked the rag doll off the top of her suitcase and handed it to Yvonne, "I brought this downstairs for you."

Beth said, "Let me see that." She studied the toy's face. "This is not a tear, Rachel. This is a blood stain." To Yvonne she said, "This may be evidence. May I take it? I'll see that it's returned as soon as possible."

Beth bagged the doll and said, "Let's go. We're done here."

Chapter 58
White House, Washington D.C.

Franklin Taylor Sandford wore a presidential cloak of satisfaction as his productive work day came to a close—crisis averted. He dimmed the lights in the Oval Office, and with a glass of Scotch in hand, gazed out the windows at the evening sky.

In a few minutes, he would be dining with Wendell Waters and the heads of the CIA and FBI. They had worked together all afternoon without the usual bickering and pissing contests, and solved the Okoro problem. Dinner was a show of appreciation for their efforts, attention to detail, and loyalty. He took the last swallow of Scotch and set the glass on the desk blotter.

Sandford's private phone rang. He looked at the ID and answered. After the usual polite small talk, the real conversation began.

Philip Vanderhagen said, "I am disappointed you sidestepped our clear understanding."

Sandford said, "Circumstances prevailed and I turned them to our advantage."

Vanderhagen said, "How exactly?"

Sandford said, "I spoke with Okoro and explained we had firsthand knowledge that an independent effort was in place to remove him from office. And that I was in a unique position to end the threat. My non-negotiable conditions were that he had to drop all blackmail efforts, reject any plans to socialize foreign investments.

Furthermore, he had to agree to measurably increase, by a minimum of fifty percent, both the amount and distribution of aid to his desperate indigenous and refugee populations.

"Okoro agreed. I emphasized that any breach of our understanding would cause a full media blitz on my discovery of the plan with an emphasis on his poor judgment, poor leadership, and unworthiness to be granted access, much less membership, to the United Nations. I also happened to mention that if he found the plane, he could keep it."

"Experience tells me Okoro cannot be trusted. Are you sure he will honor the agreement?"

"Absolutely. I just received a copy of his announcement that all disputes regarding foreign investments in Tawanda are resolved."

"Hope that you're proven right, Sandford."

After the call, the veiled threat hung in the air. While the president stared at the silent phone, his shoulders rounded, his head dropped, and he sighed. He shook his head, shuffled over to the bar, and poured himself another drink. The specter of Vanderhagen's control hung over the Oval Office. Worse, it had taken up residence.

Chapter 59
Federal Plaza, New York City

At the New York City FBI Field Office, Eric Jerrod was on the phone when the battle-worn contingent arrived. He put a finger to his lips and then held up two fingers. Beth went to her desk and sat down. Rachel and Chris, overcome with exhaustion, slumped in two uncomfortable chairs.

Eric ended the call with "...nobody talks to her. Got that?" He put the phone down, leaned back in his chair, put his hands behind his head, and grinned from ear to ear. "We got Lucy Kilmer. Trucker found her hitchhiking up the Thruway. Troopers apprehended her on Route Ninety West at the Iroquois Travel Plaza, just outside Canajoharie.

"Seems a retired state trooper drives a rig. He keeps up with the posted wanted lists along his routes and the FBI's top ten. He picked up a hitchhiker. He recognized her from our bulletin. Called his office to check in and told them he had met a woman as pretty as a picture. His office called the state troopers, who were able to track him. When the trucker arrived at the rest stop, the troopers took her into custody. She hasn't said a word."

"Let's get her down here ASAP. She gets no calls until we talk to her." Beth said. "By the way, I dropped off Ted Donovan's phones, computer, and tablet at Tech Services. They'll give us every piece of data they can find."

"What about his office and home?" Eric said. "You or me?"

"Right now, let's get the warrants and some agents to contain each site. We'll start processing them tomorrow. No rush."

"No problem," Eric said.

Beth looked into Eric's green-gray eyes. "You know I couldn't have done this without you."

Eric rolled his chair next to hers. "Am I your knight in shining armor?"

"You are. We're a great team. But…."

"No buts," Eric said. "This time, I'm not going anywhere."

Beth said, "Then let's get these warrant requests done, get out of here, and celebrate properly."

Chris' phone buzzed and woke him up. He took the call. "Yep…. We're ready…." He nudged Rachel until she woke up. "Our ride's here."

When they stood up, Beth said, "Before you take off, this would be a good time for introductions. Rachel Allen and Chris Gregory, this is my partner, Eric Jerrod."

Chris shook his hand and said, "It's been quite a day."

"Big understatement," Eric said. "Heard about the incident this morning. How are you doing?"

"A little sore, but fine."

Beth said, "Rachel took a big chance out there today."

Chris bowed his head. "I know. I saw. I'm so sorry."

"You're apologizing to the wrong person," Beth said, nodding towards Rachel.

Chris smiled. "Don't worry. I'll make the apology fit my transgression."

Rachel looked up at him. "You bet you will. First, I'd like...."

"Please," Beth said, laughing. "Do that on your own time. We've still got work to do before Eric and I can leave. Besides, I think your ride is here, literally." She nodded toward the doorway.

"Anybody here looking for a ride home?"

Rachel rushed over to Nikolai. "My hero." She gave him a hug, careful not to hurt his shoulder. "I'm so glad you're okay."

"We missed you too," Nikolai said, with a wink and a nod toward Chris. "And I mean a lot."

Rachel laughed and poked Chris. "So you missed me, did you?"

Chris blushed, cleared his throat, and said, "Let me just say I'm very glad you're back and we've got a wedding to plan."

Rachel grinned. "You're on."

About The Author

C.L. Bluestein lives in Slingerlands, New York.

Her ideas for projects are fueled by absurdity and puzzles—i.e. how, why, and how come things work—whether it is functional or mental, psychological or physical, or just plain interesting.

Look for C.L. Bluestein's short story collection and second novel in the Seduction Series 2015-17.

Available books, essays, and short stories may be found at

www.CLBluesteinauthor.com

You Want Me To Do What? is available now. Walk in the sandals of our ancestors through this engaging interactive contemporary scripted Story of the Exodus/Passover for Jewish and Interfaith Families. Targeted but not limited to tweens.

"You Want Me To Do What" is the most innovative addition to the Passover literature I've seen. This is not just another pretty Haggadah....these interactive mini-dramas will make ANY Seder using any Haggadah come alive for all ages." Cantor Charles Bergman, Los Angeles, CA

Free download at

www.CLBluesteinauthor.com

Made in the USA
Middletown, DE
15 August 2015